SHACKLED MAN
A RUST CHRONICLES NOVEL
MORGAN QUAID

FIRST PRINTING, September 2021.
Harry Markos, Director.

Paperback: ISBN 978-1-915387-66-0
eBook: ISBN 978-1-915387-67-7

Edited by: Tori Ladd

Book design by: Ian Sharman

Cover art by: Moises May

www.markosia.com

First Edition

1. The Red City

The brute bears down upon me, one eye a battered mess still spewing blood while the other narrows with hateful intent. He speaks no words as he lumbers toward me, utters no curses or promises of vengeance. There is nothing between us but hatred and a few feet of uneven ground, slick with blood and the writhing forms of the dead and dying.

I kneel atop the shuddering form of his dead comrade, holding a pistol by the barrel as blood drips from the makeshift club onto the bludgeoned mess below. I bare no particular malice against the dead soldier twitching beneath me, but war makes monsters of us all, and if I have to choose death or murder, the latter will suffice.

I try to stand, but there is no strength left within me. Twelve hours of relentless warfare have drained every ounce of vitality from my flesh. My hands shake, and my vision narrows as I see the approaching soldier through a blood-soaked fog. He stumbles in his approach, slipping atop the writhing form of a dying cannoneer and falling to his knees momentarily. I feel the curious spark of survival flicker to life within. Perhaps, if I can drive myself to my feet, I might flee this crimson hell and live on? The thought is a weak, insubstantial thing. It fades to mist the moment my enemy corrects his approach. Curious, but there is something of relief in my mind as he closes the gap between us, wielding the bayonet he intends to stick me with. Some part of me welcomes the end. No more struggling to suck in air. No more pushing worn muscles past exhaustion. No more hope of flight or freedom, just the release of this brute's savage blade.

I close my eyes and wait for the sharp release but find instead a startling new sensation.

Silence, or something close to it.

With what little will remains to me, I force my eyes open. Gone are the blood-drenched hillsides of the Crooked Vale, the battered brute set to plunge his bayonet into my chest. Lands littered with fresh-made corpses have been replaced by an impossible vista. I find myself kneeling on crimson sands, surrounded by a vast desert expanse and the eerie sonnet of distant winds.

The best I can manage is a ragged laugh as I fall to the earth, my limbs shaking. It seems that I have been spared the moment of death itself and been transported to some other, afterworld. Heaven perhaps, or more likely hell. Yet I see no demons nor angels in this vast wasteland. Just a formless expanse of crimson sand.

It may be for mere moments or long hours, but I lay helpless for a time, caught in an exhausted trance. A grinding pain within my chest forces me from this altered state, and all at once the many complaints of my flesh are made known to me. A broken rib or two, gashes in my right shoulder and forearm, a battered knee, a thousand cuts and bruises, and a nasty cut somewhere on the back of my head all throb and screech at me.

I rock myself to an uncomfortable sitting position and begin to take stock of the damage. In one trembling hand I still hold a revolver, gripped by its barrel, handle dripping with the blood of the man whose life I have so recently stolen. Out of habit, I check the weapon but find its components damaged beyond reasonable repair. I let the makeshift club fall to the sand and fumble about my waists with numb fingers.

It takes far too long to locate my own pistols, but I manage to recover first one and then the other from the holsters at my hips. Still kneeling in the dust, I reload the weapons from the few shells that still line my belt and let my dumbfounded fingers do their familiar work. The first weapon is holstered by a combination of dumb luck and the dead weight of my right arm. The second proves more difficult to holster. Half a dozen unsuccessful attempts to slide the weapon into place leaves my arm burning with a sharp pain and brings forth an unexpected chuckle. I sit for a time, focusing on the dull rasping of my breath, then make the attempt once more. Using my other hand to guide the barrel into place, I succeed and find myself somewhat pleased with the meagre endeavour.

I turn my head left and right to better understand my surroundings, finding that the crimson desert is not so barren as I had first thought. To one side stands a vast city, its walls at least a hundred feet high. Tall towers of midnight hue stretch out from the city's heart—alien and somewhat out of place among the flat desert landscape. They have the eerie appearance of a gnarled hand, reaching skyward from beneath the earth.

My first attempt to stand ends in failure, my left knee buckling and sending me hard to the ground. Spitting red dust from my mouth, I roll on aching bones and gather my strength for a second attempt. My every muscle and sinew beg for rest, but I am not yet ready for death's embrace. My sudden transportation to this strange desert landscape and its oddly placed city has stirred sufficient interest to lift me from my former malaise.

I try to stand a second time, bracing against the pain. Whether by some trick of physics or luck, I manage the feat and stand momentarily with arms outstretched in an effort to keep my balance. The world steadies around me, and I gaze out upon the distant city. Its various sounds and smells are carried away by the desert winds, so I must rely on sight alone to guide my path.

With no other clear goal in sight, I begin a shambling walk toward the red city in the distance, trying not to ruminate on just how far away the city might be. I keep my eyes locked upon the ground ahead, forcing each footfall with an effort of will. Questions float like spectres about my head, leering at me like spiteful children. Where is this place? How did I come to be here? Have I indeed passed beyond life? Am I doomed to wonder this interminable desert for eternity?

Here, as with so many other aspects of life, the stolid training of a soldier is my greatest ally. I push the questions out of my mind and drive my legs forward. I have but one purpose, one goal: to reach the red city.

***

An hour or more passes, and my body begins to remember itself. Racked with pain, my legs still do their work, carrying me across the sun-baked desert toward a city which grows more expansive and daunting with each new step. The air is thick with crimson dust. It claws at my throat and insults my eyes with infuriating force. I think not of my desperate need for water, for rest and sustenance. Instead, I force each footstep, counting the remaining shells in my belt with the fingers of my right hand—a familiar mediation designed to stave off pain and delirium.

A path of sorts emerges to my left, compacted clay cleared of rocks and other detritus. The path varies only a little from the desert to either side, yet I find myself revelling in the slight ease it presents—a little less dust, some fewer jutting stones and thus fewer jarring blows to my aching knees.

I continue on in this way for some time, drifting in and out of the moment. Thoughts of war and bloodshed drag me from the present again and again. Only the occasional buckling of a knee or jarring misstep brings me back to the here and now.

In this somewhat delirious state, I come upon a strange sight a short distance away. A figure comes into view along the roadside, perched upon a small boulder to the side of the path. The figure is shrouded in a dull brown cloak, its muted hue turned red by a thick coating of crimson dust. I judge him a man of age by his stooped shoulders and diminutive frame. He does not stir as I draw close, yet I find myself drawn to the man, as though my limbs themselves are compelled to the task.

I cease my walking and stand a few feet away from the figure, feeling my legs throb at the sudden shift in momentum. Swaying on my feet, I call out to the man, my ragged voice barely carrying above the din of the desert winds.

He moves slowly, deliberately. Thin limbs unfurl as he slips from the bolder and stands before me; an old man with weathered features clothed in his simple, threadbare robe. In my delirious state, I am unsure that I see truth and not some fevered lie. Wiping the grit from my eyes, I blink away the dust and gaze once more upon the old man.

His mouth appears to have been sewn shut, pulled tight with coarse thread which has caused the edge of his lips to pucker and redden unwholesomely. His eyes, too, have been sewn shut with a crude brutality. No surgeon or adept apothecary has plied their skill upon the old man's person. The marred flesh looks self-inflicted.

"Be at ease Idrus Kane of the shackled hand," the old man says in a voice too clear and rich to have come from his own mouth. "I mean you know harm, gunslinger. I wish only to speak my piece, and then you may be about your business."

"What business is that, old man?" I ask, the words cutting their way out of my throat. "I find myself plucked from the heart of battle and deposited here in this strange wasteland. Tell me then, am I to wander the underworld for days without number?"

The old man's face contorts in an odd fashion as laugher emanates from his deformed mouth.

"You are not dead, gunslinger, but nor are you among the citizens of that *other* world."

I move to speak, but the old man holds up a gnarled hand, and I find, of a sudden, that the impulse to speak has left me. Questions press against the walls of my mind, yet they seem locked far away for the moment. I can hear them only faintly in some far distant chamber.

"You are not native to this world, Idrus Kane, yet you are indeed a son of the red wastes. You will find and lose yourself within this arid desert, gunslinger. The fates will place you at odds with great power whilst conspiring to imbue you with that self-same power. You will pit yourself against the very gods themselves and tear this world asunder. Yet, you will act for the good and not merely the self-interest which has governed your life thus far."

The old figure takes a step closer, pressing a hand against my chest.

"Beware, gunslinger, for the Old Ones will seek to twist you to their will. Great power they will impart to you, but take care in how you use it, for the Elder Gods care nothing for the plight of mortals such as we, and to use their power in this realm is to serve as a beacon for destruction."

I feel the old man's hand retreat and sense the pull of something within my chest, as though his hand now holds something vital of my own essence.

"You will learn much and forget more in the years ahead, gunslinger. The darkness will take you for a time, and your mind will be lost amid the storm. I urge you then to heed my words, to remember this above all; *you cannot save her.* Love her you must, for we all are slave to our passions, but when the time comes for her sacrifice, you cannot, you *must not* save her. Heed these words above all, for if you do not, the cosmos will fall, and she will fall with it."

I stare at the man for a time, feeling the bonds which have held my tongue suddenly released.

"Your words mean little, old man. I need food, food and water. Not the prattling of an aged seer."

He grins, the expression gruesome upon his twisted face.

"Alas, I have no food to give, nor can I offer succour in this, your hour of need. Go to the city, take what you need to survive. Do not hesitate to act, gunslinger. A certain degree of brutality is required to live in this harsh and unforgiving land, and you must not shy away from such brutality."

My left knee buckles, and I lurch toward the old man, reaching out a hand to steady myself against his aged frame. At the moment my hands touch the roughly woven fabric of his robes, the figure dissolves before my eyes, vanishing into an ethereal mist and leaving me to lurch about and steady myself.

I'm left standing alone upon the road to the red city, my body aching, my mind fevered. Whether a symptom of my own bodily malaise or a tangible prophet come to deliver his opaque message, I leave the old man to memory and begin lumbering toward the city once again.

***

Small homesteads and ramshackle buildings begin to spring up as I draw closer to the red city. Still a distance from the hulking walls of the city proper, I reach a sprawling mass of hovels, each connected to the other with such proximity that the myriad paths that weave between the huts are often too narrow to permit more than a single soul's passage.

The stench of rotting vegetables mixes with a pungent aroma of roasting meats, thick with sharp spices that cling to the back of my throat and bring what little saliva I have left to my mouth in cruel anticipation. The sun above is still some distance from setting, but the lower city seems to welcome a false night beneath the vast shadow cast by the dark towers above. Campfires flare to life, and darkness descends quickly while the many folk of the lower city set about their nightly business.

I shamble ahead, trying to affect a casual gait despite the burning in my legs. None of the denizens of this strange place pay me the least heed as I move through the ramshackle streets. The sounds of laughter and bickering join with innumerable conversations to create a din that surpasses the constant howling of the desert winds. Already the temperature is beginning to drop, adding still further frustration to my need for survival. I consider a plea for aid, but the hard faces that pass me speak of a people unaccustomed to acts of kindness. Clothed in tattered, roughly spun garments, there is an air of desperation to them. These are not the well-to-do nor simple laborers, but the downtrodden and desperate: folk with no coin to speak of and little pity to spare for any save themselves.

My legs begin to buckle as I near a pair of tents where a group of women sit by cookpot, speaking in hushed tones while looking suspiciously at one another. The smell of stew bites at my gut, filling my belly with urgent need. From somewhere within my addled mind, a strategy emerges. I move around the corner of the furthest tent, bending down to pick up a rock from the ground. The byways are still clogged with people, yet I am unseen as I hunch down and move closer to the fire. My every fibre and sinew aches; the pain is all that keeps me from falling into delirious slumber. I take aim and launch the rock toward the cookpot nestled precariously above a makeshift framework atop the fire pit. Not waiting to see if my aim is true, I duck behind the tent, moving with all the shambling speed I can muster toward the rear of the second tent where a second pot simmers.

A screech peels through the air, and raised voices begin from the nearby tent. I seize my chance, hoping that the distraction will suffice. I duck into the second tent to find its owner immersed in a brawl with her neighbours. With no thought for the pain it will bring, I reach for the pot, snatching it away and moving off into the cluttered streets before the bickering folk notice the robbery. Merely a dozen steps pass before the pot slips from my grasp and onto the ground, spilling half its contents across the beaten earth. Without a thought, I begin scraping the food back into its place, heedless of the throbbing in my hand. Desperate, burnt, and aching for sleep, I slip the shirt from my back, not bothering to undo the buttons for fear that my fingers will stumble at the task. I wrap the shirt around one hand and pick up the pot once more, forcing aching limbs to carry me a distance from the desperate souls who are now aware of their loss.

I walk until I can walk no longer, coming to a mammoth building which stands far larger than any other among the shacks and hovels of the lower city. There is something oddly organic about the towering structure, but I care nothing for the building's aesthetic qualities. What attracts me is a small nook nestled at the base of building, a shadowed recess covered by the stretched fabric which coats the exterior of the structure like the stretched hide of some hulking beast. Careful to avoid the attentions of passers-by I move toward the nook, relieved to find it vacant.

It takes the last of my strength to climb up the jutting bone framework which serves as the odd foundation for the building and slide into the nook, still holding the cookpot. The manoeuvre takes far too long, straining every muscle and scoring more than a few additional burns about my person as the pot kisses the flesh of my thighs and arms. Finally, I manage to fall into place, nestling with the hammock-like interior of the fold and pulling the loose fabric across the gap so as to hide my body from view.

I eat with bare hands, devouring the oddly spiced stew, heedless of its heat burning a path down my throat. The food is thick with gamey meat and some kind of root vegetable which I cannot identify. I devour the contents of the pot as quickly as I am able and use my last reserves of strength to hook the pot to the insides of the fabric cover that hides the nook from wandering eyes. The weight of the pot pulls the covering taught, shielding me from view. I have no time to assess my wounds nor plan for defence against attack. The best I can manage is to reach for my revolver before sleep takes me.

***

Sleep comes only fitfully, interrupted by frequent visions of violence and bloodshed. In my addled state, I recall nothing of my childhood nor those few joyful memories which have bloomed in the hard soil of my life thus far. Instead, my dreams are beset with harrowing images of death and sorrow. I twist and turn in a fevered sweat, too disturbed to sleep in peace, too weary to rise. I know not how many hours pass in this malaise.

When I wake, it is as though I am emerging from a cocoon—reborn into a new world through the fire of tribulation. My body aches, and my mind is beset by a dreary fog, but the urgency of thirst and hunger drive me from my precious nook.

There is nothing graceful in my rebirth. I fall from the folds of animal skin which clothe the vast structure in which I have slept, hitting hard ground with a sickening crack that jars my left ankle badly. It takes an effort of will to begin walking through the city streets. They seem a little less cramped than the previous night but no less cluttered with people. In the daylight these people are stranger by far than I had guessed. While similar in shape and build to the folk I am accustomed to, they bear a range of exotic and frequently absurd markings on their skin. Hardly a soul is not marred with strange sigils or inked figures. Their every appendage seems pierced and adorned with jewellery: pieces of yellow bone, trinkets of burnished metal, and stone circles that hang low from the lobes of the ear.

While similarly adorned, the men and women of the lower city offer remarkable variety in appearance. Here the pale skinned and fair haired, there the Asiatic, the dark skinned, the short, tall, broad and diminutive. There is a certain *sameness* to the people of this city, but it derives more from the various affectations they have adorned in conjunction with their drab clothing and the pervasive crimson dusts that press against the city night and day.

Once my mind has settled sufficiently, I begin a circumnavigation of the mammoth building which stands at the centre of the outer city. It rises like a mountain, a thousand spans at the base, curving up into the sky to form a peculiar dome. There is a vast structure beneath the skinned exterior of the building, a network of curved beams which suggest an almost skeletal nature. Here and there around the edge of the building, purveyors of goods have set up makeshift stalls. They barter with locals amid the din of bustling footfalls.

The keen hunger in my gut draws me to a street-side vendor with animals, which might be lizards or some far distant cousin of the species, grilling over a small fire pit. I consider snatching one of the roasting beasts off the flame but reconsider as the vendor eyes me suspiciously. Rounding the corner, I see the full majesty of the building whose circumference I have been skirting. The mouth of the structure looms like the maw of a felled giant. Twin horns of impossible size curve up from the earth at the entrance forming a lofted arch above a vast doorway. Before the mouth of the building lies a large open square with neatly cut stones laid upon the ground. A dozen figures stand in the square, bare to the waist and darkly tanned. Each of the muscle-bound figures boasts a frightful array of bone adornments; sharp pieces of bone which pierce the skin of the chest, face, and arms. Each man brandishes a pair of large blades, and their wary eyes suggest that they are well practiced in the arts of brutality and intimidation.

I have wandered, it seems, into the heart of an illegal gambling den or some such nefarious establishment. A curious array of folk move back and forth from the mouth of the large building, under the watchful eyes of the bone-pierced brutes with their menacing machetes. Unlike the other denizens of the lower city, those who enter the hulking structure are dressed far too well. They wear fine robes with gilded trims and affect an air of superiority which dips only momentarily as they pass by the brutes at the doors.

I do not wait to be noticed but move quickly away from courtyard and its curious activities. Hunger drives me to a small marketplace a short distance from the gambling den where dozens of vendors peddle their wares. The proprietors of these makeshift stalls look hardly better fed than their patrons. A variety of roots and unappetizing vegetables are on offer, as well as all manner of insects and critters fried on crude pans above small fire pits. The air is thick with pungent spices which barely serve to overcome the rancid stench of rotten meat and night soil that hangs throughout this section of the city. My stomach churns at the contradictory array of odours, and I am forced to walk on.

Without intention, I finger the handle of my revolver, as though my hands sense some kind of danger to which my other senses are as yet unaware. It has always been this way. Years of repetitive motion under the various stresses and pressures of warfare have trained my limbs well in their given tasks. While my mind wanders and my gut churns, muscle and sinew perform their careful meditations, ever watchful and prepared for imminent violence.

I walk as swiftly as I am able, circling around the small bazaar in the hope that I might spot some vantage by which to strike and secure food. Too many people. Far too many. I have bullets enough to put an end to a dozen or more combatants, but, within the tight confines of these fetid streets, there is no space from which I might carve out a meaningful vantage.

Knives, fists, and cudgels are the weapons of choice in this kind of setting, and I have only the short skinning blade strapped to my right calf. I am alone in a city of desperate folk, surrounded by dangers of which I know too little. Here, now, there are no good choices. But choose I must, for indecision lines the path to destruction.

A shout peels out from the market. One of the vendors jabs a gnarled finger in my direction, shouting something unintelligible toward me. As one, a dozen heads turn in my direction. Whether by my blood-stained clothes or the weapons holstered at my waist, I am recognized as *outsider* and forced to make another retreat. I move quickly, vanishing into the crowded streets in search of some other source of sustenance.

***

As the sun hits its zenith, I find myself some distance from the hulking building beneath which I have set my home. I have managed to scrounge a little stale bread and some murky water from the hovels on the outskirts of the lower city. The meagre food has done little to quell my deep hunger, but it will have to suffice until nightfall.

The pangs in my stomach bring a memory of one of Griff's favoured sayings. "Only a fool fights in the daylight hours, but clothed in darkness, one man can topple a kingdom."

The words had proven themselves a thousand times over in the years I spent in the King's army. I and the band of misfits and cutthroats who had earned the appellation *Honoured Knaves* spent the bulk of our daylight hours asleep, tucked away far from prying eyes. The night was our playground, shadows our fond companions.

Mere mortals in the daylight, we were gods of the midnight hour, raining fear and hellfire on our enemies without remorse. It was then, among my wretched companions, that I learned life's most precious lesson. A year's training in gun-craft; the best tutors and

stratagems—in the daylight hours, with an enemy force
bearing down upon you, all of this counted for nothing.
I saw countless souls cut down without reason or mercy.
Shot through by misfires and panicked discharges,
undone by a loose strap or a misplaced gun-belt. The best
and most disciplined soldiers fared no better against blind
chance than the coward, the weakling, and the novice.

Serving with Griff's Knaves taught me that the best
fights are those fought with overwhelming odds on your
side. Shoot a man in the back, and he will have little
chance to offer recourse. Slit the throat of an enemy while
he sleeps, and one need not dwell on fears of vengeance.
There is no honour in such treachery; or so say those who
command from ornately clad tents, far from the battlefield.
Yet, those dishonourable deeds paved the way for victory
time and again, winning our cadre of scoundrels more
fear and respect than the thousands of honourable dead
whose bones lined countless battlefields.

It seems somewhat fitting that the moment we were
drawn into the daylight the Honoured Knaves were cut
down to a man, my own death commuted only by some
inexplicable act of transmutation. The lesson is clear:
stick to the shadows, strike from a high vantage, and
offer your enemy no recourse to vengeance. Thus, I wait
for darkness and my chance to strike.

Something stirs nearby as I huddle behind a crudely
built hut, eager to avoid attention. The sound of figures
arguing cuts through the din of the city streets. A gaunt
man darts past me, fear written heavy across his face.
Several others move swiftly from the small clearing
where half a dozen bronze-skinned brutes stand arguing.
Despite myself, I move forward to better witness the

altercation. A hulking figure stands at the centre of the group, bald and bearing a great many scars and bone adornments about his face and torso. He and the others about him are of the same ilk as the bare-chested brutes who stood guard outside the gambling den.

The figure encircled by brutes carries himself with an air of easy authority. This is a man used to giving orders and having them followed. He seems unconcerned with his current predicament, eyeing his enemies with dull hatred.

It takes a moment for me to realize what is so odd about the man. His right arm has been augmented by some kind of mechanical apparatus. The right side of his face is similarly altered, his eye affixed with a mechanical approximation which seems to glow with a vibrant red hue.

"I had thought the challenge would come from Yemen," the large figure says, wearing a crooked smile.

"Your age betrays you, Bonesmith," one of the surrounding brutes says, sliding a wicked-looking blade from its sheath and advancing.

The other men do likewise, five in all, each brandishing a machete and looking to end the matter swiftly. The augmented figure laughs—a rich, booming sound that echoes through the squalid streets.

"So that's it, eh? You lure me to the outer Fens where my support is weakest and draw weapons? Cowards one and all, you forget whom you serve."

There is a loud crack as something bursts from the man's right arm, a projectile that cuts through the closest of the men, tearing through the flesh of his chest with gruesome ease. The man cries out, clutching at his chest as he falls to the dirt. The others attack, thrusting and swinging in tandem while the bigger man attempts to fend off the blows with his mechanical arm and sheer force of will.

I know not from there the impulse comes. I am a stranger in this world; alone, wounded, and half-starved, yet something stirs within me at the sight of the betrayed brute. My revolver fires seemingly of its own will, cutting down three of the brigands in quick succession. I find myself standing at full height, gun barrel trained on the last of betrayers. The larger man seizes the opportunity, grasping his enemy by the throat and tripping the man so that he falls hard against the ground. His eyes locked on me with an expression of curiosity, the large man drives his mechanized fist into the fallen assailant's throat—a single blow of brutal finality.

Slowly he rises, walking toward me with the blood still dripping from his mechanized arm. I stand uncertainly, heart thudding wildly with the sudden heat of battle.

"It seems I am in your debt, gunman," the tall figure says, wearing a broad smile. He points to the revolver.

"An odd weapon in these parts. I would be very interested to know where you acquired it."

I slide the gun back into its holster. "From a gunsmith in the old country," I reply. "I brought it with me to this place."

The other man nods. "You are newly born to the crimson city then? A sojourner from another world?"

As he talks, the large figure walks toward the first of the brutes who had challenged him. He bends down by the man's face and pulls at the large tusk-like bone protruding from the dead man's nose. He wrenches the bone free, wipes it on the corpse's trousers, and then slips it through a belt at his waist, all the while wearing a broad smile.

"Well, gunslinger, it seems I owe you a debt of gratitude. I would have bested Jaln and his compatriots of course, but not without risking considerable harm to my person."

He eyes me up and down like a prospective buyer appraising livestock. There's a hardness to the man's face which speaks of long familiarity with violence. I recognize the man even though we have never met. He is the hard-nosed Sergeant who channels his lust for bloodshed into the battlefield, the criminal thug who has risen through the ranks to occupy a position of absolute authority—a man accustomed to wielding power, unafraid to sully his hands with blood when the need arises. I have known such men before. Some have been enemies of war, other have been comrades in arms and even officers in the King's army.

"Idrus Kane," I offer, giving him my hand. To my surprise, he is familiar with the gesture. Rather than shake with his mechanized limb, the tall man twists his left hand and grasps my own in an iron grip.

"Smith," he replies with a smile. "And you are well met indeed, Mr. Kane. Tell me, have you need of gainful employment?"

I nod. "I have need of anything you care to offer."

"Most auspicious," Smith says, beckoning me forward as he begins walking away from the small clearing and into the city streets beyond.

"I am always in need of good men, particularly those with such a talent for violence." He motions over his shoulder. "Of late, several key positions have become available, and I would dearly like you to consider filling one."

***

The Bonesmith, it turns out, is a leading figure in the criminal underworld of the red city. The vast structure in which I had inadvertently made my bed last night is owned by Smith and is indeed a gambling den and locus for all manner of iniquities and untoward activities. The bare-chested brutes with bone adornments and sharp blades are the so-called *Bonemen*: thugs and brigands who work for Smith and ply their craft throughout the sprawling streets of the lower city.

The Bonesmith's residence is the hollowed shell of a creature known only as Gargantua. The beast is said to have attacked this city some years past and been felled by the city's Empress, a ruler whose title seems to raise scorn and fear in equal parts. The Red Queen—so called for her bloody oppression of the common people—defeated the Gargantua in a past age, and the subsequent dismantling and proffering of the beast's internal qualities had brought great wealth to the red city and several of its less reputable individuals.

The Bonesmith was perhaps the greatest beneficiary of the event, building his empire at the cost of rival gangs and funding his various criminal enterprises on the back of a profitable commerce in bone and the like. It is for this reason that Smith and his followers display such gruesome bone adornments. The bone accoutrements are symbols of rank and prestige among the Bonesmith and his men though I am uncertain as to the logic behind the various adornments.

On returning to Gargantua, Smith instructs me to eat and take rest. A meal of hot stew served with a roughly textured bread is served in a private quarters laden with all manner of colourful cushions and curtains. Scantily clad women serve the food and stand waiting by the entrance to my chamber. Were it not for the desperate hunger that grips me, their appearance may prove somewhat distracting. Naked to the waist, the women are young and well kept. Like the men, their bodies are adorned with bone affectations, thin slivers of bone piercing the ears, the eyebrows, and even breasts.

After I have eaten my fill, I am led to a bathing room, where a pair of similarly clad women proceed to strip off my clothes and draw a bath. They take some pleasure in scrubbing the dirt and blood from my body, delicately scrubbing my skin with brushes fashioned from some sort of local flora. The attention of these women arouses my passion, but I dare not act upon the impulse, despite their urging to the contrary. Tiredness hangs heavy like a thick cloak over my body. I am only dimly aware of being clothed in a long robe before the women lead me to a large bed, laid out low on the floor.

I sleep and do not dream.

***

The next morning sees me fed and dressed in fresh garments which have been miraculously produced during the night hours. Unlike the loose pants and bare chests of my hosts, I am given a serviceable shirt, pants, and vest, along with a new belt for my shooting irons. A large coat is also supplied, dark and hanging only a little off the ground as I stand to full height. The clothes fit as though measured by a tailor with a deft hand. They are woven from strong fabric and do not chafe against my skin as I walk about.

The various agonies of the previous days and weeks have dulled somewhat, made more bearable for the hearty meal, soothing bath, and dreamless sleep I have lately enjoyed. I still feel my wounds like old companions, but their pangs are far less sharp than they have been in recent times. Rolling my shoulders, I cannot help but wonder whether it is the Bonesmith's art which has worked this miracle or simply some faculty of the arid deserts in which I now make my home.

Another scantily clad servant leads me to a large chamber which sits atop a vast bone staircase that has the appearance of a great backbone picked clean by scavengers and long years. It twists upwards through a second and third level of the building up to a chamber nestled atop the structure. I find myself somewhat unnerved at traversing the interior of a felled giant, such a vast complex of open halls and closed chambers adorned with bone furnishings.

"Just da head," the brute leading me upwards grunts over his shoulder.

"I'm sorry?"

"This, the Smith's Den," he motions about as if to indicate the building surrounding us. "Just the head of the beast. Body was ten times this size.

We continue up the stairs, and the brute leaves me to my contemplation. Truly this is a world of vast quantities. A desert landscape which stretches beyond sight, a red city which dwarfs any I have seen in my years, and this felled beast. I cannot help but wonder what other titanic beasts roam the red wastes surrounding this city.

"There," my escort grunts, motioning toward a chamber whose doorway is flanked by twin guardsmen wearing livid scars and dark scowls. Their eyes do not waver as I pass by, entering through an open doorway and into a lavishly furnished room of circular design. Smith greets me as I enter the chamber, sitting upon a heavy throne which looks to have been carved from a solid piece of bone. A huge scull is carved into the head of the chair, leering down at me from above the Bonesmith's head.

"Come, gunslinger," he says, beckoning me forward.

I take a seat upon a large circular cushion nestled beside the fire pit in front of the throne. To my surprise, Smith leaves his place and sits upon his own cushion opposite me on the floor.

"It would be remiss of me not to thank you for your hospitality," I offer.

He bows his head slightly. "And what think you of my little kingdom, gunslinger? How does this crimson welt compare to your native home?"

I shrug. "It is both strange and familiar."

"True enough. And you seem unconcerned despite your recent translocation into this barren world of dust and squalor?"

"There seems little point railing at the storm for the rain it brings."

He smiles broadly, chuckling to himself amid the mechanized whirring of his various appendages.

"True enough, gunslinger. True enough."

He reaches for a nearby tankard and begins pouring a dark, reddish brew into it.

"It is said that the warlord eats his own young in times of peace," Smith continues. "Very few can rule equally well in times of war and peace. I find, despite my best efforts, that I am far better suited to bloodshed than tending a flock."

He hands me the tankard, and I accept it with a courteous nod. The wine is a little bitter and somewhat harsh to the tongue, but with each new sip the taste mellows a little.

"My men are discontented," Smith goes on, pouring his own drink, "and I can hardly blame them for their discontent. We stagnate in this cesspool while the godlings throw scraps from their damnable palaces. We fight and squabble with rival crews and spend our days defending the rotting boundaries of this kingdom yet…"

He pauses, taking a long swig from his cup.

"Forgive me, gunslinger. You find yourself in the unenviable position of a confidant. A man in my position can seldom confide in others, you understand. You are newly come to this world, so your loyalty cannot be questioned. Thus, I share my frustrations too freely I fear."

I nod, drink, and do not speak. I have spent years enough listening to men such as this and have learned that they value the sound of their own voice far more than a considered opinion from another.

"I will cut to the heart of it then. I intend to rule this city, gunslinger. I intend to overthrow the Red Queen and her princelings and slaughter the priesthood to a man. This intent has only recently set within my mind. I have pondered the matter for long years now, it is true, but of late I have come to see that there is but one course left to me. Survival dictates conquest. It will be war and bloodshed and blades in the dark. In all likelihood, we will fail at this task, and my kingdom, such as it is, will be divided among the carrion birds and bureaucrats who survive the coming rebellion. Yet I am forced to action and will not be swayed from this decision. If I stay as I am, I will spend every waking breath defending my kingdom against would-be usurpers and rivals. Each day my influence will wane, and my kingdom will crumble a little more. Another decade or so, and the Bonesmiths will be little more than a memory."

He motions toward me, spilling a little wine as he waves the goblet in my direction.

"You have some skill with firearms. I wonder, what skill have you with the craft of war, with deception, with rebellion?"

I shrug. "I am a soldier, but not of a typical order. I have some knowledge of how to wage war; though my wars have been fought in shadow rather than light."

Smith nods, motioning for me to continue.

"I will not stand shoulder to shoulder upon a battlefield. Nor will I fire from trenches or nests while men kill one another in fields of war. I have seen the young, the old, the seemingly immovable cut down in moments by the machinery of war. If you wish me to fight such a battle, I must decline and risk your wrath."

Smith still smiles, but something hardens a little behind his eyes.

"I am no general nor grand strategist, but I can find a weakness and exploit it. A blade to the throat while an enemy sleeps. A drop of poison in the right bowl. A fire, set to burn enemy munitions. Give me a little time and a few good men, and I will bring an enemy to his knees while the sun sleeps.

Smith takes a long drink, wiping his arm across his mouth having drained the cup.

"If you have need of such a man, I offer my service, provided suitable recompense can be arranged."

Smith grins.

"Oh, I have a need, gunslinger."

***

Days and weeks pass as I learn the boundaries of Smith's kingdom, which stretches from the Fens though to distant settlements beyond the red city. Beyond the bare-chested brutes that surround his den, Smith employs a considerable network of informants throughout the city—men and women of many different professions and stations. Even within the red priesthood that governs the city proper, Smith has several reliable informants.

The more I learn of Smith, the more I am forced to reconsider my first assessment of the man. Brutal he may be, and he does not shy away from the shedding of blood when such is required, but beneath the surface lies a man of keen intellect and admirable desire. For some thirty years he has held the Fens in his grip, crushing foes and appeasing the ruling caste while establishing an iron grip on the gambling houses and pleasure dens scattered throughout the outer city.

His men treat me with distrust and something akin to jealousy, for I alone have the Bonesmith's ear. I am forced to sleep with one eye open, as the saying goes, for fear of sudden attack. I need only wait for a month before the first of Smith's lieutenants tries to separate my head from my shoulders by means of a wickedly curved blade. I narrowly avoid the cut, ending the man with not a little violence. Three more men attempt to lay hands upon me; three more die in the attempt.

I note that Smith does not dissuade such violence, nor does he sanction the barbarous acts of his men. It is, I suspect, a part of his desire to test me in some way. He uses the discontent of his men to hone my own skills and foster loyalty. The whole enterprise has the stink of one of Griff's hard lessons. The more I know of Smith, the more I see the similarities between the two men.

In time, more and more of Smith's operations are given over to my care. Slowly, begrudgingly, the Bonemen learn to accept my presence, respecting my shooting irons if nothing else. I learn to separate myself from the others of Smith's lieutenants, sleeping outside the Gargantua complex and keeping my own council. This seems to suit the Bonesmith, and he continues to confide in me as the months pass.

I grow accustomed to this strange city and the desolate lands which surround it on all sides. On numerous occasions I am called upon to venture to small settlements that lay throughout the crimson badlands, securing trade for the Bonesmith and ensuring that his interests are represented. The settlements are poorly furnished things, beaten by crimson sands and home to all manner of outlaws and brigands.

In like fashion, I am sent to every nook and corner of the city proper, from the lowest sewers to the highest rooftops. Only the five towers at the city's heart are beyond the reach of the Bonesmith and his brutes; protected as they are by a garrison of the Red Guard and the Red Queen herself.

Of the ruler of Rust, I learn much. She is of a peculiar race known commonly as *godlings*. She, a brute named Avernath, a mysterious figure known as Salik the

Twinned, and the Fleshmancer Calaban form the ruling caste of the city and its surrounding territories, along with a few lesser godlings who seem content to operate in the peripheries. The godlings are beings of great power, immortal creatures, it is said, that once lived in the waking world as we all did. Feared by the common folk and detested by Smith and his ilk, the godlings rule the city as capricious overlords, governed by their own obsessions rather than the needs of the people. It is this caste that Smith seeks to overthrow and, as I travel the length and breadth of the red city, I begin to see that the common people share his desire to rebel.

The common folk are oppressed heavily by the Red Queen and her godling cousins. Infractions against the crown are punished with terrible violence. Those who break the myriad laws and statues set out by the red priest are summarily executed or sent to the Fleshmancer's tents to have their body worked upon by the Red Queen's chief Fleshmancer, Calaban. From all accounts he is a monstrous figure who delights in the infliction of bodily excruciations. He warps the flesh of his victims, blending man with machine, animal with devil, and bringing about new creations that weep at their own horrific existence.

Smith himself, as he proudly says at every opportunity, is a victim of the Fleshmancer's knife. His mechanized arm and the various protrusions from his skull and back are testament to Calaban's cruel art. Unlike the many thousands who perish within the Fleshmancer's tent, unable to bear Calaban's ministrations, Smith survived his ordeal but was not content to continue in service to the Red Queen and her lackeys. In circumstances that seem to flourish with each new telling, Smith relays how he escaped the Apothacarian through various acts of personal valour, fleeing into the night and vowing never again to suffer beneath the Fleshmancer's blade.

Whether his telling of the tale is true, Smith wears his adaptations as symbols of godling oppression and the mechanized affectations seem only to bolster his claims among his followers. Others, though, particularly among the outer Fens and Ports seem to have suffered far greater indignities beneath Calaban's blade.

Whether a strict dictate of the bureaucratic priesthood, or some grotesque fancy of the Fleshmancer himself, crimes in the red city are typically punished in the most inhumane and somewhat ironic fashion. Whatever unhappy profession a soul finds themselves in, their punishment ensures that productive service to the red throne is maintained and even improved after the Fleshmancer has done his work.

Those who work the mines are furnished with coke boilers and mechanized limbs that split stone and rend earth. Farmers are fused to mechanized ploughs. Port-workers are fixed with spider-like limbs that permit rapid ascent among the many gantries and towers of the sky docks. Many prefer a quick death to a life of servitude, imprisoned within their own warped flesh, yet such a death comes with a great price. It is well known that the penalty for such an end is the brutal punishment of one's kin. What little family one might lay claim to in this strange land may be executed or sent to Calaban's tents in recompense for the suicide of one twisted soul. It is this price which keeps so many enslaved to their brutish new life; this and the distant hope of rebellion which Smith seeks to foster.

In the short time I have spent in Smith's service, I have come to see the red city, *Rust*, as a vast pit of corruption, violence, and greed. The downtrodden are many, the privileged few. Old and young alike are forced into desperate service to the Red Queen and her godling brethren, ever fearful of stepping outside the law and paying a horrific price. The red city holds little of beauty or hope. It swells with pain and suffering, sorrow and discontent—a city ripe for rebellion.

2. In the Service of the Bonesmith

"There is a fellow I wish you to seek out," Smith says, reclining upon his cushions. "He is a man of little stature. An unassuming type who runs an inkery out by Rookery Market. Litmus is his name, I believe. Find him, watch the man, and tell me what you see. Take note of the various comings and goings at his little establishment, for I believe that there is more to this Litmus than meets the eye."

"An opportunity?" I ask.

"Indeed. The man's wife was stolen by the Red Guard some years ago, accused of mancery or the like. Since that time, Litmus has spent his every free moment begging the priests for mercy, but his requests have fallen on deaf ears. He has greased the palm of every petty bureaucrat, priest, and administrator he can lay hands upon in the hope of obtaining some scrap of useful information, but all to no avail. I believe, however, that he has recently expanded his search for information to include far less reputable sources."

"He will be sympathetic to the rebellion then?"

"Oh, but more than that. Much more. I believe that this young Litmus may become the very face of our rebellion. With only a little persuasion, we may find the man to be just the heroic figure our cause requires. Go, seek him out but do not let yourself be seen. Spend a week and no more, then come back to me."

I leave Smith and set about the task in my usual fashion. I travel by night and stick to the shadows, moving alone and guarding my back. Of late, the Bonemen have ceased their rivalry against me, content to squabble among themselves rather than lay claim to my enviable position. Several of their number have shown themselves to be dependable allies, and, while I keep all at a distance, I have come to rely on some of these few souls as I go about my work.

A wily brute named Kodiac meets me in the darkened streets nearby the Litmus Inkery. He is a tall man, broad of shoulder but able to master surprising stealth when the need arises. From Kodiac I learn that the Inkery has run a brisk trade these past few days, attracting the attentions of several noteworthy priests and producing a volume of work for the various merchants and traders of the district. The city's recent prohibition against any and all writing has been relaxed somewhat. Most city folk prefer to conduct such business through such sanctioned establishments as the Litmus Inkery, guaranteeing a high level of trade for its diminutive proprietor.

Of the man himself, Kodiac reports little. He is an industrious fellow, courteous and welcoming to his customers and a portrait of subservience when it comes to the local militia and the Red Guard. I advise the brute to return to Smith with a freshly penned report. By mean of a simple code, I advise Smith that I will continue to observe Litmus myself and report back in short order.

With the coming of morning, I spy the diminutive calligrapher from my vantage atop a nearby roof. He is a short fellow, well dressed and seeming to go out of his way to offer polite greetings and salutations to passers-by. He draws his custom from both lowly merchants and more influential figures of the red city. Whether they arrive in gilded carriages or by foot, Litmus's customers left the premises in timely fashion wearing satisfied expressions, one and all.

Several further days pass, and I can see nothing untoward about the fellow. To the naked eye, the man is a paragon, his only vices a penchant for verbosity and a nip of cherry before turning in for the night. Yet there is something staged about the whole affair. Litmus makes great effort to be *seen* to be subservient to his betters. He bows deeply and smiles with practiced ease, yet the gestures are clearly well rehearsed. Even from my distant vantage, I can sense the lie in his actions.

Here is a man hiding in plain sight, masking truth with banality.

Having spoken, through various back channels, to several merchants in the local area, I have learned that Litmus was not always so mild-mannered and eager to please. On the contrary, in the days and weeks after his spouse was forcibly removed from the inkery under the charge of practicing mancery, the little man had railed at the injustice, vowing dark vengeance and testing the patience of the city guard to breaking point. Then, of a sudden, his entire demeanour had changed.

After but a few weeks of bitter frothing, the little man returned to his inkery and resumed his usual pleasant manner without a word. Companions and merchants in the surrounding streets noted the sudden change with great interest, furnishing a great many late-night discussions with the topic. They could find no reason for the sudden change, nor could they believe it genuine, and yet the man's miraculous return to normality had proven permanent. No longer did he loose petty insults and violent threats toward the ruling authority nor promise vengeance against those who had taken his precious wife. Nor did he forget Ellie or seek to supplant her by coupling with another. By all accounts, he simply reclaimed his former self in an instant and has remained so.

Only one change has entered the life of Litmus Shule since the moment of his curious reincarnation. A young lad was spotted on the day when Litmus underwent his miraculous change: a messenger from the ports. The boy carried a small parcel, which might have been a bundle of paper, or perhaps a volume or two—nothing out of the ordinary for one in Litmus's profession. Nonetheless, the arrival of that parcel was only the first of its kind. More packages arrived, all with a suspiciously bookish quality. Some were delivered through official channels, others traded in dark alleyways by staff under Litmus's employ.

It takes a great deal of digging to find the truth of this mysterious trade in packages. At a loss to the mystery, I eventually relent and break into the inkery on a rare night when its proprietor was not in. I enlist Kodiak's aid, instructing the burly boneman to keep watch while I enter the building and set about finding some answers.

In the main rooms and living quarters of the inkery I find nothing out of the ordinary, but a thorough inspection of the larder reveals a secret basement in which a vast collection of written works had been assembled. Books, scrolls, and scraps of parchment litter the room, crowding around a small writing desk where Litmus has clearly spent countless hours compiling and rewriting texts into collected volumes penned with a meticulous hand.

But this is no mere library for the sake of knowledge or the preservation of history. In all his gathering and examination of texts, Litmus is searching for something specific, trying to find his lost love through a lattice of clues hidden in ink and paper. Unable to locate his beloved and hindered at every turn by the priesthood and Red Guard, Litmus is determined to use his every possible resource to track down his beloved. Importantly, in this endeavour, the little man has not baulked at breaching the red letter: the prohibitive laws and statutes by which Rust is governed.

The knowledge gathered in his hidden library is far from benign. These texts are handwritten, forbidden, containing a great many secrets and truths about the apparatus of the red city and its ruling elite.

Using the singular gift at his disposal, Litmus has devoured every rumour and thought, every written word and supposition. He has followed strands of fact and fiction until they finally led him to the truth of Ellie's location. It sits at the heart of his penned volume, circled a dozen times, the tear-stained pages blurred.

Accused of inkmancery—the application of mancery through the calligrapher's art—Litmus's wife was taken from her home and shackled to a clerk's desk within the Administarium. The red priests, to whom Litmus daily pleaded for mercy, refused to offer a scrap of information to the man. All the while, Ellie was locked somewhere within the vast collection of buildings in which the priests conducted their cruel administrations.

As I extricate myself from the inkery and return to the Bonesmith's den, a theory settles upon my mind. Litmus, desperate and unhinged, managed to collect sufficient information to ascertain the whereabouts of his beloved wife. Having finally found her location and confirmed that she was still alive, Litmus set upon a plan. Railing against the red priests had proved of little value, yet now he had his answers. Now, he had a purpose. It is because of this purpose and its final goal that Litmus was able to perform his remarkable transformation: forgetting his anger and grief, and channelling those potent forces toward his great task.

Having found Ellie, Litmus was now in the process of devising a scheme to free her from her servitude and make flight from the red city to some safe haven or other. From what I observed, his plans were ill conceived and likely to end in a violent mishap, but they were only preliminary in nature, and Litmus had not arrived upon his final course of action.

Unwittingly, in gathering information from all manner of sources and funding his search for Ellie with proceeds from the inkery, Litmus had managed to assemble a sizable community of informants, thieves and rabble-rousers. While they owed no true allegiance to the man, they seemed to gravitate toward him, pressing their own woes and resentments toward Litmus and allowing him to shape their collective hatred into a more pragmatic weapon. This oddly formed network of delivery boys, brigands, back-alley traders, and merchants took Litmus's coin, but they gave their respect in return.

As I gather my thoughts in preparation for my meeting with Smith, Kodiak informs me that the calligrapher's activities have gone beyond the mere collection of materials, extending to the dissemination of inflammatory missives. Small pamphlets which decry the Red Queen and her lieutenants are scattered throughout the red city, carried by the self-same couriers which Litmus has employed to gather information. The small scripts of paper are nailed to walls in the dark hours, or left in fruit baskets at market stalls, on empty chairs at ale houses, and many such places. They are carefully worded—a light sedition which fosters distrust and hatred toward the ruling elite—gentle texts that have earned the movement a curious title—*the Scripts.*

The priests have been quick to condemn the missives coming from Litmus's inkery, making a grand show of hunting down the culprits responsible and dolling out cruel justice in the form of staged theatrics. In practice, it seems the red priests care nothing for such mild inflammatory activities, and Litmus is free to continue his work, slowly bolstering support among the disaffected and downtrodden.

Litmus himself is meticulous with the preparation and dissemination of his inflammatory words. Under the guise of inkery business, scripts are sent to every corner of the city, though in such a manner that their origin is obscured. They pass through many hands before reaching their final destination; an enterprise which, I calculate, has cost Litmus every spare coin his business can produce.

Hearing Kodiak's words, I reflect on the Bonesmith's orders and concede the truth of his plan. With but a little shaping, some carefully chosen words, and a pinch of deception, Litmus Shule could rise to become the hero and public figurehead of the rebellion. This little man, who could not best a three-legged dog in combat, may well topple the Red Queen and her godling princes.

Of course, a significant portion of his network of thieves and disgruntled commoners would turn on the man in moments if sufficient coin were offered. In a time of peace, discontent is easy enough to foster and cheap to harbour. If a proper rebellion begins to make itself known among the authorities, however, that cost will climb steeply, and Litmus's network will shatter within days.

Thus, while shaping the man himself will be an easy enough task, shoring up his ragtag following and insuring against betrayal will be another matter entirely. My mind works through the multitude of problems to be solved as Kodiak accompanies me out of the merchant quarter and into the Fens. There is a comfort to the mental exercise, and I find myself somewhat invigorated by the task.

Finally, among this city of oddities and freakish aberrations, I feel the ground is solid once more beneath my feet. Mind and body begin to fall into familiar rhythms, and I find a new level of clarity to my thoughts. If it is to be *rebellion*, then it we be a rebellion for the ages.

***

On reaching the Gargantua den, I report immediately to Smith, relaying all that I have discovered. My words please him greatly, but there is little surprise in his features, only the confirmation of that which he already surmised. I am sent, like an emissary of sorts, to every corner of the red city. I meet with Absinthe Annie: Madam of the great pleasure houses to the north and a sorceress of great power. I speak with Barbaras of the docking guild, break bread with a nameless fellow with rat-like features who rules the western sewers and commands a small army of under-dwellers from that region. On behalf of the Bonesmith, I make overtures to each of these and several others, gauging our support and weeding out those who may prove too risky or weak.

When the time is ripe, a missive is sent to Litmus—a letter requesting the pleasure of his company at the Bonesmith's manse. The little man arrives promptly, quivering as he enters the Bonesmith's council chamber. I watch the proceedings from my place beside the Bonesmith's throne, hidden partly in shadow, observing the Smith and his prey as they play out their parts.

"The nature of my summons," Smith says, "relates to a spate of recent, shall we say, inflammatory activities undertaken by your men."

The little man looks genuinely perplexed. "You have me at a loss sir. I have no men."

Smith let's out a bellow of laughter. "Oh, come now, calligrapher. There really is no need to be coy. I speak of the network of recruits you have garnered these past few years. The *Scripts,* is it? Truly an eclectic group. Bakers, masons, thieves, and laborers. You have managed to spread word to every nook and cranny in this fine welt of a city."

"I assure you, sir, they are not *my* men. We merely serve a common goal."

"Ah, a common goal, is it? Well, at least you do me the courtesy of not denying their existence. Call them what you will, calligrapher, you have managed to spread your tendrils wide. They reach even into the Fens, and it is for this reason that you sit before me now."

"We mean no threat to your organization sir," Litmus says, hands outstretched in a conciliatory manner. "We simply seek information about the Red Queen. Each of us has lost much at her hand and we—"

The Bonesmith holds up a hand. "You misunderstand, calligrapher. Believe me when I say that you pose no threat whatsoever. Were it so, we would not be talking as we are. No indeed, your body would be floating its way down the blood river. I am aware of your dealings, calligrapher, your collecting of information as you say. You have, I hear, acquired quite the library of artifacts concerning our illustrious ruler and her cadre."

The Bonesmith leans back, scratching at the scar below his blinded eye. This apparently casual gesture serves to emphasize the mechanized augments to his person—augments which have granted the Bonesmith unnatural strength and endurance. From my hidden vantage, I see the truth of it. Every word and gesture are carefully weighed. No action is performed by chance.

"I summoned you, Mr. Litmus, because it seems to me that we have a certain opportunity here. You have, unknowingly I suspect, laid the groundwork for a far more expansive and important venture than the mere publication of a few dissenting scraps of text. I put it to you, Mr. Litmus, that you have, within your grasp, the perfect opportunity to strike at the very heart of the Red Queen's empire; to rid this city of her wretched *justice* and revenge the abduction of your beloved wife."

The little man's eyes widen. He seems utterly struck by the Bonesmith's words.

"Oh yes, Mr. Litmus, we are well aware of your own personal tragedy. It is because of this very tragedy that I know you are a principled man, a *wronged* man seeking justice, yes? Well, let me tell you that justice will never come while you content yourself with acts of petty antagonism. Such an enterprise is vital, it is true, but without force and weighty execution, your pilfering of myths and rumours will not bring back your wife."

The calligrapher clears his throat.

"What...what do you propose?"

"An alliance of sorts. You have, as I mentioned, laid the groundwork and assembled a sizeable, if rather motley, collection of agents throughout the city. With the proper organization and an injection of force, weaponry, and personnel, we could bring down the bloody red queen."

"I... You want to lead a rebellion against the Red Queen?

The Bonesmith smiles, shakes his head. "Alas, Mr. Litmus, I lack the requisite character for such a noble enterprise. True, I possess considerable resources within and beyond the city. But even if I were to engage the Red Queen with all that is at my disposal, my efforts would fail."

He picks up his mug, moving it in gentle circles as he watches the mulled brew within.

"To lead an effective rebellion, dear calligrapher, I would need far more men. But, more importantly, I would need the populous of this great city to rise up and fight. For this to happen, the downtrodden masses must throw off a thousand years of servitude; no easy task, I assure you. How does one move the masses so?"

The Bonesmith leans forward, prodding a finger toward Litmus.

"You, Mr. Litmus, yours is a story which may ignite the passions of the dull-eyed masses and stir them to action. Already you have assembled a network of like-minded individuals throughout the red city; an assembly of the discontented, if you will. These people pay you allegiance, calligrapher, even if you do not yet realize it. Call upon them to rise up at the right time, and they will do so. Strike a blow against the Red Queen, and they will march with you. No, Mr. Litmus, I cannot lead this rebellion. It would take an effort of considerable force to have the masses follow me, but *you* they will follow out of love, out of solidarity, taking some small part of vengeance for their own loved ones."

Litmus sits in stunned silence, attempting to digest the Bonesmith's words.

"It is an...interesting suggestion," he says cautiously. "But I know little of rebellion. In truth my only interest is recovering that which was taken from me."

"And what better way to achieve that goal," the Bonesmith asks, "than to tear down this rotten edifice and lay waste to the Red Queen's rule? Think on it, calligrapher, if you were to recover your love and whisk her away to the far reaches, would not the Red Guard hunt you down? Would not the Warmaster sniff you out and cut your throats while you slept? Would it not be just a matter of time before agents of the red came knocking down your door to once more steal your heart and render you twice sorrowed? And what manner of life would you have, the pair of you, running from hovel to hovel, wandering the red wastes with only the clothes on your back? No, far better that we strike the Red Queen at her heart and, in the bargain, free your Ellie from her enslavement. Thereafter you may live in peace, working your inkery as before, without threat of violence from the Queen's brutes. I myself would guarantee such safety."

"Even so," Litmus objects, "I know nothing of rebellion, nor do I relish the shedding of blood."

Smith puts down his mug roughly, sloshing dark liquid onto the table. He leans forward. "That, Mr. Litmus, is where I can be of service. My men will fight where fighting is required. I will arm those of your followers who wish to take up arms, and," he motions in my direction, "my man will oversee all matters of military strategy and the like. You, Mr. Litmus, need only be the face and voice of the rebellion. Your story will solidify the resolve of the disgruntled, the displaced, the oppressed."

The little man's eyes fall upon me, wide with confusion. There is fear in his gaze. This is a man who knows violence, and he sees violence written heavy across my face. I find no pleasure in the calligrapher's fear. It is a necessary thing. That fear may one day save his life, so I stand in silence and let the shadows and scars speak for me.

The little man turns his attention back to Smith. "Do I have a choice in the matter?"

The Bonesmith looks down at Litmus, towering above the diminutive figure.

"You are perceptive beyond your reputation, calligrapher. You see right to the heart of it. In truth, no, you have no choice. You are, quite simply, a tool in all of this, a simple cog in a much larger machine."

Smith smiles, not unkindly.

"I am a man of ambition, Mr. Litmus," the Bonesmith says, walking to the centre of the room. "Yet I am hemmed in at every place by the Queen and her cronies. If I am to break the shackles that repeatedly quench my enterprise, I must have the red bitch's head on a platter. Make no mistake, calligrapher, we are headed to war, a war that I intend to win. Yet, with you as the figurehead of this rebellion, I can capitalize upon the heat of the moment. The discontent of the rabble is a powerful tool when wielded correctly, and I intend to use that very weapon to my every advantage."

He turns slowly, rubbing his chin with his mechanized hand. "You may rest assured, calligrapher; I am true to my word. Play your part in this enterprise, and I will see that your Ellie is freed. More than this, once power is wrested from the Queen and her lieutenants, I will see that you are at peace for the remainder of your lives together. You need not fear retribution nor strife. I will, as it were, take you under my protective wing. Simply do your part, stir the hearts of the people, and I will do the rest."

Litmus nods. He can do little else. At the slightest gesture from Smith, brutes appear from beyond the chamber and usher the little man from the room. His shoulders are hunched as though weighed down with a fresh burden.

The Bonesmith approaches me, grinning broadly.

"Now begins the true work," he says, nodding to himself.

"His network is vast but fragile. We will need to temper it and test the metal."

He nods. "Indeed. Others of our allies are likewise fragile. We must choose the right moment to act and guard our secrets closely."

There is an unspoken understanding between us. The words which are not spoken carry swift violence to our enemies and those of our allies who prove weak-willed or untrustworthy. Kodiak and the few others I have at my command will wet their blades in the coming weeks as we carefully prune and shape the tree.

"Go with the calligrapher," Smith says. "Begin sharpening his words. We must bring the anger of the populous to boil before we can strike."

I nod. "And what of this Ellie? Are we truly to free her?"

He makes a play of considering my words though I can see that his course of action has already been determined.

"We have located the girl, and I see no reason why we shouldn't at least try to reunite her with our calligrapher friend. After all, we will have continued need of his services once this business is done, and it would go well for us if we are seen to keep our bargain."

The Bonesmith moves closer, grasping me by the shoulders.

"Do well in this, gunslinger, and I will see you rule this city by my side."

I offer only a curt nod in reply. I have no wish to rule, nor do I hanker for power. If we succeed in our rebellion, I will likely leave the red city. A kingdom at peace is of little use to a hired gun. And yet, even before this endeavour has begun, I sense the folly in it. Peace won by bloodshed is a fleeting, illusory thing.

3. Preparations for Rebellion

The weeks that follow are spent in preparation for the violence to come. I spend my time locked within a small room at the heart of the Litmus inkery, sending missives and provocations to the calligrapher's network and fostering the discontent throughout the red city. I meet with allies and grease the palms of those who can be corrupted.

Litmus suffers my presence with his usual good grace though there is a hard edge behind his smile which speaks of inner turmoil. There is a strength to the little man, a fire within, born of his love for Ellie. Yet that fire will not drive the calligrapher to violence. To the contrary, he abhors the thought of bloodshed and makes great pains to distance himself from it. I find myself drawn to the diminutive fellow as time passes. We speak little, yet I learn much from his subtle manner and the care with which he rules his kingdom.

The network Litmus has established is solid enough though there are portions of the structure which must be burnt out and shored up once the dross has been removed. I know not where the bodies lay and care only that the weaker links of our chain have been removed. Noting their absence, Litmus inquires as to the locale of several of his Scripts. I offer no clear explanation, reassuring the little man that all is as it should be and our plans progress as they must. I see it clearly behind his eyes. Litmus fears me as man might fear a wolf on a leash. He accepts his place in all of this, but it leaves a bitter taste in his mouth.

On the night before we are set to light the flame, I secret myself from the Inkery and find the Bonesmith sitting on his pale throne, lost in thought.

"How goes our hero of the rebellion?" he asks, pouring a drink and offering it to me.

"He plays his part well. The Scripts have taken to him; they sense what is coming."

Smith nods. "And our allies?"

I shrug. "Annie has proven invaluable; the others will fall in line when the time is right. Barrow balks at his role, but he will not permit charges of cowardice. A little prodding here and there and he will do as he is asked."

"Good, very good. You have done well, gunslinger."

I shake my head. "The plan is yours. I have only done my part."

He turns toward me, his good eye twinkling. "Can it be? Have I truly heard correctly, or do my ears deceive me?"

I offer no reply.

"There is an air of compliment in your tone, gunslinger."

I nod. "Only the recognition of your skill in strategy."

"Still, to earn praise from such a dower spring, it warms my heart. Truly, you have given me a wondrous gift on the eve of battle. I thank you for it, gunslinger, most wholeheartedly."

We speak on into the night, carefully checking each detail of the Bonesmith's plan. Intricate wheels and levers of motion direct a hundred souls in a thousand unique actions. There is an unnerving sense of fatalism to the big man's words. He knows full well that many of his plans will unravel the moment that blood is spilt. His most stalwart warriors will falter, the enemy will not follow their usual course, and chance will spit in our eye and pull the thread of this carefully laid plan. It is for this reason that the Bonesmith has placed so many irons in the fire. Half his plans may fail, yet there may still be sufficient momentum to carry us to victory.

"One final thing," I ask, as I stand to leave. "The clockwork bridge."

Smith nods, grinning. "I know well the rumours, gunslinger, but that is all they are."

"They say the Red Queen herself controls the mechanism that drives the bridge. If this is true, if she alone can operate it, we will have little hope of making our way into the citadel."

He shakes his head. "Superstition and legend. The clockwork bridge is not beholden to that red bitch. Nor is it some etheric mystery. Like most of this city, it was built long ago by the Clockmaker God and his Acolytes. It is a machine: a device of remarkable cunning but a device, nonetheless. So many years have passed since the Clockmaker's departure that the common folk have forgotten the godling's work. It was he who built the bridge, the citadel, and the five towers at this city's heart. The Red Queen lives within a house which is not of her making. She profits off the marvels of a past age, using machines whose inner workings she cannot hope to fathom. Even Calaban and his fleshmancers cannot comprehend the Clockmaker's devices. That is why this city is in such a state of decay. We decline because our sharpest minds cannot compare to the least of the Clockmaker's Acolytes."

I nod. "And you have found a means of controlling the bridge?"

He smiles. "Gunslinger, there are a great many things of which I am uncertain, but this is not one of them. I have the means to control the bridge and make passage to the citadel. With the outer city in turmoil and the streets of the garrison quarter flooded with fell waters, our passage shall be swift and deadly."

A thought gnaws at my mind, itching to be freed.

"What is it, gunslinger?"

I consider my words carefully, not wishing to raise the Bonesmith's ire. "They say she cannot be killed."

For a moment I see the fire rise behind his eye, yet it is laughter rather than rage which he grants me.

"They say a great many things, gunslinger. But heed me when I say that I will kill the Red Queen and, if she cannot be killed, then I will bury her so deeply beneath this soil that a thousand suns will burn out before she again lays eyes upon the night sky."

***

I do not sleep this night but spend the early hours in council with those who will drive the rebellion home upon the morrow. Absinthe Annie, so named for the emerald hue of her eyes and the fine garments she wears, has become a dependable ally. The intelligence she brings from the whorehouses and pleasure dens of the northern quadrants of the city have proven invaluable. More than this, I do not doubt her resolve, nor do I question her hatred of the Red Queen and those who hold the reins of power in this dust-blown city.

Absinthe Annie owns seven of the best whorehouses in the city. Her courtesans service half the red guard and a good portion of the priesthood as well. Women, men, the so-called remade who have undergone unspeakable horrors under Calaban's knife live and work at Annie's establishments, claiming her patronage and gaining some semblance of self-respect.

Annie herself has demonstrated such a keen mind for matters mercantile that the godling Salik has only recently appointed her as Mistress of Trade within Rust and its outer territories. In her new role, Annie oversees the provision and store of vast quantities of food and trade goods. Rumour has it she reports directly to Salik himself in this capacity. And yet the woman seethes within at the mere mention of the godling race and their representatives throughout the red city.

I know not what hardships the woman herself has endured, but the tales I have heard of those in her care speak volumes. The sorrows of her "children" fuel Annie's hatred, making her all too eager to drive the rebellion forward.

It seems a supreme irony that Salik should have such a two-faced operative in his employ. Unlike the other godlings, Salik the Twinned is said to be divided into two halves; a male and female aspect who are never seen in each other's presence. Of the male aspect, we have little to fear. He is a bureaucrat and seems thoroughly disinterested in the suppression of the people. In her female aspect, however, Salik is a shadowed whisper—a knife in the dark. She is said to command a force of shadow operatives: spies, thieves, and assassins who operate in darkness and feed their knowledge back to the godling. She is a spider whose web is far too difficult to detect and, of late, I fear the strands of webbing we have accidentally disturbed.

I am brought back to the present by the scent of vanilla and rosethorn which rests in the air around Annie like a seductive shroud. While the others of our cadre make their entrances, secreting themselves within the narrow walls of the Litmus Inkery, I draw her aside momentarily.

"What is it?" she asks, impatient to be about our business.

"On the morrow, blood will be shed, and that which is let loose cannot be undone."

She nods, emerald eyes piercing.

"I ask you this only once, and I ask only you."

Again, she nods.

"Are we ready?"

She takes a few moments to consider, gazing off into the distance.

"We can make no better preparations. The bulk of the Red Guard have been sent to the Shadowlands with the Warmaster. With the bloodshed of the Rookery Riots, the common folk are fit to boil. If we delay, the rabble may take matters into their own hands and spoil our advantage. So too, the Red Guard may return, and our plans will be undone."

Her words are spoken with confidence, yet there is fear buried beneath the surface: an uncertainty that cannot be named.

"Very well." I offer her my hand, and she takes it gracefully.

Strength and subtlety are married in her grip. I feel something akin to electrical discharge pass between us as she removes her hand. This I have come to recognize as the tangible evidence of ethermancy. While I have not witnessed Annie practicing her art, rumours of her considerable abilities are too consistent to have been fabricated.

As we set about our final tasks, I cannot help but steal another glance in Absinthe Annie's direction. Her every move, her scent, the soothing tones of her voice—a mummer's farce constructed to steal the hearts of men and cloud the mind. She is intoxicating in every sense, forcing me to remember where she learned such arts.

***

The final words are spoken among my conspirators. All are confident in their abilities and sure of their plans. As they part to be about their work, I call Litmus to my side. The calligrapher looks pallid, drawn. This is the first he has heard of our plans, and the impending bloodshed weighs heavily the little man.

"I have not forgotten your bargain with the Bonesmith," I assure him, placing a hand on the little man's shoulder. "As you suspected, she is an indentured clerk within the Administratum. We have her location, and our scouts have confirmed that she is alive and well. I have a small squad prepared to apprehend her on the morrow. They will bring her safely to you here, within these walls, on the morrow."

Litmus cannot speak. His eyes brim with tears. His throat swells in an attempt to reply.

"Sleep now, a few more hours. I will wake you at morning, and we shall be about our business. Rejoice, Litmus, for we are on the very cusp of rebellion."

I watch the calligrapher shuffle from the room and climb the stairs to his bed chamber. Already the words I do no dare voice begin circling around my head. I have fought in a great many battles. I have killed many men and led shadow campaigns by the dozens. But never have I led a rebellion in such a strange city, with its peculiar flouting of normality and common sense. This is a city ruled by gods, and, though rumour and legend gift this city's rulers with wings and divine radiance, I cannot ignore the possibility that there is some truth to these tales. What little I have seen of the godlings lends credence to their supposed divinity.

Although my mind is afire with plans and potential hazards, I force myself to my own chambers. I unload and clean my weapons, letting hands and fingers do their own work as the repetitive process slows my mind. With the weapons rebuilt and in good working order, I lay down against my cot and obey the first rule of soldiery: take sleep when you can, for it may be many hours until it is once more safe to close your eyes.

I dream. I find myself sat upon a moss-covered rock, high up upon a mountain clothed in deepest green. This is no vista plucked from memory, but a mythical place which seems too beautiful to exist within the real world.

A figure sits opposite me, gnarled and age worn. He smiles a crooked smile, his eyes and mouth still sewn together as they were when I met him upon the path to Rust.

"Peace, gunslinger," the old man says, his voice sonorous and comforting. "Take your ease and speak a while with me, for the worlds turn in unusual ways, and the morrow holds great change in store for you."

I taste morning dew as I breathe deeply, rubbing my fingers together as though to test the veracity of my senses. This is a dream, that much is certain, yet I feel the truth of it, nonetheless. I am asleep in the calligrapher's inkery, my body taking much needed rest in preparation for the events which will follow. Yet, I am likewise here, upon a mountaintop with this old man.

"Still your mind, Idrus Kane," the wizened old man says, managing deep, calming tones through lips that don't move.

I look into the old man's eyes, which are at once both open and closed. Ragged stitching binds the orbs shut, yet, when I gaze upon the old man's eyes, I see the fathomless depths of the abyss within them.

"Let us speak of your fears, my boy," the old man says.

"I have no fear, old man."

He laughs, rocking back and forth upon his stoop. "To draw breath is to fear, gunslinger. You and all your kind are driven by it. Look closely and you will find the fear within, hidden beneath the very bedrock of your soul."

Even as the old man's words are spoken, I feel something shift within me. As though loosed from some internal alcove.

"I fear the rebellion will fail."

The old man nods. "Yes, gunslinger, *it will.* There can be no other outcome, for you pit yourself against gods, and the winds of chance are capricious in this season."

"And you have come to warn me of this, to urge me to turn from my path?"

He shakes his head, grinning widely. "No, gunslinger. You must continue. The rebellion must fail, for the future demands it. You must play your part in this so that you can become all that you must be."

"Speak plainly, old man. Why do you come to me on the eve of insurrection if not to sway me?"

"On the morrow," the old man says, "blood will be spilt, many will die, and the hopes of your rebellion will burn to ember and ash. As you stand upon the cusp of defeat, you will face a choice. Two roads stretch out before you; flee to the desert and forget the red city and its strife, or stay and make good your promise to the Calligrapher."

"The calligrapher? Litmus?"

"Indeed, gunslinger. I have come at this appointed time to urge you to stay within the crimson walls, even as your rebellion withers and dies. Find the Calligrapher's mate and bring her to him. Reunite these two and there is hope for the future. This rebellion will fail, that much has already been written, but the future holds another, greater rebellion which has not yet been decided. Turn from the city and you will live long and perish alone and unmourned in the barren places of that crimson land. Recover the woman Ellie and the seeds are planted for the future which may well cast you in a more heroic light."

"I have no interest in heroism."

He nods. "That much is true, it seems. Your principal motivation thus far has been one of self-preservation… and yet, you intervened to save the Bonesmith? You could not know that he would be victorious, nor that he would take you under his wing and offer sustenance and protection? Even so, you could have taken your leave at any time and the Bonesmith would not have harmed you. You could have fled to the north or tried your hand as a hired gun for some other brigand; yet you stayed, you served, you built the foundation for rebellion."

"I took the easiest path."

The old man shakes his head, wheezing with laughter. "My boy, you can scarcely conceive of the forces within that drive your actions. Consider your former life. Consider the men and women who have followed your causes, lived and died by your side when other, more appealing options might have been taken."

"I was a solider, given charge of—"

"You were a foundation stone upon which lesser souls placed their hope and salvation. Your men did not follow because of duty or threat of punishment. They followed because of *belief*, because they sensed the power within you."

With terrible speed, the old man leaps off his perch, pulling a blade from his robe and slashing upwards above his cheek. I feel my muscles tense in anticipation of what will follow, but the old man simply holds out his hand, his own severed ear nestled in his palm.

"Take this, eat it, and all will be well."

I shake my head. "I will not eat your ear, old man."

He giggles once more, and I find that the bloodied ear is now sitting in my own palm.

"Eat it, gunslinger, for it will serve as a sign that you have heard my words this night."

I know not from where the impulse comes, but I find myself raising the gruesome meal to my lips and beginning to eat, despite my distaste. The flesh is soft, laced with honey and wine, and feeling more like bread than meat upon my tongue.

"Be well, gunslinger," the old man says, "and endure. For the years ahead will shape you like an iron beneath the blacksmith's hammer."

4. Blood, Fire, Ash

I wake too swiftly, uncertain of my surroundings. Kodiak stands rapping at my door, urging me to wake in his usual, brutish manner. I push the old man's words from my mind and set myself to action, checking the shooting irons at my side and departing the Litmus Inkery as the sun's light rises with Kodiak at my side.

We are joined by a dozen of the Bonesmith's best brutes as we enter the city street. Brawny men with heavy brows and black machetes flank me as I ascend the crooked path to the citadel. We speak no words as we walk through the city, for the time for words has long passed. Threatened violence hangs thickly in the air as the common folk lock their doors and brandish makeshift weapons.

We near the Rookery Militia, where the iron tang of blood fills the street. Three of Smith's bonemen stand guard outside the Militia tents, their knives already slick with blood. Rivulets of crimson flow through the tent flaps as we pass by. A dozen guards killed in their sleep; cold murder that is echoed throughout every square and courtyard in the red city.

Cries peel out through the morning skies joined by the clamour of a disgruntled crowd. The sound fills me with hope and anticipation, despite my memory of the old man's prediction. As we round the corner my hopes are confirmed. Hundreds of souls are gathered before the Administratum. Voices are raised, along with makeshift weapons, as the common folk shout their grievances to the priests who dwell beyond the crimson walls of the temple district.

Red Guard stand watch at the entrance to the temple, stolid and resolute in the face of the rabble. Yet they are outnumbered a hundred to one, and the crowd will turn to violence before long, prodded as it is by those brigands and thugs whom we have bribed to whip up a frenzy. As I and my bone-laden comrades move past the Administratum, violence erupts, and the Red Guard are swallowed in a hail of fists and brutish implements.

Ela'ray meets us by the Larch Tower, and we are led into the network of sewer tunnels which run beneath the city. We walk in near darkness, led by the sewer rat's expert navigation through miles upon miles of interconnected tunnels and byways. The air is filled with the fetid stench of bodily waste and etheric effluvia. Here and there, luminescent scum bubbles at the surface of the foul river which flows slowly beneath the city streets, casting the curved walls in a sickly, emerald light.

Occasionally, we pass beneath grates and gutters which open up to the city above. The sounds of rebellion trickle down to our ears: a mixture of bloody cries and crackling gunfire. Some poor souls flee into the sewers in the hope of finding sanctuary. Ela'ray casts them aside roughly, driving the sickly souls into the fetid water as we pass by, walking at pace atop the stone byways which run to either side of the dark stream.

After a time, we reach our destination, climbing ladder rungs, which are brittle with rust and decay, and emerging into the bright sunlight. The Bonesmith waits for us, along with four score of his best fighters, standing in the shadow of the citadel, beside the clockwork bridge. Several rig-men from the port district stand nearby, their steam-powered mechanized arms tensed menacingly.

There are others too, scattered among the assembled host; ethermancers and mechanized brutes, hired mercenaries from the red wastes and brightly clad warriors who seem to bear the standard of the Clockwork God among their livery. Truly, the Bonesmith has called in every chit and favour to assemble such an impressive host.

"Have faith, gunslinger," the Bonesmith says, grinning. "And watch."

As if by the force of his words, the clockwork bridge lumbers to life. A thousand intricate mechanisms whir into place, dancing together in precise movements that cause the nearest bridge to descend gently, falling into place above the vast chasm which surrounds the citadel and separates it from the city proper. The Bonesmith grins knowingly as he walks toward the bridge. I walk at his side, my hands resting upon the hilts of my shooting irons. I feel an intense unease as we walk across the span of gilded metal, above the fathomless depths that hem the citadel on all sides. I cannot say from where my unease spreads, but there are eyes watching us from the shadows, I know it. Whether watching from the towers above or the depths below I cannot say.

"Steady yourself, gunslinger," the Bonesmith says, hefting a barbarous blade in one hand and flexing the mechanized digits of his other. "I sense their eyes upon us as well. This is as much for show as it is for expedience."

I nod. "I am unaccustomed to fighting in such an exposed manner."

I wince as the Bonesmith's meaty hand slaps against my shoulder.

"Rejoice, my friend, for the moment of our triumph is near." He turns to those who follow behind, raising his arms and loosing a fierce battle cry. The rabble of warriors crossing the bridge join the chorus, filling the morning air with brutal promise.

I feel it press against my gut, gnawing at me with a dread certainty. The old man's words come back to me in a rush, and, of a sudden, I see the truth of it. We are children playing at the feet of gods. For all his wicked intelligence, all his scheming and manipulation, the Bonesmith is nothing more than a tin pot ruler railing at the seas.

We reach the citadel courtyard and are greeted by a small band of finely robed servants. One of their number holds a bloodied knife, and the scent of new death lingers nearby. No words are exchanged between the Bonesmith and this cadre of citadel servants. They join our ranks as we move toward the nearest tower.

In a city rife with corruption and strife, it does not surprise me that Smith has been able to bribe servants of the citadel to allow us passage. There is a sense of unease among the gathered revolutionaries, however. A distrustful gap opens around the citadel servants, for despite their actions this morning, none of us can bring ourselves to show these people trust. Thus is the curse of the turncoat.

From above, I hear the cracking of gunfire as Red Guard pepper the rioting crowds below with gunshot, perched in their ponderous airships, circling like dull-witted carrion birds. Elsewhere in the city, I hear echoes of gunfire and the occasional boom of an explosion. A litany of activities unravels in my mind, carefully laid plans that are now born into reality. The flooding of the military district, the destruction of buildings that will block streets and byways surrounding the garrison, the poisoning of the Administratum wells; each action has been meticulously planned in the hope of furthering our chances of victory.

We are still a little way from the closest of the five citadel towers when a figure emerges from the shadowed interior of the edifice. Impossibly tall and clothed in dull black and silver armour, the figure carries a sword which stands as tall as the Bonesmith. I see no expression within the silver wolf's-head helmet, but I can feel the Warmaster grinning as he approaches. Dread fills my heart at the sight. Avernath was said to have been occupied far off in the Shadowlands, yet here he stands before us. Yet, as our host comes to a slow halt, we see the dreadful truth of it. Dozens of black-clad figures emerge from the tower, huge and brimming with etheric power, each brandishing thick blades that have the look of butcher's cleavers.

Avernath the Warmaster comes to a halt, his mammoth blade slung easily across one shoulder. Energy seems to peel off the giant figure as he leers down at us. Standing a foot or so taller than Smith, the godling threatens impossible strength, even though he stands motionless.

As one, I feel our host tense at the impossible sight. Disbelief wars with confusion among the brutish warriors that stand behind the Bonesmith, yet the man himself sees the truth of the matter swiftly. He turns to me, anger boiling behind his eyes.

"We are betrayed," he hisses.

I have no words to offer in return. I nod, pulling my shooting irons from their holsters.

As he steps languidly from the shadow, the Warmaster tosses something down onto the courtyard floor between us. I do not recognize the man's face, but Smith grinds his teeth in distaste. The severed head of one of his bonemen bounces across the cobblestone before coming to rest. Three more heads are thrown onto the courtyard by the Warmaster's butchers, and I sense Smith's rage redouble. Avernath the Warmaster does not attack nor does he taunt us with harsh words. He simply stands before the citadel towers, ringed by warriors in black cloaks, his wolf's-head helmet impassive.

"Why does he wait?" one of the lowland mercenaries beside me asks.

"There," the Bonesmith says, motioning upwards.

I follow the Bonesmith's gaze as he lifts a mechanical hand to point at a long balcony that runs the width of the nearest citadel tower. Four figures stand upon the balcony, towering over us with all the menace of broiling skies on the cusp of a violent storm. The Red Queen stands wreathed in crimson flame, flanked by her godling lieutenants. They are tall, only a little shorter in stature than the Warmaster, yet each of the godlings radiates etheric power: normally invisible threads of energy now made frightful by their art. This is as much display as threat.

The Red Queen herself pulses crimson power though her masked face seems somewhat disinterested in the proceedings, as though she has been called away from more important work to stamp out some troublesome cockroaches. The sounds of rebellion echo through the courtyard, but the air within the citadel is deathly quiet. From innumerable windows in the towers above, soft-skinned, lavishly dressed citizens peer down at our rebellious host. Some point out toward the chaos in the lower city, murmuring to one another. Others laugh and whisper conspiratorially as though observing some mummer's farce from gallery seating.

In the skies above, three airships circle the citadel spires, their weapons trained on the ground below. We are fish in a pond, cornered by giants and awaiting execution. All of Smith's bravado, all of our planning and scheming has been for naught. The betrayal of a few bonemen has unravelled months of careful planning. Yet, standing before the godling host, I can see the truth of it. Had we a decade to plan and ten armies at our backs, the rebellion would still fail.

Whether caused by godling trickery or my own fears, I feel myself wither inwardly. My grip loses, and I feel the shooting irons slip a little, accompanied by the sounds of blades falling to the ground all around me. Several of our host attempt to flee while others cower and await death. From the twisted fingers of one of the godlings, I see faint threads of shadow drifting down from the balcony and turning to a light mist that settles around us.

"If we are to die," Smith's words boom, "then let us be about it!"

The Bonesmith's words jolt me from the malaise, forcing the unnatural fear from my mind as my limbs remember themselves. Seizing the moment of freedom, I fire two shots right at the Red Queen's body. The bullets hit their mark but seem to turn to smoke the moment they reach her. The shot itself is joined by a dozen others and, within an instant, we are joined in battle.

***

I have emptied my shooting irons within seconds of the melee's commencement. Men and monsters fight with blade and claw, tearing at one another with all the savagery they can muster. The Warmaster's soldiers cut a swath through our lines, killing with etherically enhanced speed and strength, making short work of the bonemen and their allies. I am forced to draw a blade and retreat to safety, reloading with one hand and trying to pick off the enemy amid the frantic cacophony of blood and bluster.

It takes two or three bullets to put down a single of the Warmaster's soldiers, and they are driven to frenzy when wounded. Their blades dance like lethal insects, cutting through flesh and bone, driving back blades and finding the softest flesh with dreadful ease.

We are forced to retreat to the bridge, but as we approach its clockwork mechanics whir to life once more. Seized by the old prophet's words, I charge toward the bridge, running with all the speed I can muster and launching myself across the cavernous gap that is rapidly opening between the bridge and the lower city. Two bonemen follow at my heels but fall short of the mark and plunge to their deaths in the darkness below. Their screams are unheard amid the din of battle. I land hard, driving my stomach against the earth but managing to pull myself up to safety. I risk a glance back at the battle which rages beneath the dark spires of the citadel, catching sight of the Bonesmith for a brief moment. Our eyes meet momentarily, and I see no hatred in his eye as he fights to stave off inevitable doom, no bitterness or spite; only a deep, dark sorrow.

In the moment before I run, the Bonesmith catches a blade to his shoulder, driving the big man down to the ground. He brings the iron fist of his mechanized arm to bear against the black-clad soldier, beating the man's face into a pulp even as a second blade cuts into the Bonesmith's back. I turn from the sight, driven by a singular need to run.

The city drowns in chaos, its people bloodied and desperate. Here and there, throngs of common folk stab at the corpses of Red Guard, or corner a lone militia-man, intent on bloody violence. Elsewhere the Red Guard have reasserted their strength, cutting down the rabble with lethal efficiency. The streets are slick with blood, and buildings burn on every side. While fire rages through the southern districts, to the north, flood waters spring up from the fetid underseas below, drowning whole streets and dragging their aged buildings down to the abyss. Citizens and guardsmen alike are swallowed whole by the etheric tide as watery chaos claims great swaths of the city. Foul things, darkling creatures with misshapen limbs and many-toothed mouths emerge from the depths, charged by the etheric effluvia of the fleshworks and given new life by the sudden torrent of violence spilling out on the streets above.

I gather half a dozen rebels to myself as I stumble through the city: a ragtag group of survivors searching for some means of escape. They ask no questions. We cut a zig-zag path through market squares and back alleys, having to change course time and time again as the city remakes itself. We are forced to stop and hide for hours at time as Red Guard squads begin regaining control of the city, setting up barricades and patrols in those areas of Rust which still stand whole.

With the great focus of the fighting to the north and west, I and my small crew are able to make our way into the Administratum with minimal fuss. Despite the unrest I had witnessed earlier, it seems that the temple quadrant has remained largely unscathed. The dark halls of the Administratum seem eerily quiet amid the din of violence in the streets outside. I have only a simple sketch of Ellie nestled in my pocket. Penned by Litmus himself, the portrait is a fair likeness, but the task of tracking down one woman amid a myriad of indentured servants is daunting to say the least.

The Administratum spreads out before us like an impossible hive. A thousand chambers joined by dark stone corridors interconnect along a single spine that curves off into the distance. From its exterior, the Administratum seems to be a loose assemblage of disparate buildings: a haphazard arrangement which has evolved over many years. From inside, however, one gets the impression of a single grand edifice, joined together with such dark uniformity as to seem like the inner caverns of some gigantic beast.

Most of the halls and chambers are empty. With the rise of rebellion, it is likely that Administratum guards directed their charges to safety, barricading away red priests, clerks, and those servants deemed worthy of protection. What guards remain within the larger complex are distracted and easy enough to pass by unhindered. These are not the Warmaster's demons nor the highly trained soldiers of the Red Guard. Used to long hours guarding bureaucrats and clerics, the Administratum guards are little more than a well-dressed militia.

I find my way to a large chamber where a hundred or so scribes sit chained to their desks. A plump-bellied priest stands at the centre of the room, shouting at the shackled scribes with a high-pitched squeak.

"Come, come now, little ones. Pay no heed to the squabbles of the lower city and its miscreants. There is work to be done".

He slams a short wooden rod onto a nearby desk as if to punctuate the point. As one, the scribes seem to flinch at the sound.

I motion for the others in my group to guard the doors and head toward the priest at pace. He stares at me with mild interest as I draw near, somewhat baffled as to my appearance.

"What a curious fellow this is," the rotund priest says, grinning widely. "Tell me, boy, what—"

The butt of my dagger thunders into the priest's face, making a bloodied mess of his lips and cheek before he can finish the words. He falls backward, eyes wide with shock. I pounce on the man, pressing the blade against his throat with one hand while showing the sketch of Ellie with the other.

"Where is this woman?" I hiss.

The priest splutters, spitting blood but not managing to speak.

"Where is she?" I press, pushing the dagger blade a little harder.

"I…I do not know," he pleads.

I lean forward, snarling at the blubbery man. "How do I find her?"

He blubbers and cries and soils himself, forcing me to slit the man's throat and put an end to it. I show the sketch to half a dozen of the scribes, but they are too cowed and fearful to speak, and none seem to know Ellie's whereabouts. I head toward the door, fearing the time it will take to search each chamber, when a young man catches my attention.

He is shackled to his desk like the others but seems a little less fearful.

"Release me," he says, "and I'll take you to her."

I approach the young man. "If you lie to me," I advise, "I will cut your throat just like this priest."

The young man shakes his head. "Her name is Ellie, yes? I know of her. She works in the Grey Hall. I can take you there."

It takes only a few moments to free the young man from his fetters. They are weak things, fashioned from pitted iron and dulled with age. It strikes me that it is not metal which keeps these souls bound to their desks.

"Follow me," the young man offers, rubbing his wrists as he heads through the doorway.

I follow him as he shambles at pace through building, his legs clearly unaccustomed to such rapid movement. Here and there, I spot an Administratum Acolyte or guardsman wandering through the halls in search of safety from the rebellious squall. Of the scribes themselves, our presence offers little distraction. They continue their work, heedless of the bloodied thugs that come stomping through their halls. It is as if the years of dull service have softened their minds. They seem docile, like beasts who have supped from thistleweed before heading to slaughter.

After some time, the man leads us to a smaller chamber where a dozen souls labour at their desks. At the forefront is a young woman that still bears a little of the beauty in Litmus's drawing. The years have worn heavily on her face. Her cheeks are drawn, her eyelids heavy. Even so, Litmus's sketch performs its task well. I kneel beside Ellie, placing a hand upon her wrist. She turns slowly, dull eyes showing faint flickers of confusion.

"Ellie, I am…a friend of your husband Litmus. I have come to take you to him."

She makes no move to speak, nor does she acknowledge my words in any way. Slowly, like the passing of the moon in the night sky, she points a finger toward the far edge of hall. I follow her gesture to a sconce on the wall from which hangs a thick iron chain that reaches down to the floor. I follow the chain as it runs between thick iron rings hammered into the stone floor. It seems that each of the clerks in this chamber are bound by a single, tempered chain. Unlike the rotting irons I have seen elsewhere, these look to be newly forged.

Ellie nods slowly as I recognize the dilemma. She points to a doorway at the far end of the chamber.

"Administrator Kelp holds the key," she whispers. "He sits in his rectory with the guard."

"How many?" I ask.

She shakes her head, uncertain. "Three, perhaps more."

Leaving one of the bonemen to guard the doorway to the chamber, I motion for the remaining two men to follow as I head toward the door to the rectory. Only now do I notice that the lad who led us to this room has fled. I can hardly blame the boy, but I can hear Griff hissing in the back of my skull. *Should have killed the boy. Even now, he may be leading the enemy to your door.*

I push Griff's words out of my mind and press on, leaning against the door and listening. Through the din of rebellion outside, I can hear only a few muffled words. I gently test the door handle and find it rigid. With a little more time and preparation, this endeavour would be relatively risk free. But we have no time and must throw caution to the wind.

I nod to the larger of the two men at my back, and he charges at the door with all the force he can muster. The brute is all meat and gristle, standing a head or so taller than I but built like an ox. Even so, the door shifts only a little beneath his onslaught. Again, he charges at the door, and the chamber seems to shake a little as his meaty shoulder slams into the hard wood.

On the fourth attempt, the door gives way, and the boneman stumbles forward into the room beyond, slipping over splintered wood and stumbling atop the falling door. Three crossbow bolts fly through the air. The first drives into the brute's skull, killing the man before he hits the floor. The others fly into the chamber behind us, one only narrowly missing Ellie as it thuds into the desk behind her.

I crouch low through the doorway, shooting irons raised while the remaining boneman charges into the rectory with his hatchet raised. I fire, downing two guards before they can unsheathe their weapons and sighting the third just as the boneman charges into my line of fire.

The fight is over within moments. I approach the cowering figure who I assume is Administrator Kelp and holster one pistol, reaching out a hand to the sheepish man.

"The key!" I bark, jolting the man out of his horrified malaise.

Behind us, the boneman is still hacking into the body of the third guardsman. Kelp struggles to pull his gaze away from the butchery, reaching into his robes with a shaking hand. I move forward and wrench the key from his hand, returning to the chamber and the locked chain.

I manage to unlock the chain and begin pulling it through the large iron rings on the floor. The metal is heavy and difficult to move. Seeing my difficulty, the boneman by the chamber doorway moves over and begins helping me. One by one, the clerks are freed from their bondage as the thick chain snakes its way through their shackled ankles.

Ellie is the last of the clerks who will be unchained and already my arms are beginning to ache as the chain snakes ever onward. I catch a glimpse of something near the doorway and stop pulling. A dark figure enters the room with cat-like agility. The figure pauses only a moment as it spies us by the chain, dull black cleavers poised for action.

"Butcher!" The boneman shouts, putting a name to the black-clad soldier as he drops the chain and picks up his own weapon.

The butcher draws near, moving with impossible speed, and I am forced to abandon the chain. I fire three shots in quick succession, aiming for the figure's chest and spotting the satisfying pricks of blood as each shot hits its mark. Yet the butcher does not slow. He advances on me, swinging dual cleavers with terrible speed and force.

Something glimmers in the air as I roll across the aisle and duck behind a nearby clerk's desk. A long blade cuts through my shoulder, thudding into the floor and cutting a groove into solid rock. The butcher advances with his remaining weapon, and I fire off more rounds, oblivious to the sudden pain in my shoulder as I pepper the butcher's chest. Once again, the bullets hit their mark but seem to do little to slow the figure.

Three more steps and he is upon me. I have sufficient time to pull a punch dagger from my boot and thrust aside the butcher's first strike. He slashes down at me with a heavy cleaver, jarring my wrist and glancing across my arm as the punch dagger barely deflects the blow. I throw myself backward, landing hard against the floor and pulling my left shooting iron with my free hand. I fire until there are no more bullets, letting the gun drop to the floor as my bloodied arm starts to lose its strength.

The butcher staggers a little, looming above, face hidden by a mask of black cloth. He moves forward, blood running from a dozen wounds yet apparently undeterred by his injuries. Before he can close upon me, the remaining bonemen attack, one from either side. Without changing his stride, the butcher deflects the machetes of his attackers, twisting and thrusting out with his own weapon to deadly effect. The bonemen die badly, skewered beneath the butcher cleaver. But their deaths have bought me enough time to reload. I aim and fire, this time aiming for the butcher's skull. The chamber echoes with the deafening report of gunfire. The butcher staggers, still standing even after I have delivered the full wrath of my weapons. Still holding his remaining cleaver, the brute slides to the floor, breathing his last.

Driven by a sudden need to be rid of this place, I return to Ellie who is bent over, pulling the last of the chain from her shackles. I lead her through the Administratum buildings, heading out into the violent night and trying not to dwell on the appearance of the Warmaster's butcher. Nevertheless, troubling questions come to mind as I steer Ellie through back alleys side streets. How did the butcher appear so far from the Citadel and so swiftly?

Either there are butchers stationed throughout the city and our meeting was a matter of chance, or the soldier tracked me all the way from the Citadel. Neither option bodes well, but I am losing too much blood to tarry.

Despite her weakened state, Ellie keeps pace with me as we move through the city. I manage to find a few recognizable faces among the chaotic crowds fleeing from the Red Guard, and we head as a group toward the market district.

Fires rage in the lower city as the Red Guard attempt to flush out ringleaders of the rebellion. There are bodies littered about the streets, and here and there we can still hear the clash of metal or the distant report of gunfire. At the heart of Rookery Market, a Red Guard airship lies in smoking ruins, its skeletal frame wreathed in ash and smoke.

On reaching the Inkery, we are met by the calligrapher, his face taught with worry. He and Ellie embrace, weeping joyful tears at their reunion. Delirium begins to claw at my mind as I stumble to reach a nearby table. I have lost more blood than I should, and my mind is becoming enfeebled. I have sufficient sense to wonder whether the butcher's blade was coated in poison or some etheric substance. I feel myself slipping from wakefulness, pulled under by loss of blood and whatever mancery is at work in my body. I have only enough time to speak a few words in haste.

"We have little time," I manage. "They will come for us, calligrapher. We are...betrayed."

***

I wake to the stilted sounds of dawn. It is as though the morning is hesitant to rise—still fearful of the night's violence. Pain burns through my shoulder and chest, but I manage to sit up. It takes an age to clothe myself and hobble down the stairs to the Inkery's common room. Litmus, Ellie, and a handful of dejected survivors are eating a meal of stale bread and cured meat. The little man moves to aid me as I sit, smiling broadly. Ellie is utterly transformed. She has bathed and eaten. The last of her shackles have been removed, and I begin to see a little of her former self behind her sunken cheeks and smiling eyes.

I eat what I can and charge a few of our number with keeping watch at the perimeter of the Inkery. In my current state, I doubt the value a few moments' alarm will offer, but old habits linger long, and I would rather have those moments than not. We have but one course of action open to us. We must head into the badlands with all haste. I speak such to Litmus and find him more than agreeable. Provisions have already been packed, and it seems that they have waited only on my account.

Ellie and Litmus linger at one another's side, unwilling to be parted for no more than a few moments before returning to their place. Something stirs within me at the sight; could it be a glimmer of happiness, of pride? In truth, I have no reason for either. Our rebellion has failed, and Ellie's salvation is a matter of prophecy and desperation, not good will. I acted upon the old prophet's words out of some fear of mysticism, or perhaps out of habit. Perhaps this mysterious old man has taken Griff's place? Perhaps I have simply swapped one old fool's words for another?

As I muse upon my part in all of this, the door to the inkery bursts open admitting a group of Red Guard with weapons drawn. I manage to pull my irons and let of a few shots before the guardsmen are upon us. The stitching at my shoulder bursts as I lunge forward, clubbing the nearest guard with the butt of a spent shooting iron. I feel ribs crack and blood flow as they come upon me.

Once more, the severity of my injuries is a curiosity. I can barely walk, let alone fight. The butcher's blade has stolen my strength and left me helpless as a babe.

The thought has barely enough time to solidify before it is knocked out of my head by a vicious blow to the temple. I fall into darkness, harried by Ellie's screams of terror as the inkery fades into…

5. The Pit

I wake, lying in a heap upon a slab of damp stone. Darkness surrounds me on all sides but for a single, dim light glimmering far above. Hours pass, and my mind begins to roam through a patchwork countryside of skewed memory and nightmare. Images from lives past flash before me, twisted and warped by some strange force. I drift in and out of wakefulness, pressed to-and-fro by the tides of consciousness.

When I finally wake from my malaise, I find myself racked with pain and hunger. The bloodied wound at my shoulder seems to have closed, and I no longer feel the press of death upon my chest. Instead, a widespread pain assails me; aching muscles and joints which remind me of the days following battle.

Near blind, I feel about me with numb fingers, searching for some clue as to my current state. I feel hard stone, slick with moisture and the moss of long years of neglect. On aching knees, I crawl a little to one side, finding the path blocked by a wall of slick stone. By chance, my fingers happen upon a bowl of thick gruel sitting in a carved niche in the wall. The gruel has little taste, but its bulk helps to sate the violent hunger within. The meal is cold and unsatisfying, adding stomach ache to my growing list of sorrows.

Having eaten, I recline once more, letting the sleepless malaise take me. The images return, taunting me with their lies as I am forced to count the myriad of aches and bruises that cry out from my flesh. The soldier's portion of my mind counts the tally. Two or three ribs broken. A savage cut to my arm, coupled with gouges at the flesh of my chest and torso. Bulbous bruises upon my head and a finger that must, at some point, be pulled back into place or risk ill-healing.

I have no memory of taking such wounds, nor can I account for their aged nature. Were I engaged in brutal warfare a week or so earlier, I would expect such a litany of grievances. It seems the injuries of our failed rebellion have been replaced. Perhaps, like some Saint of old, I have taken on the ailments of others? More likely my mind is somewhat unhinged, and I am unable to remember the provenance of my injuries.

Lying thus, caught between life and death, I sense movement from above. Even newly fed, I am unable to muster the strength to sit up. I watch dumbly from my prone position as an object is lowered, led by rope down the narrowing slopes of the stone walls to sit gently at my side. Through some deft movement I cannot define, the rope uncoils itself and slivers back into the meagre light in the distance. The light winks out, leaving only a faint reminder of its passing.

In manage to turn my head, waiting for my eyes to focus on the object newly lowered to my cell. The darkness does not abate, and my sight grows no clearer with the passing of time. With an effort of will, I turn myself over and reach out to the darkness. My fingers find purchase atop the lip of a wooden pail, and I pull it closer. The bucket is heavy, filled with fetid water and a wooden ladle.

It is only as I move to inspect the bucket that I realize why my wrists ache. Bound to each is a thick iron shackle, joined by chains that fall to an iron ring set to the base of the wall. The metal chains rattle as I move, pulling against the shackles and casting aside a dull ache in favour of bright flashes of pain.

With slow movements designed to minimize the pulling on my shackles, I determine to make a proper inspection of my cell. Using fingers as eyes, I scour the confines of my imprisonment. Aside from the niche where sits the bowl of gruel, there is a small corner of floor which drops away. From beneath, I hear the sound of running water, smell the stench of something foul coming from below. So, this is to be my bathing chamber then?

I reach an arm through the hole and cup warm water to my nose. Despite the fetid stench below, the water is tolerable though I dare not drink it. What bathing I can manage, I shall have to do by hand. Yet the same hole will serve as lavatory, whisking away my effluent upon the steady stream which runs beneath my cell.

Exhausted by my meagre explorations, I am forced to lie back once more and consider my surroundings. This is the limit of my incarceration then: a small space, barley wide enough to lie prone, a bowl of gruel, water bucket, and lavatory. Though the dim light above has vanished, I estimate its height as no more than twenty feet. In my current state, it may as well stand a thousand feet in height.

The walls themselves are slick with moisture. They tilt slightly, widening as they rise, but of such a wicked angle that climbing them would be a perilous enterprise. I suspect that the walls are fashioned thus by cruel design. Were they sheer and without angle, they would provide no hope of escape. In their current state, however, they flaunt the possibility of freedom and thus add to my torment. I will seek to climb those walls in the days that follow, and, already I know, I will gain nothing from this exercise but broken bones and shattered hopes. Nonetheless.

***

I heal slowly with the passing of long hours. Yet with each newly knit bone, each fading bruise, I feel my mind begin to unravel. This is not the first occasion in which I have found myself incarcerated, yet there is something about this rancid cell which tugs at my sanity. Whispers flow like water beneath the slick stone of my cell, atrocities spoken in hushed tones by alien voices whose progenitors I cannot see. The stones themselves seem to move, rearranging their sequence while I sleep and showing new faces upon my waking. The differences are slight; so slight, in fact, that I am forced time and again to question whether it is they who have changed, or I.

Unlike my previous incarceration, I have been shown not the slightest hint of human contact. No boisterous guards threatening violence, no officious oaf lauding the power of law and threatening execution; there is only the stone, the fetid water, the darkness. More than this, I have no hope of rescue to which I can cling during the interminable hours of solitude. Those whom I might call comrades in arms are likely dead or long departed from this crimson city.

I am alone in this sewer, this putrid hole. I will rot in this place, unloved and unremembered. Yet, it will be a rot of the mind rather than the body, for my captors keep me fed and watered, and there is a strange agency at work within this red world which protects men from the vicissitudes of time and decay.

It is difficult to ascertain the precise dimensions of the change, but time and decay work differently in this place. I have heard rumours of prisoners taken by the Fleshmancer and kept alive despite their every appendage being removed. Cuts heal with unnatural speed. Bones knit and wounds cease their bleeding. It is said that one can count age in the crimson desert by the scars on one's body, counted like the rings on a felled tree.

Such musings drift in and out of my mind as the days and weeks pass. I find myself less inclined to bath, less inclined to eat. It seems that death is the only path out of this cruel place, yet death does not want me. I feel my muscles wither and waste as the hunger bites at my stomach. I become little more than a shadow, weak and vapid, but still alive.

There is no telling how long this will go on...

6. In Darkness, Remade

In the darkness, I am remade.

Dark walls rise up around me, yawning open like the great maw of some dire beast. I am a man subsumed—buried beneath a mountain of rotting iron and sun-baked clay.

With the passing of each day, I am lessened. The flesh drips from my bones, falling away beneath the weight of darkness.

My eyes have grown stupid and desperate, searching with manic despair through the absolute black of the pit to which I am chained. They are now organs of invention rather than mere perception. In a sea of nothing, they discern the faint boundaries of my cell; here the glimmer of fetid moisture against a steady sloping wall, there a glint of metal, a hint of form and structure in the interminable darkness. Above, the locked hatchway from which food and water are daily dispensed; a portal of hope which cuts more deeply than any torture.

My sleep and wakefulness are no longer distinct. My mind drifts, wanders through dark and hopeless paths. Yet, of late, such wanderings are infused with novelty. The canvas of my mind has become far more than the dull surface of a pond, into which I cast my memories and imaginings; a fleeting picture which holds its form for no more than a few brief moments. I have borrowed clarity and precision from some dark intelligence, some grand dweller of the pit who seeks communion.

The images of my imagination are made vivid, made strange by those beings who call this darkness home. They speak in swaths of light and colour and leave behind a host of affective impressions. I am unsure now which hand guides and which forces. I know only that my thoughts are not fully my own.

I sense their conflict, the interminably slow clashing of malevolent minds within eternal darkness. Their debates cause ripples that cast me to-and-fro like a ship amid some vast etheric tumult. I try, with all the force I can muster, to throw my own will into the fray, but such insolence is the baying of an insect at the heels of the gods.

In the darkness, I am remade.

7. A Little Kindness

The dark dream stretches out before me, seemingly without end. I am taken out of the Red Queen's cell and dwell now among the starless skies. Beings of impossible power paw at my mind with feline cruelty. I hear the dark rumblings of their wicked words but understand nothing of their meaning. All is pain and sorrow, death and excruciation. Yet, during my agony, I feel power and pleasure bloom from somewhere within.

I venture through the caverns of memory, visiting past vistas now sickly distorted by the beings who now shape my thoughts. I see the faces of those I have known in life, mixed with figures I do not recognize. Are these people I will meet in some distant future, or merely the players in some mummer's farce: shadow puppets arrayed before me as I endure this endless torture?

I dream this endless dream, skipping from place to place. First in the mind of a dire bear, devouring its prey; now in the body of an old man, withered and dying. Women, children, fish, and birds of the air; I inhabit each of these in turn at the moment of their death. I experience countless moments of passing. I sense regret, confusion, panic. I am a helpless observer, yet I feel the sensations of each body as though they are my own.

My mind buckles, threatening to collapse beneath the pressure, but I feel the will of those dark beings holding it in place.

In a rare moment of clarity, I find myself dwelling on the failed rebellion. I see the Red Queen's masked face looming above, joined by her fellow godlings. I see The Warmaster, Avernath, resplendent in his wolf's armour while the rebellious rabble stands in mock defiance. I cannot say how long I have sat in this dungeon, nor why I have been spared the Fleshmancer's art. The red city is rife with tales of those who have been punished at the hand of Calaban the Cruel, their bodies twisted and warped into horrid mockeries of their former selves. What better lesson for a seditionist than to hand them over to the Fleshsmith's blade? Yet here I sit.

To my knowledge, neither the Red Queen nor any of her associates have visited me during my stay. No jailor or tormentor has come to taunt me, no Administrator or Priest to offer judgement. I have not heard the voice of another human sole during my time in this place, nor have I laid eyes upon anyone. The bucket and bowl are raised each night and lowered each morning. Try though I might, I cannot see the hands that lift and lower the object each day.

I am utterly alone but for the dark whispers and strange visions.

***

I dream a strange dream, feeling myself pulled bodily from the depths of some vast maw. I am spirited through dark halls by shadowed figures, their words meaningless to my ears. Rough cloth is pulled over my head, and I am transported by means of some cart or other, its constant jostling jarring my bones and causing sharp pain.

The endless night wanes, and I find myself, of a sudden, above ground, blinking away tears as the light from a thousand candles cuts at me from all around. This is a dream, a vision. I have been beset by such images of late. They twist around my mind like a serpent, strangling out reason and yet, this is different somehow. There are people milling about the city streets by the hundreds. These are not the diseased imaginings of my mind, but living beings infused with life by some agency other than my own.

I stumble forward, dragging twisted feet across uneven cobblestones. Where are the voices? Where is my bucket? I determine to see this dream out to its conclusion, struggling to push myself onward, through streets that are at once familiar and yet strange. Darkness ebbs and flows, bringing shadow in place of memory. I look up and find myself outside the city proper, walking along dusty paths lined with ramshackle hovels and crowded campfires.

I stumble, falling hard to the earth. I feel its dry grit in my fingers and cannot help but breathe in the scent of roasting meat and stale sweat that hangs in the air.

An aged hand reaches out, touching me upon the shoulder. The darkness comes once more, yet I remember kindly, wizened eyes, gnarled fingers, and the humming of some aged melody I do not recognize. I am fed and bathed, laid out upon a modest cot where I stare up at a ceiling made of rusted metal and dark hide. She sings me to sleep, the old woman who has shown me unexpected kindness, and I slumber for a time.

I feel my strength return, though the waking hours are short and haunted by spectral figures. I hear the old woman going about her business, and my body seems to grow cold in those long hours when she is absent. The darkness comes upon me regularly, swallowing all sensation beneath its viscous embrace. I hear the whispers from the darkness, feel the gaze of demons upon my flesh. My body crawls with the limbs of unclean things, creatures of the abyss given life and agency by unknowable minds.

I wake to feel the warmth of a familiar broth caressing my throat. The old woman hums to me in her wavering voice, caressing my head as she ladles spoonsful of thick soup into my waiting mouth. In the moments after my dark reverie, I am helpless as a babe. My strength returns slowly, only reaching usefulness at the moment that the darkness strikes once more.

Hours stretch into days. Slowly the darkness subsides. Slowly I begin to regain a little of myself. I do not speak to the old woman but offer her thanks in the form of meagre gestures and what version of a smile I can manage in my current state. She returns the gesture with a toothless grin, offering me more of the broth that has brought health back to my body and sitting upon a wooden stool by the cot.

I eat, stand, begin to walk around the old woman's hovel. There is little to see. The shack is no larger than my cell within the pit: sparsely furnished and beset by rot and wear. I know not what service the old crone offers during the daylight hours, but it brings in sufficient coin to give her grain and root enough to make her heady broth, with a little left for a clutch of ragged street urchins that frequent the old woman's hovel each night, their grimy hands outstretched to receive what little she can give.

When finally I gather sufficient strength to speak, the old crone shakes her head with a broad grin. She motions to her ears and tongue in turns, indicating that she is both deaf and mute. I nod. I bow and thank her with mute gestures and what I hope is a kindly expression. She cooks her broth and we set about our routine, and I realize that I am a stray dog to this old crone. A wounded beast rescued from the streets, brought in and cared for until I am able to stand once more upon my own feet. That time will soon come, and, like a dog, I have no means of repaying the old woman for her kindness.

The night falls, and I am struck again by the yawning darkness. My dreams are violent, bloody. The dark voices claw at my body, driving me to brutish acts. I am confronted by a strange creature: a many-horned bird-thing that eyes me with great malice. The creature boasts a pair of vicious tusks and eyes of hateful yellow, its body covered in mottled feathers and sharp barbs. It squawks a challenge, lunging at me with talons raised. I am pulled close, pressed against the hateful beat's chest as it rakes at my back and pecks at my face.

I strike the creature, once, twice. It falters a little and I lunch forward, my hands clasped at the beast's throat, clamping against her flesh while the bird-thing squawks and flails at me with sharp talons.

Dark voices whisper in my ears as the bird-creature fights back with beak and talon. I cannot say why, but I know with a certainty that this thing is evil and must be ended. My hands do not waiver in their task, strangling the life from the beast as it flails and screeches in anger. I score a cut below my eye from one of the creature's tusks and redouble my efforts, feeling my muscles ache with the strain. After a time, the flailing ceases and the creature grows limp, its body writhing beneath my grip. I watch in confusion as the bird-creature's form is reduced to ash. The desert winds flare, driving away the ash to reveal the quiescent form of an old woman.

***

I wake, covered in sweat and bleeding from a cut below one eye. The old woman lies dead beside my cot, a spoon still clutched in one hand. I spare but a moment to reflect upon this ill deed. An old woman who has shown uncommon kindness and been killed for it. I shed no tears over the old crone, but there is a gnawing set to my heart which begins to fester.

I take a satchel and some food from the old crone's stores, reasoning that she will no longer require them. It may take an hour or two after sunrise for her death to be discovered. I do not doubt that, within moments from that discovery, every item of even moderate value will be purloined, her meagre hovel stripped bare. My thoughts stray momentarily upon the clutch of waifs who come nightly to beg for food at her table. They will likely go hungry this night though the old crone's hovel may provide some sustenance, in one form or other.

I walk through the crowded streets of the lower Fens, keeping my head down and staying to the shadows. It takes an hour or more to clear the squalid network of shacks and makeshift streets. The night is mild enough. The desert's sands claw at my throat as I head out into the night. I walk until sunrise, distancing myself from the red city and focusing on the monotony of my footfalls. The slow, rhythmic beat of my walking causes my mind to drift, forcing me to pull back to the present again and again, or risk dwelling upon dark thoughts.

I walk for several days, stopping only for a few hours of fitful sleep and to fill my belly with what meagre goods

I have managed to pilfer. The flat wastes pass beneath my feet, taking me out of sight of the red city and out into the lands beyond. I follow no path or plan, but simply walk.

The Badlands are a curious balm; their crimson flats and grey peaks blending together, sand and grit and dust beating against my body like the oppressive darkness of the pit. Wrapped in stolen cloth and hessian, I embrace the painful monotony of the desert, walking on until wearied legs can no longer hold my weight. What little food and water I have taken from the old crone vanishes within the first few days of my sojourn, and so the bitter aching of my gut becomes a constant companion.

***

I walk until I can walk no longer, falling to my knees. I lay for a time, intending to rest just a little before I continue on my way.

The desert claims me though I know not the moment in which it occurs. It may have been during the night, when the darkness abounds, or beneath the noonday sun, swept by acrid dusts from the far wastes. I do not witness the moment of my demise, nor do I comprehend the hands which lift me from that barren place and granted me succour in my time of need.

Just as the old crone plucked me from the fetid streets upon my exodus from the pit, so kindly hands deliver me from the red wastes. I am rescued, I later find, by a merchant name Eldwin and his extended family; a traveling caravan who run a circular trade from the red city to the outer skirts of the southeast badlands. He is a kindly fellow, out of place among the hard stone and blinding winds of the red wastes. In his care I am fed and well kept; able to recover a little of my strength in the few days I spend as their honoured guest.

On the third day of the journey, while my mind still reels from the weight of desolate voices that speak to me from the depths of the pit, the caravan is beset by brigands. The sharp crack of rifle fire signals a swift start and finish to the attack. That first shot takes Eldwin in the chest; the preamble to a hail of bullets that quickly cuts through the remaining merchant folk with callous ease. Rough men cheer and holler in the wake of the slaughter.

"Check the carts," one of their number orders, punctuating the words with a guttural cough that speaks of some woeful flux.

Dazed, my head still spinning, I search the wagon interior for some makeshift weapon. I am rewarded with a small, unsheathed blade: a fruit knife left atop a small chopping board. Struggling to stand, I reach for the blade but misjudge the attempt, cutting into the fingers of one hand and falling hard against the side of the wagon.

I do not see the blow that fells me, nor feel the weight of a cudgel against my head.

Darkness reigns once more, and I feel no sorrow for that fact.

***

I wake, chained to the floor of a makeshift cell, its iron frame bearded with rust. The rotting iron bars are ill-made and look as though they would give under a modest kick of the heel, but I have no desire to free myself. I sit and breathe, waiting for my mind to settle, disparate thoughts swirling endlessly amid swirling winds of confusion and doubt. Slowly, with the passing of night and the rising of dawn, I begin to be at ease.

The barbarians, who treated so violently with the merchant and his family, go about their work with surly jests and curses. They are hard men, but opportunistic and cowardly. They lack the steel of battle-worn soldiers and instead prey on the weak and unsuspecting. Yet, these self-same brigands have gifted me some measure of peace, hemming me in with walls of crooked iron and rusted metal. I find myself becalmed by my cloistered surrounds, more at home in a cell than walking free among the oppressive spaciousness of the wastes.

Days march on and I rest within myself, withdrawing from the baking heat, the sounds of men cursing, the smell of cold gruel and fetid water. I am alone again in the darkness, waiting on the counsel of dark minds. Yet the darkness no longer speaks as it did in the pit. My mind is no longer touched by the terrible thoughts of those gargantuan beings. I am alone, at least for the present.

7. The Raven-Haired Girl

The sound cuts through my malaise, a subtle noise that pulls me from the darkness, forcing my eyes open. I am in the makeshift cell, surrounded by night and the subtle murmuring of those few beasts who inhabit the red wastes. I incline my ear, shifting toward the far right of my cell. The sound of sobbing rises from what looks to be an adjacent cage. I press myself against the rotten bars of the prison, straining to see the source of this sobbing. I can make out the huddled form of a young woman, raven-haired and dressed in the attire of an outland sojourner. She weeps with strangled mews and shakes as though struck by fever.

I watch as the hours pass, but the lass does not shift from her place, and I am unable to see her face. Slowly, like the birthing of some troublesome beast, the sun rises and light dawns across the compound. The girl still lays huddled in the corner of her cell, her face hidden, but the tears long dried upon her cheeks.

Our captors stir from their slumber and set about their daily chores with flamboyant resentment. I return to the base of my cell and watch. No longer coddled by the minds of darkness, I am forced to remain awake and face the daylight. I spend the early hours of the day examining my captors, for no other reason than to stave off the silence which threatens to unhinge my mind once more.

A score of brigands set about lighting a fire, tending to pack animals and relieving those few who have stood guard the night previous. At the heart of the camp is a tent, festooned with various painted symbols and iconography. From it the Chieftain arises, a corpulent man with a prodigious beard and a habit of walking shirtless through the camp. Several women scurry from his tent upon rising; thin, battered things that look to be spoils of war—or whatever passes for war among this band of cutthroats.

The women scamper to a small well at the heart of the camp. They draw water and are forced to bath naked before the leering eyes and harsh words of the men. They bathe quickly, not wishing to draw the attentions of their captors. From a distance I can make out the cuts and bruises that they bear; evidence of a brutal lover who delights in the inflicting of pain.

I have known men such as this. I have killed several. Brutes whose fire is aroused by causing harm to the weak and powerless. The Chieftain rubs his belly, stretching in the morning sun while his men set about their work. I feel no hatred nor ire toward the brute, but only a cool curiosity. In ages past, I may have felt rage toward the object of my incarceration, but it seems that time has tempered such desires within me.

The women are accosted on their return to the Chieftain's tent, their bodies groped and pawed at by brigands as they try to make their way across the compound. It seems to be a daily game, a cruel contest wherein the Chieftain's men are permitted to fondle and accost the women, taking momentary pleasure in their discomfort beneath the watchful eye of the Chieftain himself. The game lasts only a few minutes, for the Chieftain's ire is quickly stirred where the game goes on too long.

"Fucking bastards."

The words come from the adjoining cell, spoken in a soft voice, filled with hate. I turn to see the girl sitting cross-legged at the centre of her cell, staring out at the brutish men with bright anger written heavily across her features. Gone are the tears from the previous night, replaced by a hard resolve.

"If we were back on earth, I'd tear them a fucking new one."

The girl's words are oddly spoken—filled with textures I do not recognize and inflections which make her words strange and foreign to my ears. There is steel beneath those eyes, I can sense it. This is not a helpless child content to wallow in her captivity. Before me sits a girl approaching the dawn of womanhood, a girl who is no stranger to adversity. She turns to me, frowning heavily.

"You got a name?"

Time passes, and it is only after she has turned away that I realize the need for a response. So long have I lived apart from other souls that I have forgotten the mores of common conversation. I clear my throat, speaking words that feel wooden and uncouth in my mouth.

"Kane."

She turns to face me once more. "I'm Daisy."

I nod and she turns back to watch the brigands go about their work.

"So, how we gonna get out of here, Kane?" she asks.

The question forces me to think, and once more I am driven to answer. The sensation is uncomfortable, confronting. It feels as though she is delving into my very soul, wrenching some part of me to the surface with each new word I am forced to utter.

"I have no need of freedom."

She scowls. "What the fuck kind of answer is that, dude? What do you mean do don't need freedom? These fuckers are going to kill you."

I nod.

"Jesus, dude, what the hell is wrong with you? We've gotta get out of here or—"

She stops short, seeing the Chieftain move toward us. The big man walks without haste, rubbing at the fat of his belly. He turns first to my cell, bending down a little to examine me. He grunts.

"The prisoner," he says, grinning. "First and only of your kind. Tell me little man, how did you do it?"

I say nothing.

"When we found you, we thought you barely fit for the slave pens. We travel to and from the outland baronies, you see, and a body such as yours will fetch a meagre sum at the Slaver's market."

He taps a finger to his nose, opening his mouth to show rows of mismatched teeth. "But then we hear word of the prisoner. Escaped from the Red Queen's pit and worth a small fortune in coin. I see the broken shackles at your wrist and realize that we have happened upon a miracle, sure and true. A lucky thing then that we did not kill you on the day we found you."

He waits for a response, but I am done talking. The Chieftain moves to the girl's cell, rubbing at his belly as he leers down.

"You are a pretty thing…"

"Fuck you, fat man!" the girl spits. "You let me out of here, and I'm gonna tear you a new asshole."

The Chieftain laughs, a sickly, booming bellow that causes the other men in the camp to turn and watch. He bends down toward the girl, his expression suddenly dark.

"You are pretty, little one, but not the only treasure I have secured these past weeks. You are too pale and too thin for my liking, nonetheless I will drag you from this cell in three days hence and pluck your flower from dusk until dawn. Once I have taken my pleasure, I will feed you to the men. They will make sport of you for a day or so, until they tire of kneading your flesh. They will take their pleasure until your body is bereft of life. Then, we will feed your corpse to the hounds."

The girl stares with eyes of flint, showing no fear despite the Chieftain's threats. The big man stands, twisting his neck first to the left and then the right and letting out a yawn.

"Three days, little flower."

He turns and leaves us. I watch him walk back to his tent, and soon the morning air is filled with the sounds of rutting and the faint cries of despoiled women. The girl starts to sob again, retreating to a corner of her cell to weep in solitude.

Time passes, and once more I withdraw into myself, seeking the comfort of darkness. I enter the dreamless sleep but can find no peace in it. The girl's sobbing has ceased, yet it still rings out in my mind. I see her face, cowering beneath the Chieftain's frame. Something stirs within, something old and foreign— something forgotten.

In the days that follow, the girl becomes despondent. She does not repeat her plea for aid but sets about attempting to free herself. She digs into the ground with bare fingers, attempting to burrow beneath the crooked frame of her cell. The brutes see the attempt and deliver cruel punishment. They drag her out into the open, stripping off her clothes and whipping her with a switch until she cries out in pain.

I watch the sight with detached curiosity, yet with each new beating the nascent fire within my heart begins to flare. It is an odd sensation to feel the rise of such an empathetic impulse. It is as though a single spark has flared in the ashen frame of an abandoned boiler.

The girl is returned to her cell, where she lies in a fever, silent except for the faint whimpering of her battered body. I cannot help but move closer to the girl. I do not speak, do not attempt to ease her suffering, yet with each passing moment, anger rises within me. I feel less detached from this brutality at the sounds of each sob and whimper. It is as though the girl's suffering has awakened some buried memory, as though she has come to represent some other poor soul whose face and name I can no longer remember, but whose unjust treatment I begin to feel with growing ire.

The third day arrives without fanfare. True to his word, the Chieftain comes for her, ordering a pair of thugs to drag her from the cell and take her to his tent. She struggles, kicks, and screams as they pull her from the cell, fighting to the very last. I catch sight of her eyes as she is dragged away. There is a silent plea nestled within them: a helpless call to action. I open my mouth, intent on speaking but unable to voice the words. I watch as the girl is dragged into the Chieftain's tent, moments before the head man's other women come running out to bathe at the well and endure their own indignities.

Something in the eyes of the Chieftain's women breaks the shackle within my heart. The depthless sorrow, the dying of some inner vitality... I recognize one of the women's faces. She is the kindly mother who fed me and plied my wounds with a healing balm. She is the wife of a merchant who took pity on my wretched frame while I lie dying upon the desert sands of the red wastes.

A cry cuts through the air from the Chieftain's tent. The girl is inside, as is the Chieftain. I feel power press against my chest, drawn from somewhere beyond reason. I grasp at the iron bars of the cell and wrench them aside. They crumple like rotten twigs as I stand to my feet and begin making my way toward the Chieftain's tent. Three brigands witness the act and come at me with sharp knives and dark intentions. That part of my body which remembers the past is reborn. I sidestep the first swipe, moving into the man's chest and grabbing his knife hand while thrusting my elbow hard into his throat. The figure stumbles back, releasing the knife.

I kick out at a second attacker, sending him tumbling backward into a third. I lunge forward, cutting at the man's inner thigh and kicking at the wound, before moving to the third attacker and darting forward to cut at the man's throat. Blood fills the air, flowing freely from newly opened wounds. A dozen more of the brigands have seen the melee and are now fetching weapons and making their advance.

I move toward the Chieftain's tent, setting off at a run. My legs strain beneath the sudden demands of movement, energized by some inner force. Gunfire erupts and bullets hurtle past my ears as I head for the tent. Three or four rifles fire, but I am moving too fast to be caught by their slugs. As I enter the Chieftain's tent, the big man is standing over the girl, naked and growling. Blood is dripping from his left ear, and the girl is spitting obscenities in his direction. Her clothes are torn and bloodied. Her eyes feral.

I do not hesitate but move to drive the knife through the Chieftain's back. He turns as I approach, his vast bulk knocking me aside. The knife falls to the ground, and the big man lumbers toward me, enraged by his encounter with the girl and looking to spill blood. He falls upon me, pressing his considerable bulk against my legs and pinning me in place. He roars, raising fists and slamming them down against my face with terrible force. I struggle to regain my sense, attempting to jab back at the man's torso, but finding only vast swaths of fat.

He continues to pound at my face, and I hear the sound of bones cracking beneath the blows. Something moves behind the brute, and his blows suddenly cease. The Chieftain cries out in pain, twisting aside and reaching for his back. As he turns, I see the girl clinging to the blade driven into his back. She falls aside as the big man turns and manages to rip the knife from his flesh. He advances on her, intent on red murder.

Freed from the Chieftain's bulk, I rise, turning to face a dozen brigands who now pour into the tent. I kick and punch and manage to secure another blade. The girl screams from behind me while I deprive another brute of his weapon. More of the brigands come charging into the tent. From somewhere within I feel another surge of power. The tent is filled with crimson light, and I drive my will against the oncoming horde. Crackling energy fills the tent. There is a loud boom, and the remaining brigands are sent hurtling backward.

I turn to see the Chieftain with his hand around the girl's throat. I advance with twin blades, but something catches my heel, and I am driven to the ground. One of the blades falls free while I cling desperately to the other. A wounded brute batters my chest, bleeding from a wound at his thigh but determined to pummel me to death.

I kick at the man, desperate to free myself. The girl cries out behind me while the Chieftain roars. I kick and thrash, managing to score a blow across the brigand's face and free myself sufficiently to use my remaining blade. I stab down at the figure, through the neck with one, swift strike and turn toward the girl, not bothering to check whether my blow has done its work.

A mountain of flesh topples to the floor, crushing the body of the brute I had stabbed. The Chieftain writhes, clutching at his throat as a river of blood pours forth. I turn to see the girl sitting atop the head man's bed, wearing a grimace and clutching a bloodied blade in one hand. I recognize the blade as that which fell from my left hand during the melee. The girl stares at me with wide eyes.

The Chieftain's men recover themselves and begin pouring into the tent once more. I turn to face them, covered in blood and wielding a large knife in one hand. Crimson power begins to emanate from my wrists, and I feel the rage inside redouble. Whether at the sight of their fallen leader or some other impulse, the brigands back away, moving out of the tent with weapons at the ready.

I head out into the desert with the girl standing by my side, still brandishing the bloodied knife. The other girls, still naked, seize their chance as one of the brigand wagons lumbers off into the dust.

The remaining brutes are unsure whether to go after their escaping quarry or remain and content with the crazed prisoner and the waif who has so recently slain their Chieftain. I hear words rise up from past days as the soldier in me takes control.

"Your Chieftain is dead, bleeding out in his tent."

I motion behind me with one hand, noting that the crimson glow around my shackles seems to have dissipated.

"Who speaks for the clan now?"

There is a moment of indecision as the men look at one another. I can sense them assessing the new hierarchy, tallying up the dead and wounded, seizing what opportunity they can. These are cruel men, each with their own greed and passions. The death of a Chieftain is not a matter for sorrow or bitter reflection. It is an opportunity.

A big man steps forward, rolling his shoulders and eyeing the others of his group with hateful wariness.

"I speak for the clan."

He is about to proclaim further but is cut short by the knife in his back. The big man turns in a fury, lunging out at the diminutive opportunist standing behind him. And, with barely a few words, the brutes are at each other's throats. I and the girl are far from their minds. Now is the time for conquest, for the beating of chests and the assertion of dominance.

I lead the girl, Daisy, to one of the other wagons. I'm please to find some supplies already packed, suggesting that this particular cart was destined for a journey this very day. There is sufficient food for a week's travel and enough water for the same. A few rugs, some rope, and several large knives sit in the back of the cart and the beast to which it is hitched seems agreeable enough.

We make our way into the desert. The girl says nothing and refuses to release her hold on the bloodied knife. I leave her be and drive the wagon on into the red wastes.

***

We travel all day and some ways into the night. The girl says nothing. We head further into the red wastes, driving toward the rising sun and away from the red city. I cannot say what internal mechanism pushes me away from Rust—buried memories perhaps, or some other instinctual impulse. Perhaps it is the Chieftain's words that haunt me. Word has reached these parts of a prisoner who has escaped the Red Queen's dungeon. There will be soldiers out looking for me and a thousand souls willing to trade knowledge for a golden reward.

The girl seems morose, lost in some dark malaise. She will eat and drink when offered sustenance, will respond to simple requests; yet it seems that she mourns a profound loss. I think not that the recent bloodshed with the Chieftain and his brigands is the source of her paralysis. There is some deeper reason, some deeper loss at work here.

It is a curious fact that, while the girl retreats within herself, I find my own mind clearing day by day. The unfettered nature of the red wastes, formerly a source of great distress, no longer causes me tribulation. I feel a strange sense of duty, a sense of purpose which is tied to the girl. I know not whether this protective impulse is born of necessity or whether it reflects some deeper instinct. In truth, the years past are a shadowed country, vague and indistinct. I remember only flashes of insight: an obscured face, a word spoken in hate, the warped images of bloodshed and strife. There is little sense to be made in the hall of memory, yet, in caring for the girl, I find myself somewhat whole again.

On the third day of our sojourn, the girl speaks. She utters meagre words of thanks when I offer her a meal of dried meat and blackroot. We eat in silence, but it is clear that the veil has dropped from her eyes.

"So, what's your deal," she says, biting into the meat with a little more relish than usual.

I clear my throat, unused to conversation. "I…have been imprisoned of late. Kept within the Red Queen's dungeons."

"Red Queen? Who's that?"

I study her face, reading only casual interest. "She is the sovereign of this realm. A cruel and malevolent creature who cares nothing for the souls within her charge. She rules the red city yonder."

I motion toward Rust, a swollen scab in the distant horizon. She nods toward the city, chewing her meat.

"What'd you do to get locked up?"

I cannot help the smile that alights upon my lips. Even as she asks the question, the memories come back to me in a flood. They are spectral, fleeting things, yet the mere act of her asking seems to give them greater form and substance.

"I took part in a rebellion, set against the Red Queen and her allies. We were betrayed and captured. I was sent to the pit for…"

I try to reach through the fabric of memory and decipher the precise length of my incarceration yet without success.

"…for a great time."

"So, you guys tried to kill off the queen, and she locked you up? Tough gig, dude, but at least she didn't kill you. How'd you manage to get out?"

"I cannot say. It is difficult to remember."

Even as I try to lay hands upon the events leading to my newfound freedom, they turn to dust, vanishing before I am able to bring them clearly to mind. We sit for a time, content to eat in silence. I watch the girl as we eat. She takes in our surrounds with keen eyes, yet there is a shroud that hangs above the girl; the weight of loss of whose nature I dare not enquire.

The night passes without incident, yet I feel the eyes of unseen souls watching us from the surrounding darkness. Be they animal or human I cannot say, but the need for sleep has long been lost to me, so I stand vigil through the dark hours.

At dawn, we set off once more into the great wastes. The girl makes no complaint as we ride across the arid land, nor does she enquire as to our destination. We follow the aged path of merchants' wagons that travel from the red city to outlying hamlets: a crooked line of horse tracks and wheel ruts that seems to resist the crimson dusts that sweep across out path night and day.

I learn that the girl has indeed passed from that other world, just as I did so many years ago. She speaks with fondness of a companion from the waking world, a man who acts as kin though he is of no relation to the girl. She recounts the tale wherein she and her companion are sent to apprehend a monstrous foe—a godling much like our Red Queen, though living in the waking world.

It was during their struggle with this foe that the girl was cast into the world of dreams, emerging into the red wastes some distance from Rust and its outlying districts. The girl was set upon up the Chieftain and his brigands before she could come to terms with her predicament.

"I think it happens a lot," the girl says, riding beside me at an easy pace. "There's something about that place that draws people from our world into this desert shithole. That fat prick and his bastards go there once or twice a month, pick up whoever they can find and then cart them off to sell as slaves."

Her voice hardens as she speaks of the Chieftain.

"Judging by the fact that they were all packed and ready to go when I turned up, I'd say they would have missed me if I was a few minutes later. Just my fucking luck."

We ride on, and she continues to speak of her arrival in the Traumwelt and her previous life. The sound brings me comfort though I know not why. I helps, perhaps, that I am not required to make response. She is content to talk when she wishes and to ride on in silence in like fashion—without requiring my participation in either aspect.

In some strange sense, this girl has become a touchstone to me. Having her near, talking about her old world; something about that fact keeps me lucid and at peace. The more time I spend watching over her, the more I feel the darkness within abate.

"Why do you keep doing that?"

The words cut through my contemplation, forcing me to look toward the girl. She rides beside me with a curious expression.

"You keep looking back to that side. What are you looking for?"

A smile alights upon my lips. She is sharp, this one.

"We are being tracked."

"By people?"

I shake my head. "Beasts of some kind. A pack of six or more."

"Some kind of wolves maybe?"

"Perhaps."

Her gaze does not shift. She awaits further response, but I know not what she desires of me.

"So, are they going to attack us? Should we ride faster or start a fire? What?"

I shrug. "They are perhaps curious though I will stand watch this night so that we are ready should they approach."

"Ok and by *approach*, I'm guessing you mean attack? What's your plan then?"

I pull aside the folded blanket that sits between us, revealing the weathered old revolver sitting on the seat.

She looks at the weapon with a puzzled expression.

"Where the hell did you get that from?"

"It was hidden in a small case at the rear of the cart. When we stopped, I found the weapon and decided to keep it close at hand. It may come in handy in the days ahead."

She narrows her eyes. "And you know how to use one of those things?"

I nod. "Provided my hands have not forgotten the lessons of years past."

"You haven't tested it though, so how do you know if it will work?"

I shrug. "It is an old weapon but looks to have been cared for adequately. If the need arises, we will see if it still functions."

"And if it doesn't"

I lay the blanket back over the revolver. "Then it will make a handy club."

"Can you teach me?"

The words hang between us for a time. I am new to this bond between youngling and elder and know not the boundaries of such relationships. I reach back into the barren wastes of memory for some guiding principle but find nothing other than the memories of a soldier and an assassin.

"Yes, I will teach you."

***

The girl learns swiftly. She has a keen eye and seems to know her body well. She takes to the revolver as though born to it, firing with fair precision after only a few hour's practice. She seems to feel the rhythm and rhyme of the weapon, coaxing it beyond its own physical constraints. When we come across a small trading party, we are able to trade a spare cartwheel and several bottles of gut rot for a simple rifle and some ammunition.

I continue teaching the girl, and, after a few more days, she is able to pick off a pebble at a mile, shooting with far greater accuracy than I ever managed to muster. While gifted enough with the revolver, her skill with the rifle is frightful. I have witnessed such things before: the gifts of ether which are given to precious few souls throughout the Traumwelt. It is said that such etheric gifts come from the godlings and the old gods who came before. Whatever the truth of this, it is plain that the girl is indeed gifted.

As we head further southward, I begin to see other signs of strength beyond the bounds of normalcy. No matter the task I set, she seems to work without tiring. She possesses the strength of a man much larger than her tender frame, and there is a certain shimmering that comes into being whenever she exercises her gifts. I cannot put the sensation to name, but I feel a certain rippling in the air when she fires a shot, sets her will against some immovable object. It has the crackling sensation of etheric energy though I can only see its faintest outline.

The days pass, and I begin to teach what little I know of tracking, military tactics, and the craft of survival. As with all other aspects, the girl takes to her lessons with abandon. She learns swiftly, and I am rarely required to repeat an instruction. The work gives us focus and momentum, allowing the girl to forget her sorrows and giving me some foundation upon which I may construct a new sense of self.

"How come you never see them?" the girl asks, pointing out into the night beyond our fire.

"I cannot say for certain. They seem to possess some innate impulse toward secrecy. They blend with the shadows and stay back during the daylight hours."

"But in the morning, you can see their footprints all around our camp?"

I nod.

"That doesn't make any sense. If you're staying awake each night you should be able to see something. Also, how the fuck can you stay awake all night?"

I take a strip of dried meat, easing my back against the crook of a bolder. "I recall rumours of strange beasts who were said to roam these southlands. Creatures of great cunning who hunt in packs by the rising of the moon. The wildlings are said to possess some form of etheric charm which allows them to blend into the night. Only when they strike their prey can they be seen."

The girl, Daisy, takes a strip of meat and begins chewing. "Ok, so how do you kill them then?"

"You wait for the beasts to strike and then strike in return."

"So, you wait until you're bit and hope you can take them out before you run out of blood?"

"Provided we still have wood enough for a fire, I doubt they will be bold enough to attack."

She turns to the small pile of tinder and coal sitting in the back of the cart behind us, frowning darkly.

"So, what you're saying is that we've got another couple of nights before we're screwed, yeah?"

She smiles as she asks the question. Where once there may have been fear in those eyes, I now sense hunger. Having come to terms with the brutal realities of this world, she has begun to long for violence—perhaps for the chance to strike back at the Traumwelt.

"We still have two or three nights of firelight. Then, unless we are able to secure another source of fuel, we shall be forced to trap and kill the wildlings."

"You gonna do your magic mojo trick with those shackles?"

She points to the irons that still hang from my wrists. It forces me to look down at the pitted iron bonds. I confess, they feel too much a part of me to be rid of.

"You will kill the wildlings yourself," I answer. "You have learned the use of firearms and a little of hand-to-hand combat. On the morrow, I will teach you how to wield a knife. Then, when the wildlings attack, you will put all that you have learned into practice."

"Sounds like a plan, Stan. Been itching to—"

Her reply is cut short by a strange apparition to the south. Her eyes grow wide as she points over my shoulder. A mechanical contraption, the likes of which I have never laid eyes upon, comes into focus no more than fifty feet or so from our camp. Rumbling like some brutish beast of burden, the creature sings its curious song, a brightly hued totem spinning atop the beast while its wheels slowly turn.

"You've gotta be kidding me!" the girl cries out, standing to her feet.

My hands move instinctively to the purloined firearm taken from the Chieftain and his men. It is an oddly weighted weapon, far removed from the shooting irons to which I am accustomed, yet the feel of cold metal against my palm offers some assurance.

The strange mechanized creature lumbers forward, still singing its strangely melodic tune as it grows steadily less substantial.

"I mean, what are the fucking odds?" The girl moves toward the metallic beast, despite the hand I raise in caution.

As she approaches the apparition, it fades from sight, becoming more and more insubstantial. A ghost of its former self. Light flickers around the mechanized beast, illuminating the shimmering white surface of its metallic hide. In the moments before the apparition vanishes, music blooms across the red wastes, a joyful jig played on high-pitched bells. The girl turns, her face beaming.

"An ice cream van!" she says. "What the hell would an ice cream van be doing all the way out here?"

"You have seen such a mechanical beast before?"

She grins. "It's a van, a type of car. Like a horse and cart but much more modern. We drive around in them where I'm from."

She motions over her shoulder. "That was an ice cream van. They use it to sell ice cream to kids. There's usually a creepy dude in a white apron in there... Wait, you don't know what ice cream is, do you?"

"I do not."

She shakes her head. "Jesus, we've got some catching up to do, old man. Suppose it doesn't matter anyway, the van's gone. How the hell did that even happen?"

I take a breath, attempting to organize my thoughts in a manner which will make some sense.

"This world is a thing of curious substances. It is formed partly by the dream matter of those who sleep within the waking world. The various material aspects of the world are bound together by the influence of the godlings, chiefly the Red Queen. While much of the Traumwelt is stable in form and structure, much is not. What you have witnessed is one such apparition."

She looks at me blankly, and what follows is a lengthy discussion in which I attempt to explicate the form and nature of the Traumwelt. I succeed only in adding further confusion and finally decide to leave the matter.

We see further apparitions that night: a rocky cairn, covered in brilliant green moss, a clutch of large spears laced with the bones of fallen foes, a domed dwelling which the girl identifies as a "tent," and several illusory apparitions which defy definition. The further we travel from the city Rust, the more prevalent such apparitions seem to be.

I sense the coming and going of wildling beasts throughout the night but see no physical sign of their passing, as usual. As the day dawns, I continue the girl's tutelage, offering further instruction on the use of blades and the rending of life. She learns swiftly, but there is hesitation in her eyes. Perhaps the knowledge of what must come next has set her mind at edge? Perhaps the memory of that blood she has already shed still haunts her?

I do not hide the task ahead nor does she baulk from the duty. Our fuel is almost at an end, and there are no supply wagons or settlements in sight. The wildlings will come and, with no fire to fend them off, we will need to fight.

On the night when our kindling supplies are finally spent, we eat in silence, and she clutches a blade in one hand, at all times. I do not know when nor precisely how the wildlings will attack. I suspect that they will circle their pray for a time, braying and snapping with tooth and claw in an effort to force flight. The paw marks left in the dust each morning suggest beasts with some affinity to wolves, and it is this suggestion which prompts me to think they will prefer to attack an enemy in flight.

"You will need to stand your ground. Force them to attack you," I instruct the girl.

She spears a piece of dried meat with the tip of her dagger and slips it distractedly into her mouth. She chews mechanically, her mind on the task ahead.

"They will try to draw you out, but you must resist. When they do attack, they will do so tentatively, with a swift snap of the jaw. Two or three will strike in quick succession, so you will need to move quickly once the first beast makes its move. Strike out with all your force, moving into the blow, rather than away from it. You must bury your blade deep within the beast's chest. Deal the death blow if you can. Cause it sufficient damage to render it unable to attack again if that is all you can manage."

"And what if one of its friends hits me from behind while I'm going for the bastard's throat?"

I stand, lunging forward to demonstrate the movement. "If your movement is sufficiently swift and forceful, you will cut off the secondary attack. They may strike a glancing blow against your back or side, but nothing of consequence. Strike swiftly, driving the dagger blade deep, then turn and rip the knife from the first, turning to face the others."

"Ok, then what do I do?"

I cannot help the cruel smile that alights on my lips. "Kill the pack before they kill you."

To her credit, the girl shows no signs of fearing the prospect. I sense the steel in her heart as she resolves to face an unknown enemy with naught but a pair of rusted blades. Once more I am struck by the strength of the girl. I determine not to tell her the truth of the matter—that I will rend flesh and spill blood this night also. She need only kill the first, and I will tend to the others.

"Remind me again why we can't just use the guns?" she asks.

"Because I do not fancy a bullet in the leg or chest, youngling. In the daylight hours, the firearms would be weapons of choice. In darkness, against a pack of hounds, such weapons will likely do more harm than good."

There is some truth to my words, but she senses the lie there as well. The rifle may prove too cumbersome in pitch black, but there is no reason I couldn't use the revolver. In truth, I have taken to training the girl and intend to use this attack as an opportune lesson. What better way to understand the pressures and challenges of battle than in the heat of a bloodied melee?

We finish the meal, and the girl sets herself in readiness. Hours pass, and apparitions come and go with haphazard irregularity. I feel the girl growing steadily more tired, her senses dulled by her body's need for sleep. Yet, at each moment when sleep threatens to take her, she redoubles her efforts. She stands, pacing about the camp, squatting to the earth and performing strange movements borrowed from a world I know not.

The so-called "exercises" bring clarity and ward against drowsiness. I am reminded of my time in the trenches, where men developed cruel and unusual means of performing this self-same feat. Some would cajole one another with sharp slaps to the cheek, or the twisting of ears and noses. Others would ingest ever-increasing quantities of bitter herbs, forcing their stomachs to burn for a time but rendering them a little more alert when the need arose.

I sense the attack moments before it happens, feeling the ether swell and pulse as the wildlings approach. I count five or six in their number. They are larger than wolves, sharing more in common with the hyena or some long-lost derivation of the beast though of larger size. The girl's eyes grow suddenly wide and her muscles tense, the blade in her hand jutting outwards like a fang.

I feel my own heartbeat quicken and sense the etheric power swell within me. The shackles at my wrist begin to glow with crimson light, perhaps in anticipation of the bloodshed which will follow. I know not how the dark gift works nor what agency it is that thrusts the power upon me. Yet, as violence threatens, I feel the dark power with absolute certainty. The weight of that invisible force crushes me, yet there is comfort in that self-same crushing—the familiarity of the pit.

The beasts circle, braying and snapping with barely visible jaws. They tease and tempt, staying out of reach but growing bolder with each passing moment. The girl stays her course, crouching with the knife poised to strike. I ready myself as the first beast attacks. Though fear is written heavily across her face, the girl stays true to her duty. The moment she sees the first beast lunge, she darts forward, driving the blade toward the beast's torso.

The creature lets out a bitter cry as steel plunges into the wildling flesh. Blood gushes from the wound, but as the beast retreats, the girl loses her grip upon the knife. She spins, preparing to face the next attack and giving up the knife as lost. Something keeps me from intervening. Etheric power floods through my body. I feel it bringing unnatural strength and have no doubt that I could make short work of the remaining wildlings; and yet, I hold back.

I throw my own blade at the girl's feet and, without missing a step, she scoops up the weapons and crouches in anticipation of the next attack. Two of the beasts lunge at her from behind. The girl swipes her blade across their muzzles, driving them back a step. The gruesome howls of their dying companion have taught the beasts to respect the steel fang.

Four beasts surround the girl, feinting back and forth, seeking some easy path to victory. She holds her knife outstretched, balling her free hand into a bloodied fist. The next attack comes too swiftly for the girl to counter. Wildlings attack from front and back. The girl chooses her foe and drives toward the closest wildling, driving her blade into its throat and withdrawing the knife at speed. She kicks out at the wildling behind, scoring a light blow against the beast's face and swinging wildly as a third and fourth wildlings snap at her from the flanks.

They circle her again, the first of their number now dead, laying somewhere in the darkness beyond camp with the girl's blade still buried in its chest. They alter their strategy, content to circle the girl, waiting for an opportune moment to strike, aware that there are many hours yet to pass before the rising of the sun. They will rely on attrition to take its toll; stabbing at her from the outer circle and scoring minor victories that will eventually leave her weak and unable to defend against a consolidated attack.

I see this realization in her eyes. She sees her doom as clearly as the wildlings that circle her. She must act, must draw them into action. The girl moves slowly toward the felled beast, waiting patiently for the circle of wildlings to accompany her, slashing wildly when the beasts draw too close. She stumbles against something: the twitching remains of the first wildling.

Beneath the faint glimmer of distant stars, or whatever passes for them in this retched place, the girl bends down and pulls the blade from the beast's chest. All the while, she keeps her eyes alert and knife raised toward the circling predators.

It takes the bulk of her strength to dislodge the knife from the dead wildling's fallen body. She stumbles back a few paces, falling hard to the ground as the knife gives way. She cries out, pawing at her leg in desperation. I see what the wildings cannot. The way her right leg is coiled beneath her body, ready to drive her forward at a moment's notice; the manner in which she drops the knife hilt into the desert sand, twisting the hilt and covering its slick surface with grit so as to make it easier to hold. She sits, slumped over her ankle, eyes downcast.

Clever, little one. Very clever.

The wildlings fail to recognize the ruse, two of their kind lunging toward the girl from behind. Before they are able to strike, she drives herself upwards, slashing with both knives toward the oncoming attackers. She scores a glancing blow to the first but manages to cut some vital artery with the second. Blood gushes from the wound, but both wildlings press their attack. They pounce upon her, driving the girl to the ground, jaws snapping at her throat while she tries desperately to hold them at bay, punching and slicing with all her remaining strength. The final two wildlings move in to put an end to the fight.

It is an easy thing to advance upon the beasts. They seem unaware of my presence despite the many nights I have stayed vigil over our camp. I feel the power flare as I lay hands upon the first of the wildlings, crushing the beast's skull and tossing it into the fray, knocking the others backward. The second beast is more cautious, and I am forced to snatch up the creature's leg, dragging it to ground and stomping on the wildling's head with a sickening thud.

Still struggling with her foes, the girl manages to drive her blade through the flank of a third wildling. The creature howls in pain, limping from the fight with legs that no longer respond to its master. The last wildling flees without a backward glance, driven off into the wilds by the death of its kin. I offer a hand to the girl, but she stands without my aid—bloodied and shaking, but determined. She is covered in blood and has suffered several cuts and bite marks.

She advances on the last wildling, limping in circles with one leg useless at its side and a nasty gash at one eye. She falls onto the beast's side and drives both blades into the creature's neck, drawing the beast close into a deathly embrace. The fall to the ground together, and the creature convulses beneath the girl's bloodied frame. Once all is done and the beast ceases its laboured breathing, she stands to her feet, still holding the knives.

She wears a triumphant expression, her hands now shaking with the fury of battle. The blades fall from her hands as she looks up at me. Tears begin streaming from her eyes, blood dripping from wounds at her arms and legs. I walk to her, pulling her close as she weeps.

"You've done well, little one," I offer, feeling her sob against my chest. "You are the shadow and the fang— death in darkness."

She does not hear the words and continues her weeping. Once more I am reminded of the strange clarity this youngling has gifted me. Only days earlier I was but a shell of a man, a wastrel pining for the pit. It seems that in this strange, orphaned world, we two souls have found solace amid the bloodied remains of the wilder beasts.

8. Tull's Haven

As we travel further south, the makeshift trail grows steadily more pronounced, its surface compacted by the treading of horse hooves and wagon wheels. The apparitions that have haunted our days, and nights begin to dwindle. Here and there small homesteads can be seen off in the distance, hinting at signs of life as fields of blueroot and fellweed begin to blossom to either side.

We encounter other travellers along the path: merchants and tinkerers, farmers with wagons laden with strange produce, hired thugs that guard their masters with ill-kept weapons and brutish minds. Small hills and escarpments begin to rise in the distance, cut from the same red clay that fills the wastelands to the north but interspersed here and there with spindly shrubs and crooked-limbed trees. Creatures that might be a blend of hare and armadillo scurry from their burrows to snatch up scampering lizards or insects.

There is a dull noise hanging in the air as we head further south though I cannot place its origin. The path dips steadily downward, as though we are making a long decent into some vast crater. More and more buildings spring up as we make our decent; strange dwellings made from the clay itself, which has been heaped atop circular abodes with small windows cut into the walls.

"You been here before?" the girl asks.

I shrug. "Perhaps. But, if so, the memory has been lost to me."

"Ok, so what's our plan then? We just passing through, or are we gonna try and settle down here?"

I still find the texture of her voice somewhat perplexing. I find it difficult to tell whether she asks in earnest or in jest. There is a constant tilt to her lips which taints every truth with a lie and causes me to doubt her sincerity. And yet, I sense no deception in her words, only an inflection I cannot place.

"We require food for the journey ahead. We may have to ply some service in this township to earn sufficient stores to last several months."

"Yeah, but where are we headed? Have you got a plan, or at least some idea where we're going?"

I cannot voice the impulse within the urgent desire to be far from the red city and the Queen's pit. It drives me onward, yet I cannot pinpoint its source. This is not simply the desire to be far from the site of my imprisonment nor the fear that I will once more be apprehended by the Queen's agents and incarcerated. There is some darker, more urgent force at work; a force which I can neither name nor fully comprehend.

"We head south until we reach The Unravelling. Then, perhaps we may settle."

"The Unravelling, hey? Damn, that sounds inviting. It's all cocktails and Jacuzzis down there at The Unravelling. Not ominous at all."

I don't bother speaking further on the matter. In truth, the notion has only now come to me. I know nothing of that realm other than snatches of rumour and misinformation. It is far to the south, beyond the baronies of Rust where permanent cities and settlements give way to the ethereal and ever-changing. A dangerous realm, to be sure, but perhaps furthest from the Red Queen's eye.

Our horse stumbles upon a rock as we descent further down the long path, shaking its head in consternation. Two days have passed since we offered the last of our water to the beast, and I fear that exhaustion may soon take it. We must find water and food, swiftly.

The horse stumbles a second time, and I am forced to pull the cart to a halt. I guide the creature off the path toward a nearby homestead from which the sounds of laughter can be heard. Half a dozen horses are tethered to a railing outside the building. As we draw close, I see that this is more a tavern than a simple homestead. Through grimy windows, I see that the interior of the building is interspersed with tables and chairs, half filled with revellers drinking what must be their local ale.

"Take the horse and let it drink," I instruct the girl, motioning to a trough to one side of the building.

She begins unhitching the animal, and I make my way inside the tavern. A few folks turn as I walk through the door, their hard eyes lingering only momentarily upon my frame before returning to their drink and revelry. Most I judge as farmers or merchants, but several bear weapons and have the look of hired guards. I walk to the rear of the hall, toward a portly fellow with a bristling beard and genial eyes.

"Welcome to Tull's Haven, friend," the barman says with a meagre grin. "Can I fetch you some ale?"

I shake my head, motioning toward the door. "We have a horse and cart. The beast is hard ridden and in need of water, food, and rest."

The barman nods thoughtfully, his gaze falling to the shackles at my wrists. He leans out a nearby window, inspecting the horse as the girl leads the beast to the trough.

"The beast looks a little worse for wear. So too the cart. What do you want for the pair?"

I shrug. "A little food and drink, some coin or whatever passes for currency in these parts."

I point to the gun belt hanging from a peg behind the bar. "And those."

He turns, pointing to the gun belt and double irons nestled in their holsters.

"We'll, I can see about some coin and a little supper, sure I can. But these here pistols aren't for sellin' see. Got some sentimental value."

Something stirs within me, the strange movement of etheric forces. I feel the shackles at my wrist grow suddenly cold. They begin to glow with a blue tint, and I sense the dishonesty in the other man's voice. I cannot say how I know it, but his words taste false to my ears. He intends to barter for the highest possible price and will not give up the weapons until he is satisfied with the exchange.

"Those irons," I say, pointing behind the bar, "are your prized possession?"

The barman's eyes seem to glaze over. He answers woodenly, as though unaware of the full meaning of his own words.

"No, sir. Best pair are out back. Worth a small fortune for thems that want 'em, but I hadn't thought to sell the pair today."

"Get them for me."

The other man nods, walking out toward a small storeroom around back and returning after several minutes with a simple wooden box. I open the catch and inspect the weapons. They're of a make and model I do not know but expertly crafted and well weighted. Nestled within the wooden box is a bandolier belt and twin holsters. A smaller box inside the other holds what must be a hundred rounds or so. I undo the makeshift belt and aged revolver taken from the Chieftain and his brutes, laying the weapon on the benchtop and sliding it toward the barman.

He stares down at the worn revolver with a puzzled expression as I pick up the new gun belt. The smell of oiled leather kisses my nostrils as I buckle the belt in place. I feel a strange sense of wholeness accompany the familiar weight of the belt and pick up each of the shooting irons.

"These weapons are in working order, yes?" I ask.

He nods.

"Do you have a rifle to trade?"

He shakes his head.

"Fine, then I will take what dried meat, bread, and water you can spare, plus sufficient coin to buy lodgings in the city yonder for a month or so. You may take ownership of the horse and cart out front as well as this weapon." I point to the pilfered revolver. "Are we in agreement?"

The tender nods woodenly, confusion written heavily about his face. He sets about gathering supplies and packing them into a large satchel. All the while, my shackles glow with a slight blue tinge, cold to the touch as they perform their strange etheric task.

I find myself just as puzzled as the barman by the whole affair. I am capable of persuasive argument when the need arises, but this is something wholly different. From what source have my shackles absorbed these strange abilities? What are their limits and scope? More troubling still, what intelligence grants these gifts and what service to they expect in return?

I push back against the thoughts, letting the shackles do their work as the barman hands over a sizable sack of food and a small coin purse with roughly cut coins nestled within. I thank the barman for his time and exit the tavern, signalling for the girl to leave the horse and follow. She takes only the clothes on her back, the knives at her belt, and the rifle as we continue on down the road.

9. The Arena

The path dips dramatically, falling into a large valley, overshadowed by towering rock on every side. A thousand clay dwelling spring up from the ground, clustered tightly together as though fearful of solitude. The large road widens, splitting into a dozen smaller paths which are filled with people of all colours and creeds. The common folk wear plain tanned robes and various head wrappings of brilliant colour. There are hues of purple and bright yellow, pinks and greens, all tarnished by the ever-present crimson dust that flows in from the surrounding wastes.

The people of this hamlet walk with purpose, as though the devil himself drives their work. Yet they seem content in their bustling. Several of the merchant class are surrounded by slaves in thick iron collars, their heads shaven and branded with scars of ownership. The slaves walk naked, but for a slim cloth about their loins and a coloured sash through ear or shoulder held in place by rings of brightly polished bronze. So it is that those merchants who boast bright yellow colours in their turbans, mark their slaves with thin sashes of the same hue.

The girl does not voice her disapproval, yet I see the distain written plainly across her face. Whether due to her recent incarceration or as a simple matter of principle, she abhors the sight of so many slaves.

"A man once told me," I offer, "you cannot fight a world."

She turns to me, frowning deeply.

"I mean to say, there are some battles we are able to fight and some which are beyond us. The cruelties and injustices of this world are vast. We must choose our battles wisely and fight where we can win."

"Sounds like a cop-out, dude. I don't think it's right to pussy out just because things might get sticky."

I see the steel behind her eyes and remember feeling that self-same resolve. Long years have passed since such idealism bloomed in my heart.

"We are sojourners in this land and must respect its customs lest we risk a fight we cannot hope to win." I motion to a nearby group of slaves, bound hand and foot and led by a corpulent woman with brilliant emerald adornments upon her person.

The girl nods. "We're not here to free the slaves, yeah I get it, dude. It's just, shit, it's kinda hard to see it up close, you know. Also, wasn't that long ago and we were both headed here—or worse."

The girl speaks truth, and I offer no words of rebuttal. The sight of so much slavery rankles my own spirit as well. In my mind's eye, I see Griff shaking his head. *You cannot fight a world.*

We move on through the city, toward a vast arena which seems to occupy pride of place at the very centre of the mammoth bowl into which this hamlet has been seeded. Banners of different hues line the outer shell of the vast area, fluttering in the breeze, each standing higher than a dozen men.

People flood to the arena from the surrounding streets and dwellings. Many are accompanied by several house slaves. Many such folk walk alone. There is a buzz in the air. A sense of tremendous anticipation. I begin to see guards of a sort, stationed at the entrances to the grand arena. They are clothed in simple leather armour, each wielding a simple short-sword and buckler.

"Seems a bit odd, doesn't it?" the girl asks, pointing toward a pair of guardsmen.

I swiftly clutch her hand, gently guiding it downward so as to avoid suspicion. I move the girl away from the guards, down toward a vast archway to one side of the arena.

"In my experience," I offer, "it is rarely advisable to point at guardsmen."

She frowns. "Yeah, I supposed. It's just, doesn't it strike you as a little weird that the guards here have swords and shit?"

"I do not understand your question," I reply, watching the guards from the corner of one eye. Their attention seems fixed upon the large milling crowds.

"I just think it's weird. Kind of like that old saying about bringing a knife to a gun fight?"

She points to the irons at my belt.

"Why are those guys armed with swords when there are guns around? I mean, what are they gonna do if they get in the shit with some bastard who has a six shooter?"

I smile as understanding dawns. Many years ago, in a different life and a different world, I might have asked that very same question. While Griff might have slapped me for such a query, I have in mind a different form of instruction for the girl.

"Bladed weaponry can be remarkably effective in close-quarter combat. It is more likely that guards in a hamlet such as this would use short swords or daggers rather than shooting irons. Besides, the blades make an effective show of force without having been drawn."

She tilts her head to one side, eyes fixed upon me.

"Still a bit weird though, yeah?"

I nod. "Perhaps. But there could be a simpler explanation. Firearms are expensive tools in this world. They required careful maintenance and a steady supply of ammunition. Swords must simply be kept keen and clean. It may be a simple matter of cost? Or it may be that the sovereign in this land prefers their city guard to brandish sword and buckler rather than rifle or revolver?"

She taps the hilt of one of the knives in her belt. "Yeah, but why not both?"

Before I can respond, we are jostled by the incoming crowd. The streets have swelled so that even the back alleys are filled with people. The girl is swallowed by the tumult and carried toward the hulking stone gateway at the side of the arena.

I follow, trying to press my way through the crowd but only managing to catch up to the girl when we are already inside the arena. She reaches out and grabs my arm, pulling me close as we are driven toward the layered seating which lines the circumference of the vast structure.

"Jesus, it's like Black fucking Friday up in here!" the girl yells as we are dragged further into the press.

Amid the sudden mass of humanity, I feel a growing sense of unease. I feel the eyes of each person as a burning brand upon my flesh. Something claws at my skin, pawing at me from the tumult. I feel the power rise within me, dark and all-consuming. A black hunger that longs to devour, to bring silence to a world rife with flesh and blood and—

"You ok, boss?"

The girl's hands upon my wrist are an anchor, brining me back from the cusp of the abyss. She walks ahead of me, guiding me by the hand through the throng, past great clots of humanity, up a stone staircase; up, up, and higher still, nesting among the highest rows of stone benches that command an expansive view of the arena below. Only when we are seated does the girl release her grip. She leans close toward me, inspecting my eyes with concern and interest.

I offer up a smile as meagre thanks. The swelling of darkness within me has abated for the moment, but it troubles me that such a simple thing could ignite the dark passions within. Once more I see the value in this young woman who has called me back from the precipice.

"I am well, Daisy," I say with all the confidence I can muster.

"What happened back there? You were freakin' out."

I sit for a time, breathing in air thick with red dust and the smoke of cook-fires. There is another scent in the air: the metal tang of spilt blood.

"It has been some time since I have had to endure the company of so many souls. It is…troubling."

She nods. "Yeah, you got yourself some classic PTSD there, chum. Need to get yourself a therapist, stat."

The words are lost to me, but her sentiment is clear. Once more I find myself indebted to this young girl from a world not my own.

"Citizens of Tullhaven," a voice calls out above the din. "The Grand Collector bids you glad tidings and rich bounty."

The girl points to a small balcony on the far side of the arena. A short figure dressed in flamboyant robes is speaking into a mechanized contraption which seems to amplify his voice to thunderous proportions. In the private platform behind the figure, there sits a monstrously fat man, reclining upon a cushioned palanquin. A score of salves surround the corpulent figure, their muscled bodies glistening with gold paint that reflects light with painful severity. Others surround the sovereign: smaller figures coated in silver and bronze. They wait upon the mammoth figure, supplying food and drink while his emissary continues his speech.

"We gather on this most auspicious day to make preparations for the blood gala and fight for honour and rich reward."

A loud cheer rises from the crowd, many of whom are still entering the arena and making their way to seats. The girl turns to a short woman sitting nearby and strikes up a conversation while the speaker continues his speech.

"Prepare yourselves, citizens! Gird your hearts and put forth your very best, for only the victor shall be rewarded."

Another cheer erupts from the crowd as the figure turns and shuffles toward his rotund master, inclining an ear with overzealous deference. He returns to the balcony once more, raising his hands to either side.

"Citizens, I bring exquisite tidings! The High Lord Tull, Great Collector and Primordial Sovereign has granted a special boon. A thousand chits will be awarded to the victor of this day's supplication."

The crowd erupts, and the speaker is forced to wait while the noise dies down.

"More than this," he goes on, "the sponsor of each male and female victor will take their place within the Collector's Court."

The noise that bursts forth from the crowd at this point is deafening. The ruler's emissary does not bother continuing. He simply turns to his master, bows low to the ground, and takes his place at the large figure's side. The roaring of the crowd continues for several moments, punctuated with the occasional fire of gunshot. Once more I feel the press of people around me: a disquieting sensation which threatens to awaken the darkness I harbour within.

Once more the girl's touch brings me back from the tempting darkness.

"Ok, so the old lady there tells me that this is some kind of fighting contest. The fat dude over there is Tull. Rules this city and some of the areas around here. He's big on the whole slavery thing and likes to have these big contests once a month to keep the punters happy."

She points to the pouch hanging from my belt. "Can I see that?"

I hand her the pouch, and she pulls a single chit from the bag, examining the flat bone disc with a mixture of disgust and fascination. She holds it up to me, leaning forward so that her words are not overheard.

"You see this? It's like the official currency over her. They make it by cutting down bones in the arms and legs of dead humans."

She points to the arena floor below.

"Fuckers are going to kill each other down there, and, when it's all done, that fat bastard will have the bones cut up to make more money. That's how it works here apparently. Some kind of annual festival which they kick off with a death battle in the arena down there. The poor guys who lose get turned into fucking coins!"

I nod. "So, a thousand chits is a handsome sum?"

"No, dude, you're missing the point. They're going to force slaves to kill each other while these fuckers just watch. It's worse than what the fucking Romans did. Once it's all done, they're gonna cut the poor fuckers up and use them as *money*. Also, it gets worse. Once the fight's over, that fat fuck over there has all the dead people roasted and then he fucking *eats* them."

I take the chit from her and slip it back into the pouch.

"We need to get the fuck out of here, boss. I can't watch these fuckers kill each other."

I motion to the crowds, now beginning to sit upon the steps of the arena. Every nook and corner of the arena is filled. Down below, the guards stand watch beside large iron doors, now closed and locked.

"We have little choice."

The girl tries to protest, but her eyes see just as clearly as mine. We have wandered into the hornet's nest and cannot make our escape until this business is done.

A loud trumpet call rings out across the arena, sending the crowd into an ecstatic frenzy. From above, a small orb descends, obscuring the midday sun. As the orb descends it takes the form of a large air balloon; its bulk is bound with large ropes that hold a small sailing vessel aloft. Blades of crude metal spin to either side of the airship, cranked by strange engines which belch smoke and hiss steam.

The craft hovers above the arena, releasing several smaller vessels, which drift gently toward the crowd. The miniature craft are only a little larger than a handspan, evincing the same propellers as the larger ship but in smaller detail. From each craft hangs a long crimson banner. Three such craft descend to different sections of the arena. Their movement is smooth and subtle, yet it seems to lack precision. The swirling eddies of wind that spiral about the interior of the arena drive the smaller aircraft this way and that, such that their final destination is a matter of pure chance.

When the first of the three craft lands—its trailing banner striking the head of an aged merchant with a bright blue turban—the crowd erupts once more. The old man bows in the direction of the balcony where his corpulent Lord sits. He makes a gesture with one hand and taps the largest of his slaves on the shoulder. From this distance I cannot make out the slave's features though he seems of strong build and well-muscled. Towering over those around him, the brute makes his way down toward the arena floor, to the accompanying cheers of the crowd.

Two more slaves are selected, and both are led to the arena floor. The ruler of this hamlet seems utterly unconcerned with the events that now transpire. He lies upon his oversized bed, gorging himself on delicacies and luxuriating in the lavish attentions of his gilded slaves. At a raised hand from his emissary, the slaves gathered below are given their leave by the soldiers. From the larger ship above, a basket is lowered into the centre of the arena floor. The glint of steel flickers from the basket as it falls hard to the earth, its ties to the ship above severed.

"They've got no choice," the girl says, shouting in my ear above the din. She points to the old woman next to her. "She says that the soldiers just kill them if they don't fight. They've gotta try to kill each other, or they'll all end up dead. If one of them survives then they get to fight again the next time; so, you're kind of fucked either way. She says there are about fifty of these before it's over."

So many souls killed for the pleasure and petty advancement of the rabble, while their portly sovereign looks on with disinterest. Is this what the southern wastes holds then? Needless bloodshed and barbarity. More of the same, it seems.

"Tull!" the girl calls out.

"Pardon?"

"The fat bastard that runs the show here. His name is Tull. She says he's a godling, like that Red Queen bitch."

The word cuts far deeper and more quickly than I would have imagined. I force myself to nod. I cannot say why I had supposed this particular settlement would be without a godling benefactor. There are dozens scattered throughout the Traumwelt, many of whom do not see eye to eye with the Red Queen.

"She says he's a kind of sorcerer or something like that. Says he can't be killed, and he's got some kind of wicked power."

I stare across the arena, unable to make out the godling's features. I know not this Tull, yet I know his kind and cannot help but set my will against him for that fact. If he is allied with the Red Queen, we are in grave danger. If not, he warrants a wary eye, nonetheless.

"Anything that lives can be killed," I say, still staring out toward the godling Tull.

The girl shrugs. Her reply is cut short but the sudden rise in shouting. In the sands below the three slaves take up arms; pawing desperately at the weapon basket and striking at one another the moment steel and iron are pulled free. The fight is over quickly. The crimson merchant's man is far more skilled with the blade and taller than his opponents. He draws a long spear and uses its length to good advantage, felling the first of his competitors in seconds and finishing the strike by plunging the spear into the man's chest.

The second opponent is more cautious. He has managed to acquire a small leather buckler and short sword. He circles the crimson warrior warily, swiping out here and there as if in warning.

"See the large man?" I ask, unable to resist the impulse to teach.

She nods, forcing herself to look despite the displeasure it brings her.

"See how he does not waste his strength on needless feints? He waits, he watches. The other man has grown used to his opponent's lethargy. He will make his move shortly."

No sooner have I spoken the words than the shorter of the two men darts forward, cutting at the larger brute's legs and driving forward with wild strokes of the short sword. The other man steps aside, thrusting his spear forward with a viper's speed, cutting into sword wielder's thigh before withdrawing the spear to circle around his victim. The swordsman cries out. Blood gushes from the wound as he staggers and slumps to the ground.

"The spearman knows that he does not need to deal the death blow in one move. He needs only to injure his opponent, to weaken the man with a few well-placed jabs of that spear."

The swordsman slashes out at his opponent, half kneeling, half standing while blood continues to pour from his wound. The tall spearman skips three paces at speed, his spear lancing out to cut a blow across the other man's upper arm. The wound is not fatal, but now blood flows from two places, and the swordsman's swings are growing weak and careless. It takes one more strike of the spear to render the swordsman senseless. Too weak to mount an adequate defence, he lies back in the sand, awaiting swift death as his opponent towers above. The fight is over with one swift thrust to the heart.

Cheers erupt from all around the arena. The blue-turbined merchant dances for joy, receiving hearty congratulations and looks of jealousy from those around him. Chits exchange hands all across the arena as bets are paid and profits made. The merchant receives a pouch of coins, delivered by arena guardsmen. He hefts the prize above his head, remembering only belatedly to turn to the godling Tull and offer a deep bow.

"Fucking sick," the girl spits.

"That it may be, but there are lessons to be learned here, little one. If we must endure the sight of such wanton slaughter, then we should learn its lessons at the very least."

The next choosing commenced immediately, miniature craft drifting through the crowds to land upon three figures. To our right, one of the crafts selects a burly figure dressed in black. The slave he selects is mountainous—a brute of enormous size and dark countenance. He towers above the guardsmen who lead him to the arena floor, dark muscles rippling across his back as he takes his place. The other two combatants take what weapons they can find and prepare themselves, facing the spearman with obvious intent.

A cry comes out from the crowd; the owner of the dark-skinned barbarian raises his voice to be heard, turning toward the pavilion and making a show of his proclamation.

"Lord Tull, I give you a rare gift this day. Behold, I offer Rook the Wrathhammer, greatest of my slaves and a warrior without equal. He will win this day's fight and bring great honour to your name, Lord Tull."

He raises a hand toward the dark-skinned brute standing on the arena floor below. The crowd grows curiously quiet, all eyes turning to the slovenly godling lying upon his palanquin. A single, grotesquely corpulent hand rises from the godling's bed, a sign of two raised fingers made for all to see. The crowd erupts at the sight, and the black-clad merchant bows with a wide grin.

"What the fuck was that about?" the girl asks.

"This Rook is his champion. By claiming the victory at this early stage, this merchant seeks to raise his honour higher. If his man should succeed, he may secure even greater wealth and prowess for the victory."

"What if he dies on his ass?"

I shrug. "Then equal shame will fall upon the merchant and his house."

As the fight commences, the figure named Rook does not take up a weapon. He stands casually, twisting his arms to the left and right as though limbering up for what lay ahead. Two sword-bearers attack the spearman at once, reasoning that he is their greatest threat. The pair are not without skill, but they do not fight well together.

"He will wait for an opportunity as before. See how the swordsmen do not strike in unison? They hamper one another when they should be working in concert."

The spearman seizes his opportunity, swiping the butt of his spear across the face of the first swordsman and twisting with speed to slice the blade of the spear through the gut of the other. Before either foe can recover, the spearman delivers deep cuts to their legs and abdomen; finishing them off with dreadful ease as he turns his attention to Rook. The giant appears to have finished his stretching. He bows gently as his foe approaches, an odd

gesture which brings to mind the chivalry of ages past—
something out of place in this wretched world.

"Why hasn't the big guy got a weapon?" the girl asks.

"I suspect it is because he does not need one."

The spearman circles his foe, and Rook does not
bother to spin around as the other moves to his back.
The spearman jabs forward experimentally but garners
no reaction from the dark-skinned brute.

"If this is as I suspect," I offer, "Rook will defeat the
spearman in one swift blow. By doing thus without
weaponry, he strikes fear into the hearts his opponents
and drives up the value of his master's bet."

The spearman moves in close, jabbing a mere finger
width from the brute's flesh. Rook does not react.

"See how the spearman has been forced into the weaker
position? He must act first; must initiate the battle."

"Is that important?"

"In this instance, yes. Normally, to strike first is to strike
last, but in this instance such a move will prove fatal."

My words are made truth by the spearman's next attack.
He dives forward, falling to his knees and driving the spear
toward the big man's gut. Rook moves with impossible
speed, defying reason as he thrusts his back toward the
ground, hitting the earth with a thud as the spearman's
weapon jabs through the air, narrowly missing the big man's
flesh. Rook grabs at the spear with both hands, wrenching
the spearman off balance and pulling him further in the
direction of the spear jab. With a spare hand, the giant grabs
at the spearman's throat as he passes overhead, then rips
the flesh of his neck and drives his hulking form upward.

The manoeuvre takes only a second, but, when it is done,
Rook stands above the spearman's body holding his torn-

out throat in victory as the other man squirms in the sand nearby, his lifeblood gushing onto the ground. As before, sound erupts from the arena, the name *Rook* is shouted again and again as the miniature airships begin their selection once more. The big man stands impassively, letting the gore fall from his hand. There is no joy, no bloodlust in his eye; only a far-gazing expression which speaks of loss and sorrow, of a task which must be done for lack of choice.

Even from this distance I can recognize a kindred spirit. The man standing upon the arena floor is a soldier out of war. Years spent in the application of despicable acts of violence have blunted his desires, made him more machine than man. Yet some part of the brute longs to leave his bloodied history behind. To live as others do, at peace and in contentment. The man before me is a soul who has come to realize that such hopes of rebirth are mere fantasy. All there is for men of our ilk is blood and violence.

The next three combatants are better trained than the previous slaves, though they attack too fiercely and without reason. Their skill with bladed weapons is plainly obvious—evidenced by the enthusiastic manner of their swordplay—but they are unaccustomed to the pain of lethal combat, and this begins to show the moment the first wound is struck.

"See how they fence with one another," I lean toward the girl, pointing to the pair of slaves still thrusting and parrying with one another as the third lies bleeding from the stomach a short distance off.

"They seem pretty good to me."

"They are skilled, that much is true. But these are duellers, not soldiers. They fight for sport and do not seek to kill their opponent outright."

"I don't get your meaning?"

"Look at the brute. See how he sits and waits in patience for the others to expend their energy? He has the right of it. Whatever your skill, the dealing of death is an exhausting business. When one can kill with a single stroke, it is folly to kill with three or four. If this were a duel between two opponents, then such vigour would be perhaps warranted. But, as you have already said, the victor of this battle must win a dozen more bouts before the sun sets, and that is after they have bested the Wrathhammer."

One of the combatants slips on the flailing limb of a fallen foe. The man stumbles and is run through by his opponent. At his moment of triumph, however, the fallen slave strikes out with his own blade, such that the pair are gutted in tandem as they slump to the earth together. Rook watches impassively.

"You see. By making such a fierce impression with his first fight, the brute has forced his opponents to waste their strength against one another. He wins this round without striking a blow."

She turns to me, eyes narrowing. "Dude, you sound like you admire the guy?"

"There is much to admire in a keen mind. You would do well to learn what you can from this Rook."

Three further slaves are selected. This time a woman is among them. Lithe and dark-skinned, she prefers a pair of small daggers to the longer blades and blunt weaponry. She does not content herself with the newly arrived slaves, but heads directly for Rook, circling the big man and striking like a viper. The brute is forced to twist with impossible speed, jumping to his feet and stepping out of harm's way as the woman's needle-like daggers cut through the air, narrowly missing his dark flesh.

She strikes again, and once more the big man narrowly avoids her strike. Rook backs away a little, moving closer to the hapless pair fighting with swords and bucklers behind him. One of their number sees the big man backing closer and attempts to seize upon the opportunity. He lunges toward Rook, just as the woman darts forward for another attack. Moving with deceptive grace, the big man manages to sidestep the thrust from behind, grabbing the man around the neck and thrusting him toward the outstretched daggers of the dark-skinned woman. As she pulls back, Rook presses his considerable weight down onto the wounded swordsman, driving him to the ground and taking the woman's daggers with him.

Forced to pull back or risk broken wrists, the dark-skinned woman retreats, but Rook is on her too swiftly, meaty hands grasping her throat and squeezing with inhuman strength. The big man turns, spinning her flailing body around just as the second swordsman slashes out at Rook's frame. The blade cuts into the woman's torso, and she lets out a muffled howl of pain. In the seconds that follow, Rook bludgeons the remaining swordsman with meaty fists, as the lifeblood flows from the other two combatants. With a grim expression, the big man plucks a sword from the swordsman and neatly cuts the throats of the dying slaves. This done, he tosses the weapon to the ground and resumes his spot, seated upon the arena floor.

Through raucous cheering mixed with other sounds of disapproval, the airships begin choosing their next victims. One of the small ships draws close to where we are seated, hovering uncertainly as though held in place by a gossamer thread. The craft drifts steadily higher, drifting closer and closer, its tail banner fluttering in the breeze as it draws near. The girl catches my arm.

"Ah…Kane are you seeing this?"

I feel the beating of my heart increase as the banner drifts and falls across the girl's shoulder. The folk around us erupt with applause and violent shouting. I feel hands slapping at my back and shoulders as guardsmen move from further down the stairways, eyes locked upon us.

"What the fuck do we do?" the girl asks.

I note the brown cloak about her shoulders and hit upon an idea. I stand, shrugging my own cloak off my shoulders as I lift my shackled wrists for all to see.

"What are you doing?"

"This is the only path," I say, slipping off my gun belt and handing it to her as the guards move closer.

"Kane? Kane, what the fuck!"

Her words die down as I am led through the crowd toward the arena floor below. The throng jeers and bellows as we pass down each row, shouting unintelligible slogans. The smell of sour liquor fills the air as denizens of Tullhaven begin uncorking skins of wine and ale, settling in for the long afternoon of bloodshed. As we reach the floor of the arena, servants clothed in dark garments scurry from hidden tunnels below the ground, dragging the remains of fallen slaves down into the darkness. They leave sickly smears of blood in the sand that crisscross the arena floor.

Two other slaves enter from the opposite side of the arena. They waste no time in acquiring weapons, snatching up sword and spear in turn. I begin stretching stiff muscles, squatting to the ground in an effort to ready my body for what is to come. I walk to the basket at the centre of the arena, pick up a short sword, and swing it experimentally. The weapon is ill-weighted and crafted of poorly hammered steel. A quick glance at the other weapons tells a similar story. Why waste the best weaponry on slaves who are set to kill one another?

A trumpet call rings out, and the fight begins. I feel the surge of energy which precedes bloodshed, but none of the etheric power that has arisen of late. Two slaves, tall and well-muscled, square off against me. They are not without skill, but these are brawlers and brutes, not men whose skill has been honed over long years of combat. The memory of my early years is still little more than a fog, yet I can feel the strength of those years as the swordsmen set upon me. It is as though memory has become a physical thing to me; an instinct which is at home only when violence ensues. In this moment, beset by enemies that threaten deathly violence, I am more at peace than at any other time. I cannot help the smile which alights upon my face as the first blow is struck.

It is a small thing to sidestep the first few strikes. My enemies slice and cut for the torso, but they move too slowly and pose no serious threat. I use the time to bring warmth to stiff muscles, ducking and diving beyond their strikes in preparation for the true battle which is to come. Off to one side, Rook watches with little interest, sat cross-legged upon the ground, a martial statue cut in dark granite.

As I duck and spin out of reach, I feel the limits of my flesh. Years spent in the Red Queen's dungeon have rid me of a great deal of muscle, and my reflexes are not as sharp as they once were. The weeks spent traveling to Tullhaven have been restful and allowed me to regain a little of my former strength, yet I am far from what I was.

The pattern emerges swiftly, amid a rain of jeers from the crowd. The taller of the swordsmen favours his right side and overcompensates when he is pressed on the left. The shorter man moves more swiftly, but his blows are tepid things that lack resolve. Always his weight is held back, as though each strike is little more than a feint.

I lean back as the larger man thrusts and kick out at the side of his sword, driving the weapon into the path of the other man. An odd moment ensues when both swordsmen are entangled, their weapons jarring against one another, anger flaring in their eyes. That moment of uncertainty, when the pair debate whether they should abandon their attack against me and move instead against one another, offers a small window through which I press my advantage. I pull the hidden blade from my sleeve and drive it deep into the taller man's neck, pressing down hard against his back so that his full weight drives the shorter man back onto his heels and to the ground. I drive the heel of my boot against the shorter swordsman's neck and feel the satisfying crack of bone. A simple cut to the neck of both men sees their struggle end.

I wipe the blade against the meagre loincloth of the taller man and turn my attention to the brute, still sitting off to the side. I walk slowly toward the man, slipping the knife back into its hidden sheath. Dark eyes slowly turn toward me.

I am the first to speak. "I confess, I see a kindred soul in you, my friend."

Rook says nothing, yet there is a hint of mirth to his features as he stands to full height, flexing his muscles in preparation.

"I should like to know how a man of such strength and skill came to slave for a petty merchant in this backwater hamlet. It seems a story worth hearing."

He looks down at the broken shackles on my wrist and grins widely. Yes, I have a story of my own though I can remember so little, it is not worth the telling.

He strikes with frightful speed, lunging toward me with his full bulk. I twist aside, but the big man anticipates the evasion and strikes a hammer blow to my chest as I spin and duck out of reach. The blow hits me like an anvil, almost knocking me off my feet and crushing ribs with the contact. I back away, waiting for the big man to turn and face me once again.

In those few moments, I feel the curious sensation of bone beginning to knit. The pain which has momentarily crushed my chest gives way, and I feel myself somewhat restored. It is, perhaps, another etheric gift granted by the pit and those dark beings that whispered dark words for all those years? I have no time to contemplate the odd sensation.

He lunges again. This time I move ahead rather than retreating, driving my knee into the man's chest and kicking out with all the force I can muster. The sensation is akin to kicking a boulder with bare feet. The impact causes Rook no discomfort, and I am forced to dive away in order to avoid a second blow from his mighty fists. A sound like the rumbling of distant storm clouds rises from the other man's chest. Laughter perhaps, or something like it.

I look down at the iron shackles on my wrists. They do not flare with etheric power, nor do I feel the strength of hidden forces infusing my body. It is simply I against he, and I already know with certainty, that I cannot win this fight if I abide by the rules of civil combat. Even with this newfound capacity to heal swiftly, I doubt my body would recover if the brute were to snap my neck and remove my head from my shoulders.

I do not wait for a third attack, but feint ahead, then dart to the left, ducking beneath his mammoth hands and slipping the dagger from my right wrist to drive the blade through the flesh of his calf. I feel the thunderous impact of a fist to the back of my neck as I roll across the ground, stumbling to my feet as the world spins around me.

I turn to see Rook standing with a bloodied leg. The injury does not seem to slow the man as he charges toward me, but his earlier mirth has all but fled. We clash again, and once more I strike a blow across his flesh, cutting deep into his left arm and catching a glancing blow against my cheek as I stumble away. The brute's strength is impressive beyond words. As the moments pass, I score several more cuts, but fail to slow the brute down.

The brute swings a meaty fist toward my head. I manage to evade the blow, striking out with a dagger that cuts deeply into the man's hand. Yet, as I spin to pull free the blade, he catches it, wrenching it from my grasp and tossing it into the distance. Blood drips from his fist as Rook circles around me. I cannot help but admire the brute's resolve. There is nothing of desperation in his movement, only the snarling confidence of a born predator.

"You are a man of great talent," I call out above the din. "Tell me, why do you fight in such a contest? A man with your skill could command an army."

A dark grin crosses his lips. "I have no choice, shackled man."

His voice is deep, like the rumbling of thunder clouds.

"Every man has a choice," I counter.

He nods, still circling around me, fists clenched.

"True enough," he says, twisting his neck to one side to the cracking of bone. "Yet it is not only *my* life in the balance."

I consider his words. There is no play for time here. He is not nearly so wounded as I had first suspected. When the time comes, he will fight with all the force he can muster. Something flares within me, and I feel the ether begin to rise. The shackles at my wrists glow faint emerald, and I am momentarily puzzled by the strange hue.

Rook strikes with a flurry of blows that drive be back. I catch a glancing stroke to the shoulder and cannot help the cry that escapes my lips as the thunderous fist cracks bone and causes fire to flare across my arm. I manage to keep my feet, staggering away as my body begins its curious work. Bones knit, muscles are soothed, and the pain subsided. This healing is swifter and more profound than the first. I feel myself renewed, reborn. Muscle and sinew have been refashioned, and I feel the strength of days long past return to me.

Three more blows the giant rains down upon me. I catch a glancing blow to the temple and narrowly avoid two swift jabs. I am about to counter when the brute's knee thunders into my face, snapping my head back with such force that I feel my neck break with a sickly crack. I stumble backward as the shackles flare with emerald light. Bone and muscle reform, cracking back into place as I shake my head and advance upon the giant.

The big man's eyes narrow as he witnesses the miracle. Already he knows the truth of it. Superior though he may be in strength and skill, I will win this fight. It seems that the fates have chosen me for their cruel jest, and they will not let me die until they have taken their pleasure.

"You speak of others whose lives you hold?" I say, rubbing my jaw and feeling it click back into place.

He nods, circling once more. "The Pirate Lord Yulenbane has my wife and daughter. While I fight for him, they live."

He drives forward, striking again. I parry his first thrust, duck beneath his second, and manage to land a blow against his stomach before diving to freedom, narrowly escaping his grasp. One might as well fight a mountain. I feel the ether swirling through my body, longing to be freed. The shackles swell with emerald light, yet I hold back the tide of power, a notion coming to mind.

"You will need a blade," I offer, nodding to the spilled contents of the basket at the centre of the arena. "Cut deeply across my neck but take care not to sever the head entirely."

The big man narrows his eyes, considering my words.

"I will make a show of death and wait for them to carry me away." I nod to the shackles at my wrists. "I do not claim to understand this power, but you can see as well as I that a death blow will not kill me."

He stares at me for a moment, his heavy fists unclenching, drops of blood falling to the ground below.

"You would do this thing for me?"

I shrug. "It is no great sacrifice. In truth, the notion of fighting to the end of this day does not appeal to me. Better that I die and enhance your reputation still further."

"You are sure?" Rook asks.

"I am."

He nods. "I will not forget this kindness."

Rook does not wait a moment longer. He charges toward the fallen weapons, picking up two short swords and advancing at speed. It is no great thing to make a show of survival. The big man wields the blades like clubs, swinging them through the air—great steel claws that threaten to rend and tear as much with brute force as the sharpness of their blade's edge. I counter where I can, picking up a fallen spear and batting away the swords until the spear's haft splinters and cracks.

I fall hard to the ground, and Rook takes his opportunity, pinning me to the earth with a mammoth knee and knocking the spear half from my grasp. I feel the full weight of his body pressing me against the sand, a falling mountain set to crush the world beneath its weight. He leans forward, pressing a sword blade against my throat.

"Thank you, friend," he says, in the moment before he does the work. "I shall repay this kindness in time."

I hear the rasping of steel against flesh, and blackness swallows me from somewhere within. The pain is sharp and vivid, yet I am drawn into the warmth of darkness. It sooths and comforts me, calling me ever downward into oblivion. Moments pass, and gradually my senses return. I hear the roaring of the crowd; feel myself dragged across the ground, pulled down into the cool tunnels beneath the arena. Calloused hands lift me, tossing my body into the heap as severed limbs and corpses are piled atop my body.

The roaring of the crowds has become a distant din. Sounds of movement close by begin to recede as the bloodshed begins once more in the arena. I drag myself from the carrion, my neck still leaking blood, though from a much smaller wound. I descend from the meat cart, landing warily upon hard stone, alone but for a snoring guardsman on a nearby stool. The ghouls who dragged me from the pit have returned to their places. They watch the fighting with rapt attention by the mouth of the tunnel, eagerly awaiting their next entrance upon the field of battle.

I approach the sleeping guardsman, slip behind the man, and cut the breath from his throat. He struggles violently, but the arena din drowns out his flailing. I pull him into the darkness, strip the corpse of clothing, and enter the tunnel proper once more. My thoughts fly to the girl. I have little time to waste.

"You there!" I shout to the closest ghoul. The wretch spins, his grotesque features a mix of surprise and fear. "Come with me!"

I grab the wretch by his arm and drag him down the tunnel. He strains beneath my grip, protesting that he will be treated harshly for abandoning his post. A swift jab to the stomach silences the ghoul. I force him to lead me to the surface, through twisting tunnels, and up a narrow shaft which leads to the bottom level of the arena seating. Once we reach the surface, I release the ghoul, who bows and scraps, shielding his eyes from the sun as he retreats down the hole and into his beloved tunnels.

I am surrounded by a sea of souls, all shouting and jeering at one another while the bloodshed continues below. From a distance I hear the sound of Rook's name repeated over and over. A short walk brings me in sight of Rook's master, and, from there, I see the path to my former place high up in the arena stands. Still garbed in the makeshift armour of a guardsman, I push my way up the cluttered stairs. She does not see me as I reach the highest step. My face is obscured by the leather helm, and the girl seems stunned with remorse, staring out into the arena like a lost soul.

I call out, but my words are not heard above the shouts of the crowd. I push my way toward the girl, earning looks of scorn and outright hostility from those I push past. She turns as I draw near, her eyes wet with tears. It takes but a moment for recognition to dawn. She moves to embrace me, but I forestall the gesture, reaching out to grab her by the arm and drag her roughly from her seat. The crowds shout and spit as I pull her from her place and lead her back to the stairs. She plays her part well, struggling to free herself but with insufficient strength to accomplish the task.

We make our way to the lowest level, moving through the press toward an iron door guarded by two men. They offer puzzled looks as I approach, hands drifting toward their weapons. I feel the ether surge within, sensing the power rippling through my arms as I drive a hand toward the closest adversary. There is time enough for the other guard to sound the alarm and draw his weapon, but his cries go unheard amid the tumult in the arena beyond. Several folk turn from the arena, watching the melee with mild interest, but otherwise unconcerned. This is a squabble between guardsmen and nothing more.

We are well away from the arena when the girl finally speaks. "I thought you were dead. That big guy cut your throat."

I lift the helm from my head and show her my neck, still bloodied but otherwise whole.

"How the hell?"

I put the helm back in place. "I cannot explain. There is a mark upon me, a death mark placed by they who dwell in darkness. I know not what purpose this mark serves, but only that mortal weapons cannot harm me as they once did. I know not how long this boon will last, nor do I know for what nefarious purpose the dark ones have chosen to impart such a gift."

She nods, and there is deep understanding within the gesture. "Yeah, I used to have something like that. Not now though. All that changed when I got sucked into this fuck hole. It's like I lost something...like I lost my best friend and my family all at once. Now I'm just as weak as everyone else in this place."

I shake my head, grasping her shoulder. "There is no weakness in you, child. None whatsoever."

She leans forward, and we share an awkward embrace. Once the moment has passed, she lifts the gun belt from beneath her robe and hands it to me. I take the belt but find no means of strapping it to my waist, given the bulk of the guardsman's armour.

"So, where to now, boss?"

I let her words rest a while between us. The drive to continue on has not lessened, yet there is something that holds me to this place. I stare out at the sun-baked buildings that huddle against one another around the vast bowl of the valley.

"We stay for a while." I fish the purse from my pocket and throw it to her.

"What the hell? Where'd you get this?"

"From the man who wore this armour and his two compatriots at the arena gate. Combined with our earlier purse, it should secure sufficient accommodations for a month or so. We shall stay here a while, take our rest, and then move on once we have gathered sufficient wealth to ease the journey."

She nods. "Ok, sounds like a plan. How the fuck are we gonna get more money though? We're out of horses and carts, and you can't just go around knocking people on the head all day."

I smile. "We shall continue your education. It is time you learned the skill of thievery."

10. A Thief's Business

We find suitable rooms for hire at a small tavern cut into the upper wall of the clay bowl into which Tullhaven is set. Nestled beside a pleasure house and tinker's hut, the tavern boasts twelve rooms of modest size and a communal hall at the base of the dwelling where food and drink can be found. Prices seem to have risen in response to the recent arena festivities, so a week's payment depletes our funds almost completely. We are forced to take a single room between us and eat sparingly.

We spend two days making a survey of the strange city, skirting its circumference and noting its various districts and curiosities. It is a city like any other, built up over long years and showing the haphazard signs of growth and development. The people of this city are just as varied as those found elsewhere throughout the Traumwelt, yet there is a similarity of attire and attitude which unites them.

Tullhaven, for the most part, is a city of merchants and slavers. It is a *haven* on inasmuch as it represents one of the larger trading hubs to the south of the red city. While aligned with Rust in principle, the city does not shy away from trading with other principalities and kingdoms, welcoming traders from all corners of the Traumwelt in the interests of amassing wealth.

While they trade in gold and gems of all types, the locally prized currency is that of the polished stone disks fashioned from the bones of slaves killed in the arena. Once a year the barbaric festival is held, wherein a week of feasting and celebration follows the bloody events at the arena. During this time, the godling Tull is said to feast constantly, dining upon the flesh of the fallen and thus bestowing his blessing upon the remains which will later be fashioned into precious chits.

It is a curious and barbaric custom, but one which the common folk of Tullhaven seem to relish. There are other oddities about this city and its people, but I resolve to solve our own troubles before exploring further. On the third night of our stay at the tavern, we eat a meal of thick stew and dark bread and drink several tankards of chippa, the local ale brewed from a curious grey root grown upon the ridges that line the outer limits of the city proper.

The girl grimaces as she drinks, clearly unaccustomed to strong drink and the particularly bitter brew they serve in these parts.

"I can't believe they drink this shit," she mouths, slamming her tankard down against the table and returning to her stew.

I nod. "It has a bite to it, and no mistake."

"Stew's good though," she says between mouthfuls.

I cannot help the smile bloom upon my lips. "Indeed."

As we eat, the sun falls below the lip of the ridge which surrounds Tullhaven. The bowl city is cast into sudden darkness as the false dusk falls. Revellers in the city below begin to grow restless, spilling out from countless alehouses into the city street.

"Sleep a while," I advise the girl, "for there is work to do this night, and it will require a great deal of you."

We head to our room, and she takes her place upon the meagre cot to one side of the quarters and falls swiftly into a deep slumber. I watch her for a time, puzzling over the girl's inner strength, her capacity to adapt to new circumstances. Though I can remember only portions of my life before the Red Queen's pit, she strikes me as something remarkable, something unique among the many souls I have encountered thus far. Though she speaks in strange twists of the tongue and seems to flare into indignant rages on a whim, there is much to admire in the youngling.

I take my leave and head to the upper floor, opening a large window cut into the thick clay wall. I sit for a time and simply watch the city below as the arena erupts with the final bout of the day. While the ceremony proper has ended, there have been lesser contests run within the arena walls. This city seems to thrive on bloodshed, and the bouts have been a constant feature in this week of celebration and excess.

As torches are lit around the vast edifice, I find myself thinking of the giant Nubian who had slit my throat. Perhaps Rook has triumphed in the end? Perhaps the burly slave has fallen to a lucky blade or been dragged to the sand by his many wounds? I find myself wishing for the former.

Denizens of the bowl city spill forth from innumerable ale houses and pleasure dens, moving like ants through the tightly woven streets of the inner city. I am informed by the tender of this tavern that these souls will not return to their homes this night. Instead, they will follow the broad path which leads north and south out of the city and onto the sandy wastes beyond. Vast fires will be lit, and celebrations shall ensue, wherein the folk of Tullhaven will drink and make merry; throwing their lot with havoc devils until the night has waned. It is more than a custom among this people. To attend the feasts of blood is law for all but a few citizens of the bowl city. Only the tavern keepers, sojourners, and those servants and slaves left to tend the godling's palace are excused.

It is to be a night of debauchery and abandon, when the godling Tull is said to feast upon the flesh of those slaves who died in the arena. It has taken two days of preparation to construct the various tents and furnishings to accommodate Tullhaven's vast ruler and his entourage; two days to strip meat from bone and prepare fallen slaves for the godling's dinner plate.

I have seen such travesties of nature before. In times of war, when famine and pestilence reign, a man can do terrible deeds in the name of survival. This, though, is a matter of godling perversion and gluttony. To feast upon the arena fallen is simply unforgivable. Tull, like the others of his kind, are a plague upon this sunburnt world.

Even from this height, I can see the godling's procession as it ascends the singular straight path toward an expansive palace, cut into the wall of the bowl directly behind the arena. It is a mammoth thing with an almost skull-like quality, haphazard and misshapen in places but equal in grandeur to the arena itself. Towering statues line the entrance to the palace; grotesque, monstrous figures plucked from nightmare and displayed for all to see. A line of stairs ascends to a grand archway some fifty feet high. A score of gilded slaves are forced to carry the godling's palanquin, with the corpulent ruler lounging atop his bed. Countless more servants trail behind, each glittering with metallic paint, naked and shaven like living statues.

The Collector they call him, this godling Tull. Collector of bones and human misery—an overlord whose excesses keep the common people bound in poverty while cruel merchants pander to his every whim in an effort to increase their own wealth and political standing. The godling breed are a cruel and selfish race, and I find my heart stirred to ire as I watch the procession below.

I wait a while, watching the revellers snake their way upward around the lip of the ridge and onto the sandy wastes beyond. I hear the sounds of their debauchery as it drifts upon the night air. It seems that the day's violence is not yet at an end, judging by the sounds I hear from the distant revelry. I wake the girl, careful not to startle her. Sleep hangs heavily upon her as we make preparations.

"Come, it is time we began your lessons. Take your cloak and knives and stay quiet."

***

We keep to the shadows, moving with stealth through the bowl city while revellers make merry far off in the wastes above. I teach the girl the various hand signs and gestures needed for communicating in silence. I show her how to walk, how to climb and move in the shadows. The girl learns swiftly as though her body were fashioned for precisely this purpose.

"Why aren't we wearing cloaks?" she whispers, ducking down beneath an upturned barrel.

"Cloaks have their uses, but one moves more swiftly without a billowing piece of fabric at one's back. There is also less risk of getting it caught against something in the dark. The key to a successful enterprise is preparation, strategy. Where such is not possible, as in this case, then speed and stealth are our best allies."

The meagre dwellings of the city offer little in the way of spoils. Likewise, the taverns and ale houses have little of true value and such establishments are more likely to notice their purloined wealth and report it to the city guardsmen. For this reason, we head east, toward the godling palace and those lofty dwellings that surround it.

"An Overlord will never enjoy his wealth in solitude," I whisper, leading the girl up a makeshift ladder and onto the roof of a simple dwelling. "He must surround himself with a cadre of privileged souls, whether aristocracy or merchants of wealth. There must be some to whom he can demonstrate his power; some to fawn over the godling and witness his various activities."

"So, that's where we're heading now? To the house of one of those privileged bastards?"

"Indeed. On this night they will doubtless all be in attendance at the godling's palace. There will be a small guard set about the house but nothing of consequence. In truth, our real enemy will be the local thieves' guild or opportunistic brigands. The significance of this night will not be lost on them, and they will be far better prepared than we."

As it happens, luck is with us. The closest and smallest of the grand houses is guarded by three guardsmen of dubious skill. It is a grand building in contrast to most of the houses and buildings in the greater city. Standing next to its fellows, however, beneath the shadow of the godling palace; this merchant manor is a meagre thing.

We are able to slip into the house by means of an open window on the second floor and find the building's interior dimly lit and free of guards. Three men have been stationed at the entrance below, but there is no one patrolling inside the house. Doubtless the owner of this property has forbidden the guard from entry; a petty prohibition which renders their task as defenders of the house somewhat useless.

As we begin moving through the house, we see signs of ostentation and greed. Large statues and oil paintings line the walls while gilded furnishings of all kinds litter each room. There is no sense of logic or structure to their arrangement, only the brash desire to show wealth. We move to a large study at the rear of the house, and I am struck once more at the desperation I see in every aesthetic choice. The building screeches to be noticed, trying desperately to assert its place among far grander and more richly appointed dwellings.

Wordlessly, I direct the girl to begin looking for smaller objects of value which will fit neatly into the dark sacks we have acquired for the night's activities. She moves through the house with adequate stealth, eyes wide and muscles tensed. I find, nestled behind a case of leather-bound volumes, a stash of chits and gems which glint in the faint moonlight.

The girl returns with a handful of jewels purloined from the bedside of what must be the lady of the house. I select a few items and instruct the girl to replace the rest. She gives me a puzzled expression, but obeys, nonetheless. We make our exit without being seen and head back toward the tavern. The sounds of feasting and revelry echo across the city from the red wastes beyond as we move from rooftop to rooftop.

Once we are back in our room, I spread out the night's plunder, and we begin taking stock.

"I don't get it," the girl insists, as we make tally of our newly acquired wealth. "We took like, not even half of the stuff that was there. We could have had three times as much money, and no one would have noticed."

I toss her an emerald gem, cut into a faceted rectangle. She snatches it out of the air and examines it with mild interest.

"Were we to rob them of all their wealth, they would know for certain of our presence this night. The other Lords of this city would be alerted, and they would take pains to double their guard and remain vigilant, making our task that much harder. But here, we take only a little of their wealth; enough to serve our needs, but insufficient to raise their ire. The wealthy, for the most part, are not fastidious when it comes to the precise nature and whereabouts of their wealth. Provided their copious needs are met and their standing with their fellows is not impugned, they will overlook petty theft almost entirely."

She looks down at the pile of chits laid out across the bed.

"This is petty theft? There must be a couple of hundred chits here."

"A few hundred out of ten thousand. And that was only the first cache we were able to find. The petty Lords of this city will doubtless keep the bulk of their wealth hidden away, buried deep beneath their dwellings or housed at the heart of some grand labyrinth. What we saw tonight was merely the necessary coin made ready for sundry needs."

"Ok, so we sneak in and only take a few bucks from the guy. So even if he notices that something's missing, he's probably going to think he just misplaced shit or one of his guards took it?"

"Precisely. It is for this reason that we approach the lesser Lordling's residence and not those further up the hill. The more prestigious and lofty houses will have skilled bookkeepers who will account for every chit. Those of old money are often misers who resent the spending of even a single coin. By contrast, the owner of the manor we robbed this night was concerned only with the appearance of wealth and prestige. Their house was cluttered with needlessly expensive items, and its owner is likely not the sort to count every chit and copper before bedding down for the night. Thus, we stick to the lesser Lordlings and take only a little of what they have to give."

She nods, tossing the emerald back to me.

"Ok, so what now? Do we get some new digs? This place is a shit hole."

"We remain here for the moment. To relocate to loftier accommodations would raise suspicion. Also, there is little better accommodation to be had. Better that we remain as we are and behave as normal for the duration of our stay in Tullhaven. Perhaps, when we are set to leave, we might make a more extravagant claim upon the wealth of this city?"

The girl makes no reply. She is lying upon the cot, her eyes heavy once more. I let her lie and set about hiding our newly acquired wealth. On the morrow, we will find a suitable clothier and commission some more fitting attire. I will test the metal of the shooting irons at my side and continue the girl's tutelage. In truth, I know not what force keeps me bound to this city. There is a darkness here that weighs against my heart—a wrong that must be righted.

To set one's will against a godling is a foolish game, yet I find my own will fixed upon the ruler of this wretched city. I cannot rightly say from where my ire truly comes. Perhaps the Red Queen's justice has bred in me sufficient hatred of the godling race to cause my present animosity? Perhaps the sight of needless slaughter and slavery beneath the godling's gaze has raised my ire? Of, perhaps it is the will of those dark whispers in the back of my mind which I am confusing as my own.

Whatever its progeny, one driving thought compels me to action.

Kill the godling Tull.

11. The Ivory Key

The weeks pass swiftly. By daylight we explore the city proper, mapping each corner and crevasse, every meagre dwelling and lofty mansion. We mark the coming and going of the guardsmen, the collection of taxes from merchants and tinkerers, and the various ceremonies and laws which govern society within the dust bowl of Tullhaven. By night the girl hones her craft, pilfering coin and jewel from the lesser nobility and learning to move with stealth and strike with deadly force when required. She fashions for herself a curious garment of wrapped cloth. The dark fabric is wrapped tightly about her arms and legs, like a second skin, giving her the aspect of a prowling cat as she scours the night in search of treasure.

I find a smith of some worth in the lower reaches of the city and commission a series of throwing knives, daggers, and short swords. The weapons are fairly made but costly. Apart from the weapons and clothes, we refrain from further purchases, not wanting to raise attention. We keep to the small tavern atop the hill and keep our own company wherever possible. It is not until four weeks have passed that the trouble first begins.

The girl has become proficient enough in her trade that I allow her to walk the city streets alone at night. In only a few weeks of tutelage, she is now able to choose a suitable house, enter its walls without raising alarm and pilfer a portion of jewels and chits that represent a small fortune. This she does without my supervision. Indeed, she has become more adept at the skill than I myself. Each night she leaves as the sun dips below the horizon and returns in the early hours with her plunder.

On some nights the takings are meagre. Either because of bad luck, excessive security, or a merchant or slaver with insufficient funds to pilfer. We learn that there is a great deal of deception at work within the petty nobility of Tullhaven. Many of the well-to-do have little actual wealth but have grown expert in the mummer's farce required to deceive their fellow noble. Their dwellings are empty facades whose treasures have long been sold off to pay bad debts. This fact itself represents a significant opportunity for future endeavours but does nothing to further our immediate needs.

As the sun begins to rise, the girl returns to me, fresh from her latest endeavour. She empties out a small pouch of jewels and coins onto the cot and smiles widely as I inspect the goods.

"What is this?" I point to the object nestled at the base of the stack of coins: a long, ivory key ornately cut with gems studding its haft.

The girl frowns, stooping to look at the object. "I dunno. I don't remember picking it up. It must have been in with the cash."

The object resonates with etheric energy. I can feel the tang of power as I pick up the key, examining it from each side. The power emanating from it is weak but of a curious order.

"Which house did you visit this night?"

"Lord Munek, I think. The big bastard with the dud eye."

Munek, one of the lesser Lords in Tull's court, is a large fellow with a series of maladies that have turned his face into a grotesque mockery of its former self. To mask his ugliness, Munek is known to don fanciful masks and elaborate costumes that hide his various afflictions.

So successful is the corpulent Lord in this endeavour, that Tull himself has been known to mimic some of Munek's outfits, speaking of the minor Lord's various flamboyances in affectionate terms.

"Does it matter?" the girl asks, motioning toward the stolen key.

I shake my head. "Most likely not. Though we must take care to keep it hidden. A key, however fanciful, is for but one purpose. A man does not fashion such an object unless he wishes to keep something of value hidden."

The tension leaves her body as I say the words. Yet, even as they leave my lips, I know them for the lie they are. The ivory key tugs at my mind, pressing against me with dark humours. I know not how the key will bring strife, but there is no doubt that strife is coming.

"Take your rest," I instruct as the girl sits on the cot. "I have some tasks to be about. I will return a little later."

While the girl sleeps, I walk the city, letting my legs take me where they will. It feels good to be clothed in those garments to which I am accustomed. The weight of the shooting irons at my belt serves as an anchor to my soul, dispelling the troubling thoughts that seem always to wait about the edge of my mind's eye.

I find a simple tavern nestled among a row of merchant dwellings and decide to take my ease. The tender is a short fellow with a furiously over-zealous moustache and a cheerful demeanour. He serves me dark ale and hard cheese, and I sit on a stool in the darkest corner of the common room. I take my time, drinking slowly and letting the warmth of the liquor do its work. Before long the tavern is filled with burley workmen and merchants of common goods. Those with slaves are required to leave the poor souls outside, treating the shaved and shackled men and women more like dogs than the people they truly are. The sight raises my ire somewhat, but warm ale and pungent cheese have done their work, and I cannot hold to the anger for long.

"Leave Tullhaven?" I overhear one of the workmen say from a nearby table.

"Aye, and right quick too. Lord Tull had Munek strung up outside the temple, clear as day for all to see. To hear Emit tell it, he was in a black rage. Said he was gonna turn out every house and stable in the city till he finds it. Got the other Lordlings in a might state."

"But we ain't done nothin' for it. Ain't no trouble comin' out way, surely?"

"Don't be daft, boy! We're at the bottom of the pile, sure enough. It ain't the Lordling's gonna hang for this. They'll come down on us like a storm, sure and true. Better to find work in the outer hamlets, stay clear of Tullhaven while the Lord's anger is stoked."

As if in response to the man's prophetic utterance, a horn call rings out through the night—two long blasts that pierce through the din of the tavern. With a meaningful glance at his companion, the workman downs the last of his drink swiftly, then takes his leave, followed closely by the other man. Other patrons similarly finish their business and make to leave.

The door to the tavern bursts open, admitting a fist of armoured thugs bearing torches and blades. The diminutive tender raises his hands, walking out from behind the bar with an obsequious grin. Before he can open his mouth, the first of the guards storms forward, thrusting a grimy clay tablet toward the man.

"By with will of our Lord and sovereign, we are instructed to search this premises in a manner most thorough, in accordance with land and law."

The tender reads the tablet with a worried expression. The guards do not wait for his response but begin turning chairs and tables, smashing bottles, and roughhousing patrons in a manner which seems more punitive than exploratory. The tender pleads for mercy and receives a cudgel blow to the side of the head for his troubles. The little man falls heavily to the ground, blood streaming from his wound while the guards continue their sport, moving toward the rooms beyond the common. Several guards stay behind and continue frisking the tavern patrons.

A pair of the burly guards approach the corner where I sit. "You there! On your feet."

I stand, enduring their wicked grins while they begin looting my person. They pull the small purse from my belt, the dagger strapped to my left boot, and the shooting irons, laying the weapons out on the table with great interest.

"What's the manner of your business here in Tullhaven," the more articulate of the two asks.

"I represent a merchant house from the red city. I have come to source new supplies of grain and ale."

The guard nods with little interest, inspecting the barrel of one of the shooting irons, while his companion attempts to strap the belt around his copious waist.

"May I enquire as to what you gentlemen are looking for?" I ask.

The larger of the two grunts, continuing his inspection of the weapon. Clearly neither man has any idea why the godling Tull has authorized a sacking of his own city, and neither man cares. My mind turns to the girl, and I resolve to act quickly.

"Gentlemen, I'll be needing those weapons back, if you please."

The large of the two grins wickedly. I forestall his reply, thrusting a hand toward the man's bare throat. He gags and recoils, dropping the shooting iron. I snatch the weapon out of the air, advancing on the second guard before the man has an opportunity to act and jamming the butt of the weapon into his face in a series of rapid blows that send him reeling with a bloodied nose. I pick up the second iron, slide the dagger back into its sheath, and make my leave. Several of the tavern patrons seize the opportunity to do likewise, fleeing into the night.

I move swiftly through the shadows. The sounds of guardsmen harassing the city folk can be heard from every corner of Tullhaven. Here and there, the screams of women pierce the air, their violation rising as musical accompaniment to the night's brutalities. I pass old men being beaten in the street, houses burnt to ash, and guardsmen revelling in the bloodlust of their brutal debauchery. The sight of a young woman molested by three guards, gives me pause. Something dark tugs at my heart, giving rise to a black rage which flares with sudden, etheric power.

The darkness takes me momentarily. I do not remember taking to the guards with either knife or shooting iron, yet, when the momentary fog lifts, I stand above three bodies. The men are battered and bruised, their necks clearly broken, yet there is no bloodshed, and I hold no weapon. The girl, cowering and bloodied looks wide-eyed toward me. I offer her a hand, but she shies away, quivering in terror.

I feel the etheric charge leave the shackles at my wrists and cannot help but wonder at what dark mystery has taken me this night. They are there, nestled in the outer recesses of my mind: faint but insistent whispers that speak of the pit and of dark days ahead. I shake my head and clear my mind of the madness, leaving the girl and heading back to the tavern on the hill at a steady run.

The carnage passes me by as I move through each street and narrow passage. Half the city is aflame, and there will be great bloodshed this night. What kind of a ruler would permit such treatment of his subjects, much less demand it?

I reach the tavern and feel my heart clench as the flames rise from its windows. Black smoke billows from the building, thick with the acrid scent of burning oil and scorched flesh. I stand before the blaze, lost in that moment of meaningless destruction. The sight takes me back to another world, another time. Watching the city burn, its people perishing beneath the flames while I and my brothers watch. There is no art to this, no skill or honour—only destruction for its own sake.

A stone strikes me from behind. I turn, drawing both shooting irons by instinct. A shadowed figure stands in the narrow passageway to my left, firelight dancing off her shadowed form. I move closer, letting the guns slip back into their holsters as the girl's bloody smile comes into view. She is wearing her thief's outfit, bearing a large satchel and heavy cloak. There are cuts upon her face and arms, and she seems somewhat unhinged.

"There were only three of them," she says, her voice quavering. "Dopey fuckers, but one of them could fight. I managed to get out before the fire took over the place, but I couldn't get anyone else out."

Tears fall down her cheeks, cutting a path through the soot and ash.

"It's the key, isn't it? That's why all of this is happening?"

I nod.

"Fuck! Can I take it back? Maybe if…"

She does not finish the thought, already knowing it to be a vain hope. The city burns beneath the unquenched anger of its sovereign, and no act on our part can dampen his ire.

"Come," I say, drawing close. "We will find a place to await the passing of this night. On the morrow, we shall decide our next course of action."

She nods. "Are we leaving the city?"

"Not yet. First, I would dearly like to know why that key is of such profound value and why it rested in such a precarious place."

***

The city sacking passes well into the daylight hours. The city guard, some thousand souls, are let loose against the Tullhaven citizenry, and only those with sufficient wealth to hire mercenary soldiers and house guards are left untouched. We spend the remainder of the night and most of the following day nestled in the detritus of a lofty rooftop, not far from the tavern which had been consumed by fire.

"I just don't fucking understand it," the girl says, kneeling at the rooftop, staring out at the open welt of the city below. "Even if the key is worth a fortune, why the fuck would he do this to his own city? I men, Jesus, it looks like a war zone down there."

"And yet the people will recover, and coin will flow through the city streets once again. A few thousand souls may be extinguished. A dozen mercantile concerns will be burnt to the ground. But more people will come to the city, and businesses will spring from the ashes of those that have perished. In one night of bloodshed, the godling proves his absolute authority over the people and Lordlings alike. By unleashing the hound, Tull has taught his people a bitter lesson, and one that they will not soon forget."

"So, what? You're saying that he used the key as an excuse?"

I shrug. "Consider what we have witnessed these past weeks. Lord Tull is rarely seen in public. He prefers instead to work through his Lordlings and emissaries while he spends his time steeped in debauchery and excess. Yet, it is an excess of rumour rather than fact. The arena was the last time the people witnessed Lord Tull at his leisure. There are rumours of his consumption of human flesh, his rampant debauchery and cruelty at the festivities following the arena slaughter. Prosecute the matter though, and none can truly boast of seeing these things with their own eyes."

The reasoning becomes clearer as I talk, as does our next course of action.

"Most noteworthy among his attributes is the godling's tendency to fly into a rage at the slightest provocation. Thus, we are presented with a mercurial sovereign who revels in excess and tends toward flights of violent anger. Such aspects of the godling's character are well established throughout the city, yet none of its citizens have witnessed their sovereign in person and up close. The Lordlings, by contrast, may have had occasion to observe Tull's wrath and excess—sufficient at least to propagate the image he wishes to promote. Or perhaps they are complicit in this and simply fabricate and bolder the lie so as to keep the common folk at heel?"

She turns toward me, her face a thoughtful mask. Already I can see her reason it out, knowledge dawning like the rending of a thick curtain before her eyes.

"It's all for show," she says, in disbelief. "All the ceremonies and the arena and the rumours; it's all to paint the right picture for the people to believe."

"Precisely."

"So, all of this is just to reinforce the image he's built up? He's had his own city sacked just to prove what a bastard he is?"

"As I see it, the reasons for the sacking are twofold. Firstly, as you say, the brutality of the purge serves to bolster Tull's reputation as a capricious and malevolent ruler. It begins with the hanging of Munek. That has the added benefit of bringing the Lordlings to heel; showing the privileged that even they are not safe from the godling's terrible wrath. Consider also that the royal guard serves as the hand of their ruler. While Tull sits in his palace chamber, the guardsmen prowl the city streets, enacting his justice in whatever brutish manner they please. To the people, those guards are the living embodiment of their godling overlord. It is as if Tull himself walks the street, bludgeoning old men, raping women, putting the city to the flame. He need not leave his palace, but the impression is most poignantly made."

"Damn."

"Secondly, the purge serves a more practical purpose. Cities such as this grow wilder with each passing year. The more merchants set up camp, the more people make

Tullhaven their home, the more tinkers and tailors and slavers who come to this city, the harder it is to control. If a city is permitted to grow beyond certain bounds, the authority of its ruler begins to wane. Others rise up and begin to take power for themselves, cutting out small kingdoms within the larger empire. Before long, rival groups begin to clash; squabbles break out and soon blood spills onto the streets. All the while, the ruler of the city must devote their strength to putting out the fires of rebellion. This makes them vulnerable and weakens their claim."

"But if someone like Tull lets his soldiers loose on the city and cleans it out, the city stays a manageable size for a while longer?"

"Indeed. Growth is halted, and the ruler's power is consolidated. From this position of authority, he may choose in which direction he wishes to permit growth. It would not surprise me in the least to find a number of criminal factions wiped out in the course of last night's bloodshed. In addition, one or two of the more powerful Lordlings will likely not have lived through the night. Under the guise of the chastening of this city, Tull will likely have removed any who pose a legitimate threat to his power."

She nods, chewing over the words as we watch the smoke spiral upward from the eastern quadrant of the city. Though most of the fires had been put out, the air was still thick with smoke, clutching at the gullet like the claws of a bird of prey.

"I gotta ask you a question. Don't know why I haven't asked it before. I guess I was still just trying to make sense of everything. It's killing me now though. I've gotta know."

I sense her hesitation.

"Ask your question."

She breathes deeply.

"Who the fuck are you? I mean, you're this badass killer and…well, I've seen you take apart a dozen guys with just your bare hands and the freaky magic shit that comes from your wristbands. The ether or whatever you call it. You're a killer, and I don't mean that as an insult. Fuck, you're the only reason I'm still breathing, the only reason we got here in one piece. Sometimes, though, you sound more like a philosopher than a killer and…shit, it seems like you know everything about everything sometimes."

I consider the question, trying to unravel the knotted words she has spoken. Though the precise nature of her query eludes me, I get the sense of the question.

"I have lived long and have not always been the killer you see before you. As to knowledge, what little I have has been garnered from the lips of far greater souls than I."

"What about the magic bling?"

She motions toward the broken shackles at my wrists, and I find myself somewhat unmanned.

"They are a memory of the pit, of whispers from the darkness."

"It's ok, you don't have to talk about it. Didn't mean for things to get weird. I was just curious, that's all."

She turns from me, staring out toward the city below. I begin to speak, but words fail me. They are inadequate to the task, unable to represent the true horror, the majesty, the truth of that darkness which dwells within. Unable to speak more of that which troubles me, I opt instead for an easier path.

"On the morrow, I will enter the godling palace and seek audience with Tull."

She turns to me, eyes wide. "Seriously? You think he's in a talking mood right now?"

I shrug. "In my experience, those who hold the reins of power are always in need of a mercenary or two. After all, he has a problem which I am in a unique position to resolve."

She smiles, nodding. "You're gonna find his missing key."

I find myself returning her smile. "Indeed."

***

I leave the girl to guard our purloined wealth and make my way to the lower city where a few well-placed bribes yield only a little information. Rumours abound in the wake of the purge, but there is little of substance, and few souls are willing to speak freely to a stranger in such a time of strife. After a largely fruitless day spent moving from tavern to tavern, I finally happen upon a drunken sod whose tongue waggles freely for the simple price of a tankard of ale. It takes some time to wade past the murk and nonsense and get to the heart of truth in the drunkard's words. Yet truth there is, buried deep, but not less valuable for the fact.

As I had suspected, the godling Tull had used the purge to mask more pointed activities: attacking three of the four largest criminal guilds in the city. Of those three, two were shattered against the stone, their backs broken, their members slain or scattered to the winds. Only the Scorpion Brotherhood evaded the attack, surviving largely because of their knowledge of the many tunnels and caverns that crisscross the hollow heart of Tullhaven.

An offshoot of a larger guild which operates in Rust and the northern hamlets, the Scorpion Brotherhood are said to control the bulk of trade between Tullhaven and the red city. Likewise, they control the supply of fellweed and various etherically enhanced liquors upon which the city's vast labour force relies. Boasting a sizable number of recruits, the guild's greatest asset is their illustrious leader: an aged pit boss known only as the Scorpion. It is because of his gift for strategy that the guild has survived so long, threatening the godling Tull's hold over the city and surviving the great purge with relative ease.

The only other surviving guild which might hope to threaten Tull's power is the Slaver's Guild. While not as numerous or well-structured as the Scorpions, the Slaver's Guild boasts considerable wealth and exercises complete control over the exchange and purchase of all slaves within the city. It seems that Tull is less concerned by this group, largely because vast quantities of coin are tithed to his coffers by the guild and its leaders make great pains to show their allegiance and supplication to the godling ruler.

I thank the sod for his words, leaving the man with two more tankards of ale and making my way back to the girl. My mind spins of its own accord, setting forth a strategy in loose threads and binding my feet to a certain course of action. I cannot say if it has always been so, but the detailed workings of my mind seem to put me at ease. The planning of words and deeds into the days ahead seems a perfectly natural and harmonious course of action, so I give in to the process and let my mind do its work unhindered.

As I finally ascend the rickety ladder to the rooftop where we have made our camp, my mind has settled, a plan laid out with crystal clarity.

"You took your time!" the girl says, sitting up from her makeshift cot. "I've been going out of my mind up here."

I take a seat opposite the girl, reaching for the pack which houses a goodly portion of dried meat and cheese—supplies pilfered from a neighbouring tavern in the wee hours of the morning.

"On the morrow, we will walk to the palace and seek audience with Tull. We will offer our services as traveling mercenaries and request only modest means and suitable accommodations."

"Ok. Not the smartest thing you've ever said, but I'm guessing you've got a plan?"

"We will hide a little coin and some supplies here upon this rooftop. Should matters grow dire, we will meet here and flee the city."

She narrows her eyes. "Not really filling me with confidence there, boss."

I cannot help but smile.

"Take some rest. On the morrow, we will make our first move. I wish to see this godling face to face that I might take his measure."

She nods, standing to full height and stretching her arms wide. "You can rest if you want. I've been lying on my ass all day. I need to get out and do something."

In a single bound, she springs from the roof, rolling down upon a small ledge below and pouncing, cat-like, to the street beyond. Within moments she has vanished into the night, leaving me alone with my thoughts. I take the opportunity to fetch the ivory key from its hidden pouch and sit for a time, worrying the curious object between my fingers. Of the key itself there is little substance, yet the ether buzzes around the strange object, hinting at great purpose.

It brings with it an odd memory: a night of flame and sorrow, of failed rebellion and loss. I see glimpses of faces, torn and bloodied. I hear the report of rapid gunfire, smell the scent of ash and etheric discharge. A woman, impossibly beautiful, clothed in a long jacket of emerald green, her fingers taught with etheric power. A name rises on the tip of my tongue, roughly hewn and oddly shaped. Absinthe Annie.

The images pass as swiftly as they come, hinting at a past I cannot yet recover. They leave a bitter taste in my mouth.

12. Lord Tull

"Why are we doing this during the day?" The girl squints beneath the noon sun, clearly uncomfortable out in the open.

"I mean, if we were going to walk right through the door, I could understand it, but this is nuts."

"It is a matter of reputation. To steal into the palace in the dead of night and make our petition to the godling would be a great feat. To do so in broad daylight is miraculous. We are unknown to the godling and must gain his interest swiftly, so a powerful demonstration is necessary."

"Ok then, so how the fuck are we gonna be able to scoot on into the guy's bedroom without anyone noticing?"

I offer a smile in response, leading her down a short passageway near the eastern edge of the great arena. We pass servants laden with large baskets, their heads lowered as if they are so used to subservience that they no longer dare look another soul in the eye. I wait for a suitable pair and draw them out into a small nook beside the passage. The girl nods as she looks the servants up and down.

"Ok, I get what you're throwin' down here. Not exactly the most innovative approach, but it's worth a shot."

It is a simple matter to incapacitate the servants, strip them of their clothes and assume their roles. The male servant's breeches and shirt are a little tight, and I have some trouble hiding the shackles at my wrists, but we manage to enter the servant's manor without incident, mimicking the downcast gaze of the other servants.

The interior of the manor is abuzz with activity. A hundred souls bustle about the building, busily going about their tasks with the singular purpose of ants. We make our way through the lower levels, ascending to higher floors amid the bustle and managing to avoid the attention of our fellows.

The girl motions toward those servants attending in the upper halls and chambers of the palace. Unlike their drab cousins in the rooms below, these are dressed in modest finery, so as not to offend the eyes of their masters.

"What now?" the girl whispers.

By way of answer, I find my way to a hidden alcove and set about stripping the simple servant's garb from my body.

"Bring me two more, dressed in the house livery."

The girl frowns momentarily, considering my words. I see the question in her mind without the words being uttered. She wonders if I wish the hapless servants dead or delivered as they are. I do not answer that question, for I confess my own curiosity as to how the girl will approach the task.

She smiles, turns, and walks out into the hallway, returning a few moments later with two servants in tow. Clearly of higher rank than the lower servants, these two grow rapidly indignant upon seeing my unclothed form squatting in the corridor. I strike quickly, silencing the pair with rapid blows to the throat and dragging them into the darkness. The girl follows, disrobing quickly.

"This is fucking ridiculous," she spits, struggling to pull new garb over her head.

The uniforms are garish and elaborately adorned: pristine white jackets festooned with garish stones and gilded buttons, stretching to the floor. The britches are of a rough woollen texture, dyed pitch black with stripes of gold and silver running from hip to toe. The outfits are absurdly cumbersome, such that walking in a straight line is a feat of some skill. Newly garbed, we locate a series of silver trays housing a variety of ornate goblets and vessels filled with exotic fruits and nuts. We each select a suitable tray and continue our journey.

We climb several flights of stairs, careful to put out an air of privilege as we pass lesser servants and slaves. I feel the etheric force of my shackles begin to charge, as though in response to our need for anonymity. A slight amber hue emanates from the cuff of my jacket, drawing the girl's sudden attention.

"What are you doing?" she whispers, pointing a gilded jug toward my wrist.

"Be at peace, little one," I reassure her. "The shackles aid us."

"What the hell is that supposed to mean?" she asks in her curious dialect.

The question goes unanswered as we move through a thick curtain, out into a vast chamber of polished stone, filled with towering columns of white rock. The chamber is filled with revellers; Lordlings and their entourages, playing at frivolity while the city smoulders beyond the vast walls of the godling palace. A hundred souls are gathered in the great hall, laughing and talking raucously while servants pass by, boasting serving trays filled with all manner of delicacies.

"No! No! No! It cannot be thus!" A voice bellows from the large circular dais at the far end of the chamber. A man of impossible size, hemmed by rank upon rank of gilded slaves, luxuriates upon a many-cushioned throne so vast that it occupies a similar space to many of the smaller houses scattered throughout the city streets below.

"You shall not have it, Tobias! Even should the sun burn itself to ash and the moon cease its slothful sojourn!"

The godling's voice booms through the chamber, bringing hushed silence to the crowd of nobles. They turn as one toward the gilded throne, their faces adorned with false smiles that barely hide the fear etched beneath. The godling raises a small piece of stone above his head, straining against the copious weight of his arm to complete the gesture.

"Tobias thinks to best me at squares," the mammoth godling booms. "But it shall not be so, for I have seen through his scheme!"

The godling thumps the square piece against a large rectangular table. The noise of stone striking stone rings out through the chamber, echoing off its vast stone walls. As one, the gathered nobles cry out in delight, shouting their praise of the godling with cries of, *Bravo* and *Tull*. Unctuous praise fills the great hall. It is clear that the Lordlings in this chamber well understand that their sovereign speaks only in jest. Even so, the fear of sudden violence hangs so thickly in the air that one might almost reach out and touch it. Soldiers line the edge of the hall, standing to attention while the revellers continue their frivolities; less ceremonial than practical, I begin to see. Should the godling have a sudden need to separate a certain Lordling from his head, the city guard are close by to oblige.

The girl and I begin moving through the crowd, offering our refreshments to the inebriated Lordlings and their fellows. As I move closer to the throne, I see clearly the rotund figure that lounges upon it. Tull is every bit the monster of caprice and violence that rumour paints.

Heavy brows conceal dark, hateful eyes. The godling's face is powdered pure white and etched with colourful markings that bring to mind a poorly painted whore from one of the less reputable pleasure houses in the lower city. His garments are elaborately sewn kingdoms of wool and silk; many-colored and indistinguishable from the bright hues of the cushions that line the length and breadth of the throne.

I watch the godling closely, but sense nothing of what I expect. This has the feel of mummery, rather than truth. Once the items on our trays are depleted, I lead the girl back down a servant's corridor and into the heart of the palace.

"I thought you wanted to talk to Tull?" she hisses.

"That was not Tull. I seek the puppet master, not the puppet."

We move through the halls and corridors, keeping a steady pace and affecting an air of purpose. I scour every doorway and wall, scanning each new room for some sign of affectation.

"Do you have any idea where you're going?" the girl asks, her voice growing tight.

"A little. I was able to acquire a rough outline of the palace from an old merchant by the Eventide gate. It holds true for the most part, though there have been changes made to many of the rooms and corridors."

I find what I seek a moment later, but keep the realization from my eyes, continuing to move through the temple underbelly with the girl in tow. A few moments later, I pull the girl into a small larder nestled beneath a narrow staircase. We stand for a moment, cloaked in shadow.

"What is it?"

I point across the hall to one of the large kitchen chambers.

"The doorway there, by the pantry. Tell me what you see."

She squints, ducking down and peering across the hall as servants move to-and-fro.

"A couple of guards… Is that what you mean?"

I nod. "Guards in a kitchen? Does that not strike you as odd? And tell me, what is your impression of these guards?"

She looks intently into the other room.

"They look different to the other guards."

"Different how?"

"Jesus, dude, is everything a lesson with you?"

"Answer."

She lets out a deep sigh. "I dunno. They look meaner. Like they can handle themselves better than those other jokers. Also, they've got shields, big-ass ones, resting against the wall there, and bigger swords too."

"And what does this tell you?"

"Tells me these fuckers are ready for a fight. I'm guessing they could hold that doorway for a while, just the two of them, even if there was a bunch of badasses lookin' to get past."

She speaks in an odd timbre but sees the truth of it. I see, once more, that my lessons have not gone unheeded.

"You have spoken true, little one. I'll wager that the puppet master lies beyond that doorway. Doubtless there will be more guards once we are through, but for the moment we need to find a way past those men without raising the alarm."

The girl smiles. "Damn, son, you're just crushing the 80s action film stereotypes today."

The words make little sense to me.

"A distraction! You need a distraction to divert their attention so you can slip past. Something like a kitchen fire. While everyone is coughing their lungs out, we slip past the soldiers and—"

I shake my head. "These men are well trained. They will not be so easily distracted. Besides, I'll wager the door is barred from the inside. No, there is no way through this impasse without shedding a great deal of blood. We will need to act swiftly."

"Wait, you wanna kill them all? Won't that set off the alarm?"

"Indeed, it will. We shall have to kill every soul in that room, then light fires to block the entrances."

"Wait, you're gonna start killing cooks and cleaners? What the fuck, dude? I mean, I'm cool with taking out a few guards and that greasy fucker Tull, but we can't just go around killing innocent people."

"I see no other option, do you?"

She holds up a hand. "Just, give me a minute, ok? I'll think of something."

I wait, watching as she presses her mind to the issue. I read the tension in her posture, the striving of her mind against impossible circumstances. It is a cruel test, but necessary. In the days ahead, if we are to survive, she will be tested thus time and time again, and I may not be nearby to render aid.

"Ok, how about we just wait. Sit tight here for a while and wait to see if anyone goes down there. I mean, he's gotta have food and drink right? Someone's gotta go down there some time. So, when we find out who has the job, we'll knock them out, steel their uniforms and wander through without a problem."

"And when the guards see our unfamiliar faces?"

Her expression falters somewhat. "We make up some shit about the other guys being sick... Or you can pull your Jedi mind trick or whatever and put the whammy on them?"

She sighs. "Ok, so it's a shit plan. I just need more time, and I can come up with something."

I place a hand gently on her shoulder, feeling the knotted muscle tense at my touch.

"Steady yourself, little one. We need not kill these folk. Remember, the goal is to impress Tull with our stealth and utility, not to slaughter the innocent and lay waste to his guard."

"Ok, what do we do then? Bribery? Some kind of poison that knocks everybody out for a few hours?"

"Such a poison would be a welcome trick, but alas, I have no such concoction."

"What's the plan then?"

I turn to her, the smile no longer laid upon my lips. "You are young, but of age, yes?"

"What the fuck does that mean?"

"You have been with a man before?"

She snorts. "Depends what you mean by 'man.' I've had sex if that's what you're talking about, not that it's any of your fucking business."

"Then you are aware of the pull a young woman can exercise over a man?"

"I really don't like where this is going, dude. No way in fuck am I tugging off a pair of guards just to get to Tull."

"The choice is yours, little one. Distract the guards with feminine wiles, and I will slip past unseen and meet with Tull on my own. You need not pleasure the brutes, simply distract them."

"And what if I refuse?"

"Failure."

The moments pass with painful slowness as she considers the path ahead. She paces within the confined limits of the pantry, worrying at her fingernails. As if to mark her decision, she tears off the long jacket and thrusts it to the floor.

"Ok, I'm gonna play the whole woman in distress angle, ok? So, I need you to make it look like I've taken a beating."

"And what if the guards do not take the bait?"

She shrugs. "Jesus, dude, I don't fucking know. I'm doin' the best I can here, ok. I've got fuck all for tits and my ass is practically non-existent, so there's no chance of me walkin' in there and seducing a couple of guards without some kind of backstory. I figure I'll play on the whole damsel in distress ticket. This whole place is stuck in the fucking dark ages, so I'm guessing all the men here assume women are weak as shit and need their big ball sacks to come help."

I nod, sliding the dagger from my boot and cutting a shallow groove into the flesh of my right hand. I dab blood against her face and chest, tearing at her garments such that her nakedness is all but laid bare.

"Move them to the left, if you can," I offer, wiping the remaining blood off the knife and sliding it back into place.

She takes a deep breath, her chest heaving. I place a hand on her shoulder, pulling her face toward mine.

"You have your blade, yes?"

She nods.

"All is well then. If this should fail, kill the guards and make your exit. I will proceed alone if need be. Remember your training and keep your head."

She smiles, tilting her head to one side and letting forth a blood curdling scream as she darts forth into the corridor, trailing blood. I move swiftly, passing through the eastern entrance to the large kitchen and feeling the flow of etheric power through my shackles as I move toward the guarded doorway. The girl wails and falls to the floor, mumbling an unintelligible complaint as the other servants gather around and attempt to comfort her.

At first the guardsmen are unmoved, watching the spectacle without consideration. But the girl draws close, grabbing at the tunic of the first guard, imploring him with tear-stained words while she tugs at his clothing. In the final sum, it is not her beauty which draws the guards from their place. Rather, her hysterics that prompt movement. She begins to thrash and rant, spitting and frothing, lashing out with hand and fist. The guardsmen move to contain her, dragging her writhing form from the room. I move to the doorway, driving a foot forward with all my might and breaking the doors wide open at precisely the same moment the girl lets forth a shrill scream.

I move swiftly into the corridor beyond, closing the door behind me. A single guardsman lies in a heap upon the floor, knocked senseless by the door's sudden bursting. I lean the man against the doorway and move on through the corridor, stripping the outrageous steward's uniform from my body as I move.

The shackles glow with soft amber light as I traverse the dimly lit corridor. Something in their glow brings me back to the memory of the woman with raven-black hair and the long, emerald coat. Was it from her that I first learned of the ether and its various proclivities and uses? Another face rises from the past, hard as polished stone and bearing the marks of the Fleshmancer's art. His features are stern, yet there is trust and something akin to fondness in his hard eyes.

I push the memories away, moving down several flights of stairs into another corridor. The light dims suddenly, such that the corridor is draped in a thick, impenetrable darkness. Where such sightlessness may bring angst to another, it sits well with me. The years spend in dark solitude have bred within my soul a certain comfort with darkness. I feel it wrap around me like the womb and move on through the corridor.

A further three guardsmen are stationed in the murky underbelly of the temple catacombs. They are sharp-eyed and suspicious, yet the etheric energy emanating from my shackles performs an odd working in their midst. I walk with all the stealth I can muster, yet any keen-eyed soldier should be able to detect my approach: the slight scuffing of shoes on the ground, the rustling of clothing, and so on. But while the shackles glow amber, these guards hear nothing—see nothing. I pass by without the need for sudden violence. Only the last of the three senses something as I pass, reaching for his sword with a grim expression and poking tentatively at the darkness.

It is only as I move past the third soldier that I understand their true value. The three are blind; most likely blinded by the cruel godling who rules this city. They rely on sound and scent rather than that sense, which can so easily be misdirected. It confirms to me the completeness of the shackles' work. To pass by such honed instruments of detection is a boon that I am only now beginning to comprehend.

A large door, guarded by two men, stands brightly lit at the end of the final corridor. Here lies the final test. I cannot simply approach with the hope of being unseen as torches line the walls of the corridor and the men stationed at the far side are armed with spears and short swords. I feel the shackles flare brighter as I draw close to the light. It runs against the grain of my training to put such trust in an untested trick, yet I move slowly into the light, crouched and ready to run if the need arises.

The shackles' power holds, and I am able to draw right up beside the two guardsmen, passing behind the pair and lifting a cudgel from a nook in the wall. I strike swiftly and decisively, yet the blows hit home without making the slightest sound. As the guardsmen fall to the floor, I cannot help but stare in wonder at the glowing shackles upon my wrist. What manner of gift are these? What price must I pay when their use is done?

The doors give way to a large chamber, a vast room filled with light and purpose. Large tables are cluttered with maps and scribbled pieces of parchment. The walls, too, are littered with finely hewn maps and intricate drawings of various mechanical contraptions. There is an air of charged power in the chamber, as though lightning has only recently struck.

A quick glance about the room shows me a small bed and bathing tub, a library of sorts, with countless volumes placed in neat nooks cut into the stone. One side of the chamber is a workshop devoted to various mechanical oddities. Tools and trinkets lie scattered upon large tables lit by etheric lamps. The sounds of labour ring out across the room.

I approach slowly, observing the rhythmic blows of a hammer as they rise above the furthest bench, their fall punctuated by a sharp clang of metal. I stand for a moment, observing the godling at his work. He is a thin man, thin but fashioned with taught muscle and sinew.

His hair is cut short, and he wears only a simple pair of breeches, preferring to work with his chest bared to the heat emanating from a small forge nestled against the far corner of the chamber. The man before me is a machine-smith, not a corpulent brute lounging in excessive comfort in the halls above. Yet, in this man, I can feel the pent-up power of a thousand worlds. Etheric charge sits so heavily about his person, that I must hold myself to task, simply to remain standing. Doubt begins to rise from somewhere within. What vanity could make me think that I could kill a creature such as this?

The hammer blows cease, bringing silence to the chamber. The godling Tull stands to full height, sweating profusely and labouring for breath. He lays his hammer down carefully.

"Who is it that disturbs my work this day?" he asks, his voice sharp and direct.

I smile. "A weapon. A tool. A sharp instrument for hire."

He turns slowly, sharp eyes looking toward the chamber doorway.

"I see. And your sudden appearance is intended to impress, I gather?"

"Merely to show my worth."

He nods, picking up a cloth on a nearby bench and beginning to wipe the sweat from his chest and arms.

"Tell me, how many of my men did you kill?"

"None."

He looks up at this, eyes narrowed.

"Truly?"

I nod in return.

"Then you have indeed shown your worth. Tell me, what is it you wish of me?"

"To work. Nothing more."

"I see. Am I to guess then that this work of yours comes at a significant cost?"

"It does indeed."

"And may I enquire as to what you wish to do with such wealth?"

"You may ask, but I shall not answer. My reasons are my own. I promise only that I shall not harm you or your interests whilst I am in your employ."

Tull laughs, a rough, hacking sound. "It amuses me that you think yourself able to render me harm. Truly, you are a bold soul, if somewhat deluded."

He leans against a nearby table, smiling. "Tell me, what makes you think I have need of a mercenary such as yourself?"

"Your need is plain. You would have killed me the moment I stepped foot in this chamber if you had no intention of securing my services, or at least considering the matter. It is likely that you already knew of my approach before I breached the first doorway. The matter is already done; all that is left now is to agree on a price."

"I see. And what price did you have in mind?"

"Gold, silver, precious stones. I have no need of chits."

"Very well. And what are the limits of your service?"

I shrug. "I stay in Tullhaven for no more than a year. During that time, I will render whatever service you desire, provided it means not to harm to myself or my kin."

"If I wish you to murder a babe in its cot?"

"Then I will do so."

"And if I bid you start a revolution, slaughter every beast that takes in air upon the great wastes, or kill a rival godling?"

"All but the last are acceptable. To kill a godling will cause me harm."

He stands in silence for a time, chewing over my words as though mulling over a fine wine. I feel thin tendrils of etheric energy twist their way around my mind, prodding and poking, trying to find their way within. Through no effort of my own, the etheric cords are rebuffed. It seems that the darkness that haunts my dreams will suffer no other tormentor within the hallowed halls of my mind.

"Very well, shackled man. As it happens, I have need of someone with your particular talents. You are aware of the Scorpion Brotherhood, yes?"

"I am."

"Then your task is simple. Bring me the head of the Scorpion, and you will be paid handsomely."

He moves to a small wooden chest sitting beside the simple bed. Tull pulls a small pouch from inside and tosses it to me. Inside the pouch lie several diamonds, rubies, and emeralds—a small fortune.

"Double the price once you bring me his head."

There is an unnerving confidence to the godling's voice, which hints at foreknowledge. I consider the wealth nestled inside the small pouch. A significant enough amount to secure my services, but not so much that I would simply take the gems and flee. It seems a little too convenient to have such a sum at hand the moment I walk into his private chamber.

"One question, if I may?" I ask.

He nods.

"You are a godling, with all the power of your race. Would it not be a simple thing to hunt down the Scorpion yourself and put an end to him?"

Tull smiles, considering my words carefully. He walks over to the nearest workbench, lifting a small mechanical contraption with innumerable dials and cogs that whir and rattle as he lifts the strange device.

"You have heard of the so-called Clockmaker God, yes?"

I nod.

"Truly a genius, a being of infinite magnitude. He and I were…close once. Brothers, if you will. We worked side by side when he built the red city. We spoke of many things and made many plans; all of which were thrown into disarray by Eva and her obsession. Once the council was broken, the Clockmaker set himself apart from his kin and grew secretive. The great strength of his mind was put toward obscurities and myths."

He looks at the small mechanical contraption, something like sorrow written across his face.

"But I digress. To answer your question, I do not venture beyond the bounds of this chamber firstly because it is necessary for my true self to remain hidden. There are forces at work within the cosmos which are at odds with my kind, and I have no wish to court their attention. Thus, the corpulent puppet who rules in my place; a well-crafted shadow-play to keep the citizens of this little hamlet in check."

He places the device carefully back down upon the table, moving toward the far end of the chamber and pulling aside a thick, black curtain.

"Quite apart from my need for anonymity, I am possessed of a singular obsession; one that the Clockmaker and I shared long ago."

As the curtain moves aside, I see a second chamber open up, its walls lined with shelves and glass chambers lit by dozens of etheric bulbs that hang from above. It is a museum in miniature and, as I step closer, the bizarre nature of its exhibits become clear to me.

"You are familiar with the Shadowspawn, yes?" Tull asks.

"I am."

"They are a fascinating breed, truly fascinating. While monstrous in size and brutality in the north, those who appear this far south tend to be of a more fleeting and diminutive nature."

Within the large glass tanks, black creatures of nightmare skitter and claw at invisible bonds. The largest of the brood is only a little taller than I, but each beast writhes with tooth and claw, salivating from their various maws.

"There is little rhyme or reason to their physical properties," Tull goes on, walking ahead through the rows of glass jars and chambers, stroking them lovingly. "They spring to life in a moment and are gone shortly after. Yet their variety and ubiquity are staggering."

I move toward one of the closest specimens, an oily black creature with gnarled features and a many-horned head. While no larger than a cat, the Shadowspawn spits and claws against the glass like a rabid beast.

"I truly believe that, within these creatures lies the secret to this world and those beyond. If one can comprehend the inner working of the Shadowspawn, one can unlock the secrets of the cosmos."

His words take on a fervent edge, eyes burning with fiery zeal. I tap the closest chamber, sending the Shadowspawn within into a frenzy.

"I had thought the Shadowspawn only fleeting things? Yet you have devised a means of capturing them?"

Tull nods, smiling. "You have heard the appellation *Collector* no doubt, yes?"

I nod.

"It is one of the few truths I have allowed to spread in the world above. For in truth, I am a collector of sorts, though my doppelganger in the palace above is seen to collect only petty baubles and worthless trinkets. Yet, my collection is not a matter of miserly acquisition. I collect only that I may study and unlock the hidden truths within. For it is with this great work that I may understand the true enemy and seek a means of defending myself against their intentions."

He seems to remember himself momentarily.

"Come, there is another, swifter path to and from this chamber. I give you leave to use it when you return with the head of the Scorpion."

He motions to a small nook beside the museum entrance and a tightly winding flight of stairs that spirals upwards.

"Understand I cannot offer any official recognition or privilege. You must undertake your work without sanction."

"As it should be."

He considers me a final time, nodding. "Very well. Be on you way, shackled man. Return with my prize swiftly."

***

"Ok, so what's the plan here, princess?" the girl asks, sitting upon her perch, overlooking the city below. "We gonna kill Tull or what?"

Her words bring a smile to my lips. "Are you especially keen to kill a godling?"

She shrugs. "I thought you had a thing for them? Weren't you locked up by the Red Queen and her bunch?"

I pour myself a cup of ale, watching the amber liquid flow gently from the jug.

"For my part in the rebellion, yes. Though, in truth, I remember little of those days. I have other reasons for my animosity toward their kind."

She nods. "Got it. You're an old-fashioned racist, huh?"

The word is unknown to me. It draws a puzzled expression, but the girl waves it away with a smile.

"So, like I said before, are we gonna kill Tull or what?"

"We are going to bide our time, work for the godling, and gather resources."

"So, not only are we not killing the bastard that torched this city and had his goons rape and pillage their way through the streets, we're gonna work for him?"

"True enough."

"Ok, so why? Why the fuck would we work for a prick like that?"

I pour a second cup, handing the first to the girl. She takes the drink, sniffing it with a grim expression.

"Of late, the past is a strange country to me. I remember only a little of what has come before, and those memories are scattered and murky, as though seen through dark glass. The darkness of the pit has taken much from me. It was a thief that stole sanity and lucid thought for many years. Now that I begin to grow whole again, I am left with a fractured mind and a bloodied soul. Yet, I feel much, in my gut if not my mind. I remember the feel of shooting irons, the touch of a naked blade against the skin of a foe, the shedding of blood, and sudden violence. I cannot say why such horrors bring me solace, but they do. It is only among such dark remembrances that I feel truly myself."

I take another sip, looking out over the scattered lights of the city below, unable to look the girl in the eye for fear of what I will see there.

"I am no saint, little one. Nor have I ever pretended to be thus. I am a soldier, a mercenary, an assassin. I have lived upon the knife's edge, killing for profit at the behest of wicked men. I know not how to work the loom nor sow seed or harvest crop. I am no merchant or tinkerer. But in matters of war and bloodshed, I have knowledge enough to fill a thousand bloody tomes. So, as I came to this city, a scheme arose within my heart, unbidden and growing more substantial with each passing day. I see it more clearly than the daylight sun. This godling and his petty kingdom are ripe for the plucking, little one."

I pull the small purse from my pocket and throw it toward the girl. It lands upon her lap, and she begins rifling through its contents with growing interest.

"A small fortune, and that is but a tenth of what the godling will offer should we continue to render aid. In his service, we will put down rabid dogs and frustrate his enemies. We will bring him the head of the Scorpion and lay waste to the guilds and pit crews that threaten his control. We will make ourselves an invaluable tool to the godling and then, when the fruit is ripe, we will cut him down and decimate all that he has built from the ground upwards."

The girl slaps her thigh, letting out a sharp *whoop*.

"Fuck yeah! That's some old-school vengeance shit there, bossman. You work the guy so you can get nice and close to him, then jam a blade in the fucker's back."

I hold up a hand to halt her words.

"Understand, little one, we will leave this city a broken furnace. Many more will die with our passing than ever would have perished if we left the godling untouched. If we kill Tull and destroy all that he has built up, a great many souls will perish. Some in fire, some in blood and blade. Women will be despoiled, the old and infirmed will be slain, and the streets will run red with blood and sorrow."

She stares at me, unblinking, uncomprehending.

"Ok, then…why do it? Why not just leave the bastard alone and take his money? I mean, if we're just gonna make it all worse, why would we even do it?"

I feel the ether stir as my iron bonds begin to glow with crimson light. It takes an effort of will to suppress the anger that rises from within, an unnatural thing that goes beyond the dictates of my own temperament. The shackles settle, and I take a deep breath.

"Because I cannot suffer the godlings to live, child. They are a scourge upon this land and that other, waking world. They must be purged from the cosmos without remorse or regret."

Even as I say the words, I wonder how much of them has come from me and how much from the darkness within. I feel the guidance of dark hands upon my soul as I voice the threat. I cannot say whether the anger and certitude I feel are mine alone or borrowed from the voices in the dark.

"The path ahead will be troublesome. We will fill this world with blood and terror, such that all the wealth in the cosmos could not outweigh our guilt. I tell you this because you have a choice to make, little one. I have taught you much in the little time we have had together, and you have learned well indeed. I do not doubt that you could find valuable employ as a caravan guard or at some such trade; but this may not be necessary. I offer

you the purse at your feet as fair price for the gift you
have given me. For it is you who dragged me from the
pit and forced me to climb into the light. I cannot forget
such kindness, and so I offer you this choice: take the
gems, buy yourself a life of ease until the coin runs dry.
Part ways with me, and we shall share no regrets. Stay,
and you must partake in my blood debt."

I wait for her reply. The girl looks out over the city,
weighing the purse in one hand. In my mind's eye, I see
the path that lies before me should we part ways. It is
a dark and miserable path; a return to the pit which I
cannot avoid. Some part of me cries out in the silence
that rests between us, begging for the girl to stay. Yet I
utter no sound. I must offer this to the girl freely and
without regret.

"I lost something when I came here," she says. "I
lost something that made me feel powerful, important.
I didn't really know it at the time. Took the thing for
granted if I'm honest. Then I got shoved into this shitfest,
and I lost it."

She turns to me, eyes burning brightly.

"I'd be dead or worse if you hadn't done your magic
mojo trick and kicked three kinds of shit out of those
bastards back in the desert. You taught me how to fight,
how to protect myself, and, for the first time since I got
here, I'm starting to feel powerful again. It's not the same
as what I had; it's kind of better. I know what I am now.
I know what I have and what I can do. This place is a
shithole, but it makes you realize what you have."

She tosses me the pouch, smiling.

"Anyway, I'm not going anywhere. For starters,
someone's gotta keep an eye on you, or you'll end up

tearing the universe a new asshole and setting the whole damned thing on fire. Secondly, I ain't finished learning everything you've got to teach."

I nod, feeling the muscles of my body relax a little.

"Very well then."

She holds up a finger. "Just a couple of things though. I don't care what you told that prick Tull, we're not killing any kids or people that don't deserve killing, and if I see an asshole that needs his face broken, I'm gonna do it, even if it means rocking the boat a little bit; got it?"

Somewhere beneath the darkness, I feel warmth rise within. She is a firebrand, this one—a jewel in the rough.

"Very well. Though we may have to employ a great deal of subterfuge to maintain such rules."

She claps her hands together sharply.

"Great. So, where do we start?"

"On the morrow, we begin hunting our Scorpion."

13. The Hunt Begins

"Seven kills. It is not enough to make an assassin, but you will lose your hesitation. You will no longer feel the guilt of shedding blood. To kill the Chieftain who tried to brutalize you was one thing, but it is quite another the end the life of a man who never sees you coming."

With those words, I set the girl upon her path. I feel no guilt, no culpability for the trajectory upon which her feet are now set. In this hard, unforgiving world she will learn to kill, to survive, to thrive on the blood of her enemies. This is the only gift I can offer.

Yet, I cannot say to what extent I am driven by the darker impulses that dwell within. Do I wish to teach the girl in order to pay her back for the light she has ignited within, or does the darkness seek to use her as its puppet? There is an expediency in the girl's tutelage which serves our immediate goal; but there is a more far-reaching purpose which drives me forward. I have not love for the godlings, that much is true. But neither do I possess the requisite folly to make war upon their wretched race. It is the first duty of the assassin to preserve one's own existence. War upon the godling race is anathema to that goal, yet I find myself irreversibly drawn into such a war, dragging the girl with me, albeit as a willing accomplice.

I am aware of these disjointed tensions within my soul, yet still feel no guilt, no remorse at the blood that will be shed and the innocent souls that will be brutalized as a result of the coming war. Perhaps, if I were properly furnished with a full suite of memory, I might be capable of resisting the darkling urge that drives me onward? Perhaps not.

As it is, we proceed.

The plan is laid out within my mind, in every detail and with frightful clarity, as though some other intelligence has placed it there. I see the *why* and the *how* of it; the branching paths that twist and turn as matter changes and time passes.

"We must establish ourselves as a viable threat to the Scorpion," I advise the girl as we explore the boundaries of our new abode—a lesser lording's residence, recently vacated by a noble who happened to fall afoul of the godling Tull—or his puppet.

"The purge offered Tull an opportunity to disband the Clockwork Embassy and Lumber Guild's both. There is thus a gap in the city's trade which needs to be filled. The Scorpion intends to fill that void, so we must frustrate their efforts and establish our own reputation."

The girl moves out onto a spacious ledge which overlooks the arena and a thousand cluttered dwellings in the lower city. She leans over the balcony, assessing the drop to the street far below.

"Sounds like you want to set up shop here, start your own guild?"

"Indeed, that is precisely what we must do. Or, at least, we must promote the appearance of a rival guild newly born from the ashes left by the Tinkerers and Lumber rats. The Scorpion is secretive, and too well protected to attack directly. It would be difficult to do so without raising suspicion of Tull's involvement."

"And I'm guessing he wants to keep out of this?"

"Yes. In truth, he does not want the Scorpion Brotherhood eradicated altogether. He simply wishes to cut off its head and sew disarray for a time. In this way, he can halt the advance of his enemy yet maintain the mercantile interests which the Scorpion Brotherhood controls. Trade will continue to flow through the city, but any designs the Scorpion may have had upon Tull's leadership will wane."

She moves back inside the spacious house, running hands along the polished stone walls.

"Ok, so how do we set up a rival guild with just the two of us?"

"By the judicious application of deception. The right words whispered in the right ears will serve us well. A few pointed kills and some well-placed disruption and our legitimacy will be assured. We must move swiftly and with care. For a time, this will be enough, but before long we will need allies to serve as proxies. Brutes and coin men, tinkerers and thieves. We must stay relatively small in number. We need only to garner the Scorpion's attention, not to take over their entire enterprise. Guilds such as theirs do not suffer competition lightly. A few pokes of the stick and the beast will attack. That is when we will have our opening."

"What's the deal with this place then? I mean, don't get me wrong, I'm not complaining. This place is way better than our last joint. They've even got a toilet! Like, a proper toilet, not a damned hole in the ground."

"This house will provide respite when it is needed. Our operations will take place elsewhere. There is an abandoned warehouse by the skyport. We will work from there and reserve this place for sleep."

"You don't think they'll come after us?"

"I am counting on the fact. For this reason, we can never enter this residence in view of the street below. Always by rooftop and always in the dead of night."

The girl nods. "Got it."

"There is another reason for such a locale."

As if anticipating my words, the giant and his entourage enter the house. Though bare chested, the arena brute, Rook now wears pants of fine silk and a jewel-encrusted sash that hangs across his mammoth frame. The big man nods as he sees me, then bows a little to the girl. She spins to face me, confused.

"Rook and his family have been granted their freedom by the godling and given the status of minor Lordlings. They will live at this house and care for it."

A woman with dark skin and a tall, thin, frame enters behind Rook. A young girl clutched at the woman's dress, wide-eyed.

"My wife Ashanti, and daughter Kya," the big man says, motioning to his family.

Others enter the house as well: servants dressed in plain brown robes that set about various preparations, each one knowing their task as though born to it.

"Daisy," the girl says, holding out her hand for the big man to take. "I figure you already know old tall and brooding over there?"

She moves to Kya, smiling as she bends down to hold out a hand to the girl.

"Hello, princess. Aren't you a sweetie?"

The girl blushes, moving further behind her mother's legs. With a little coaxing, Kya begins to talk with the girl. I draw Rook aside as Ashanti watches over her child, still uncertain in our company.

The big man clasps my shoulder as he draws close. "Thank you, brother, for this kindness. Though I have been elevated to the status of Lordling, I have no wealth, no lands or income to draw upon."

I nod. "It serves us well to have you living here, my friend."

"Still, you have my thanks. It has been too many moons since I have held my wife and child in these arms. I have you to thank for such good fortune."

"You may not be so thankful as time passes."

He smiles. "I am no stranger to suffering, brother. When the time comes to spill blood, I will not shy away from the task. Know only that I seek to keep my family safe from harm. This goal stands above all others."

"I understand. Yet, there is more that I must ask of you. This house, your new station. You must play the part of new-made Lordling in every possible way. Our new enterprise will see us well stocked with wealth and you must spend a portion of that wealth with great flamboyance if you are to play your part."

The big man frowns. "Such a thing will surely draw attention to this house."

"Indeed, it will, and that is, in fact, your purpose. You must play your part among the lesser nobility. You must attend balls and festivals, adorn your wife with precious gems, furnish this house with exotic furnishings. You must become a Lordling in more than mere title; though it may leave a bitter taste in your mouth to spend so frivolously."

The giant's brows furrow. "And what if others should enquire as to the sudden source of my wealth?"

"I do not doubt that the other Lordlings will find you an irresistible curiosity. You are new-made and that is suspicious enough. You are also of a foreign land and, more than this, a former slave and champion of the Arena. They will whisper daggers at your back and speak shrewdly to your face with honeyed words willed with hidden barbs. In truth, your sudden wealth will be the least provocative of your traits. When they do enquire, tell them that you have secured a lucrative trade agreement with a benefactor who wishes to remain anonymous, and simply leave it at that."

He nods, solemnly.

"Make no mistake, friend Rook, this is not a cessation of hostilities. You are not giving up the life of a warrior so that you may run to fat. It is simply that the terms and locale of the battle have changed. Now you must fight with words and nuances rather than fists and blades."

"I have no skill with such weapons."

I place a hand upon his arm. "You have more skill than you know, friend. Speak little and let your stature talk on your behalf. It is said that even a fool seems wise when he says nothing. You are no fool, so your silence will speak volumes."

"Will not such a course cause offense?"

I cannot help but smile. "Your very presence will cause offense. You are the first slave that the godling has seen fit to elevate to the status of Lordling. Your fellow nobles cannot help but hate you for that fact. Their animosity will only increase when they see that you are not the pauper they suspect. Throw a little wealth around and their hatred will blossom to even greater heights."

"And this is a good thing? You wish to set the royals against me?"

"Just so. You are already an anomaly, friend Rook. That is precisely why the puppet godling chose to elevate you, that and the order given by Tull. But it seems clear that this corpulent puppet king has taken a fancy to you. If you simply fall into step with the other Lordlings, he will soon forget you. But make yourself unique among their company, distance yourself from the others, and the puppet will continue to show you favour."

"And this is important?"

"The more attention you and your new house attracts, the less visible our true work becomes. While you parade about in the light, we keep to the shadows, sawing at the struts and pillars upon which this crooked city has been founded."

He takes in a deep breath, face uncertain. "You still intend to kill the godling then?"

"I do."

He nods. "I have heard your words and will do as you ask. But in one respect I cannot mimic the Lordlings. I will not suffer the keeping of slaves. No man should wear a collar, much less a woman or child."

"Friend Rook, you shall have great wealth, and you now have a title." I reach into a coin pouch and pull out a small emerald, handing it to the man. "Take this and go on the morrow to the Slaver market. Buy yourself as many as you wish and take them into your house. Free them, make them servants rather than slaves. While within your house, they are under your protection and no Lordling can make claim over them."

The sound of laughter comes from the adjoining room, drawing our attention away. The girl approaches, smiling broadly. Rook bows a little and takes his leave, returning to his wife and child, the emerald clasped tightly in his hand.

"They're amazing," she says, drawing close. "Ashanti and Kya came here together, and then Rook followed after. They were a family before this place. Somehow Rook figured out a way to get through to the Traumwelt. Some kind of voodoo magic or some shit like that. Amazing!"

The sound of a child's laughter continues from the other room.

"Ashanti told me a little about her home world, and it sounds nothing like ours."

"Does it surprise you, little one, that this place of dreams may connect to more worlds than our own? We have not spoken much of our world; perhaps we, too, are from disparate worlds, drawn to this place by some curious power?"

"Yeah, I kind of figured. Just some of the stuff you say every now and then doesn't really make sense. First, I thought you were just some old western dude, but that doesn't work."

"Indeed."

"I wanted to ask you as well; how come there are no kids in this city? I mean, there are a couple, but hardly any. No babies and no pregnant women."

"I cannot say why, but it is a defining characteristic of this world that children cannot be born within it. A child may pass to the Traumwelt but not an infant. I presume that the mind needs to be sufficiently mature to permit the sojourn."

"So, no babies at all?"

"Indeed. The families that you see around you are formed by those who come to this world, not those who existed prior to their journey here. Children who are drawn into the Traumwelt are often adopted by existing families. Those self-same families are formed by souls who met here in the world of dreams. It is a matter of solace and expediency."

"But not with Ashanti and Kya though. Like I said, they came through together."

"On rare occasions, I believe such things occur."

"And then Rook somehow managed to find his way here too?"

I smile. "I do not doubt that friend Rook would tear the world asunder and devour the sun if it took him from his family. Perhaps, in his world, such things are possible? Perhaps it is simple a question of the man's indominable will?"

***

We leave the house and begin our true work, heading first to the dock house which will be home to our new enterprise. The building is dilapidated and filled with the stench of rotting fish, but it offers the necessary seclusion and anonymity for what lies ahead.

I send the girl out day and night to reconnoitre and spend my days in the various taverns and ale houses throughout the lower city. Tullhaven lacks the grandeur and scope of the red city, but its various social and cultural structures are no less intricate for that fact. I learn much as I spread a little coin and offer drink to local merchants and workmen. There is unrest in this city, a discontentment which is fostered by the Scorpion Brotherhood and their mysterious leader.

Of the Scorpion himself, little is known. He acts always through proxies and is never seen in person. Some say that he dwells perpetually in the dank underbelly of the city: the network of sewers and tunnels that runs beneath Tullhaven. Others place him in a lofty airship, flying in the skies above and never touching solid ground. Of particular note is the fierce reputation the guild leader has fostered among the city folk. Much like the godling who toils away in solitude beneath the garish palace, the Scorpion has established a powerful image which inspires fear and awe.

I take special note not to dwell on the matter when talking with others; never raising the guild in conversation and keeping to general questions about the state of affairs in the city proper. I pose most often as the regent for a mercantile house from the red city but feign great secrecy when asked precisely which house I represent.

I continue the girl's education, instructing her to continue her thievery as the nights pass. We plunder the Lordling manors and stock Rook's strongbox with all manner of precious jewels and an abundance of chits. The girl is careful to take only those goods which will not be missed, and nothing that can be clearly traced back to its owner. As her skill increases, we begin to explore the criminal locales throughout the city. These are far better protected than the Lordling manors, and each chit and sliver of gold is carefully weighed, so their absence is always noted.

A few well-placed thefts and soon the Slaver's Guild and Scorpion Brotherhood are at each other's throats. The tenuous peace the two groups had been able to foster over the past decade begins to crumble as we leave incriminating suggestions at the site of each theft. Tensions begin to rise, and soon bloodshed spills onto the streets, prompting action by the city guard.

Upon a balmy night some weeks after our enterprise commenced, the girl sidles into the small chamber to the rear of our makeshift thief's den. She sticks to the shadows, clinging to the walls as she walks soundlessly toward me from behind. She has grown deadly quiet these past few weeks, taking to the thief's art as though born to the role.

"You return early?" I ask, scribbling notes in a small ledger.

"God damn it! How the hell did you hear me?"

She moves out from the shadows holding a small satchel, clothed in her customary black fabric wrapped tightly about her slender frame.

"I heard nothing."

"Then how the fuck did you know I was here?"

"You reek of sweat."

She sniffs beneath her arms, frowning.

"I jest, little one. You forget, I was reborn in darkness. It is my native state. You cannot hope to avoid notice whilst skulking in the dark behind me. Not so with other men though. Your skill continues to grow."

She drops the satchel upon the table, falling to a nearby chair and pulling back her cowl with an exasperated breath.

"Ok, well that's it then. I don't think we can go pinching shit from the Scorpions again. They're out for blood, and they've got a triple guard at all their safe houses. Slavers are all beefed up too and so are the Orn Merchants and the city guard."

I nod. "Good. You have done well."

"So, what's next then? You any closer to finding out where the Scorpion is?"

"I have not, but nor did I expect such. The Scorpion values secrecy above all else. He acts only though lieutenants and keeps his identity from all but his most loyal soldiers. One could drown the Scorpion Brotherhood in blood and not come close to learning their leader's identity. It has caused me to wonder whether the Scorpion is one man or simply a figurehead, an idea propagated by those who rule the Brotherhood."

"Ok. You want me to steal some more shit?"

"No, little one. It is time for you to learn a different lesson."

I clap my hands thrice, loudly. The sharp sound rings out through the building, echoing off tattered walls. Figures step from the shadows, clothed in black and dark brown, each bearing hidden knives and cudgels. They have the look of experienced thieves and cutthroats. Five men and two women; all slight of build and hard as iron.

The girl says nothing as the figures surround her. She smiles.

"You are not surprised by our guests?" I ask.

She shakes her head. "Figured you'd explain why they were here soon enough."

There is no lie to her words. She has grown so accustomed to thievery, to moving in the shadows and assessing her surroundings, that she likely spotted the seven figures before entering the building. Even now, standing cross-legged and leaning against a post, she holds both hands by sheathed daggers; ready to draw the weapons and strike at a moment's notice.

"I have secured the services of these individuals for the next few months. They will work for you in whatever capacity you deem necessary and, in return, will receive a healthy portion of our profits."

She nods.

"As you know, I have business of my own to which I must attend, so I will leave you to divide their labour and pay their fee."

She turns to the figures, assessing each with a critical eye. And here the mummery begins. We have spent long hours rehearsing the words and deeds which follow. She plays her part well, strolling to the tallest of the group:

a broad-shouldered man with heavy scars on his cheeks and dark, sullen eyes. One by one, she numbers them off.

"We won't deal in names. You don't know mine, and I don't want to know yours. While you work with us, you'll get a number, and that's how we'll do it. You can be one, big man. You're two, three, four, five, six, and you can be seven, princess."

She smiles, moving in front of the group.

"You refer to each other using your new name. You refer to me as Shadow." She points a finger in my direction. "You call him Shackle."

The newly named *One* raises his hand. She nods in his direction.

"What are we to call this guild?" he asks in a heavy accent.

She shrugs. "Call it whatever the fuck you want. Maybe, the Shadow Guild, or something like that. Keep it vague and don't get yourselves into a situation where you have to talk about who or what we are. Just do your job and get in and out as quickly as you can."

Three raises her hand, talking without waiting for the girl to acknowledge her.

"And what is it we are required to do? The...Shackle was not clear on our responsibilities."

Shadow, as I must now come to know her, smiles. She unrolls a large piece of parchment on one side of the table, unfurling a roughly marked map and beckoning the group closer. She jabs at the map with one finger, punctuating her words with repeated jabs.

I leave her to the work, moving to the furthest corner of the room and standing in darkness. She speaks well, ordering her troops to definitive action. When it is done, the cutthroats leave as they came, and Shadow finds me sitting in darkness. She waits for the last of the crew to leave before speaking, and only then, speaks in hushed tones.

"How was that?"

I nod. "Excellent. You have established yourself well. Now, we must hope that they fulfil their part of the venture."

"And what do I do if one of them steps out of line?"

"You discipline them, harshly."

"What if they all decide they want to take me on?"

"Then you put them down like rabid dogs and we begin again."

She nods, but I can see that understanding is yet to dawn. I wait for a time, to see if she is able to work through it.

"Back when we first started," she says, staring out through the ruined window of the dock house, "you told me that I'd have to kill seven people before I really knew what I was doing, before the hesitation went away?"

"I did."

"Ok, so I'm thinking it's not a coincidence that we've got seven bastards working for us. I don't think it's a coincidence at all. In fact, I'd go so far as to say that you brought these pricks in to do our dirty work, just so that you can have me kill them off once we're done with them."

"You have an astute mind, little one."

"Jesus, Kane, you're like a parent that won't let his kid name a pet rat. You make me give them numbers instead of names because you know I'm gonna have to put the bastards down eventually."

I turn to her, seeing the conflict waring behind her eyes. I wonder, somewhat woodenly, whether I too had struggled with the matter so firmly when first called upon to kill.

"I can give you their names if you wish, or, at least, the names they go by. If it helps, these are not good people as you would say. They are cutthroats and brigands each. Most have come from the Scorpion's own ranks, too unruly and blood thirsty for even the criminal guilds of this city to abide. They care only for coin and would slit the throat of their birth mother if they saw the slightest advantage in it. They are thieves and liars, but much more than this. They kill for pleasure, not merely expediency. Even now, I dare say the bulk of the group has designs on murdering you while your back is turned."

She snorts. "How much of that shit is even true? You're just telling me what I want to hear so that when it comes time to kill them, I don't go all weak at the knees."

"It is truth, whether you choose to believe it or not. I have kept your requirements in mind and ensured that those you slay are not innocents."

She nods. "Ok, well I'll get the job done when it's time."

I nod. "Very well."

11. The Scorpion

For the next month, I insinuate myself into the criminal underbelly of Tullhaven. Working my way through various crews with ruthless efficiency. I perform every task given me with resolute perfection and ask nothing but the agreed price for my efforts. When asked the reason for my diligence, I reply only of my hatred toward the godling Tull and his crooked regime.

I find myself warming to the narrative as the days and nights pass. I invest the story with new details, using the shackles at my wrists as totems and symbols of my previous oppression. I am a slave reborn, a man with fire burning within and a drive to make the godlings pay in whatever small way I can.

At first, I am set to pilfer minor objects from rival crews. Proving adept at this task, I am soon set to guarding safe houses, running small operations, and eventually killing rival brutes where the need arises. My lack of ambition serves me well as I rise through the ranks of one of Tullhaven's lesser criminal gangs. The Smokehouse Brawlers are a small and inconsequential outfit, specializing in petty theft and extortion among the lesser merchants and travellers who frequent the southern portion of the city. Their reach widens considerably as I am permitted greater responsibility and, though their coffers overflow with coin, before long the grizzled bear of a man who runs the crew begins to grow suspicious despite my protestations at having no designs upon his position.

They come for me in the dead of night, three Smokehouse thugs with blades drawn and faces masked. I hear them in the distance, their clumsy, fumbling movements too difficult to ignore. I watch from the darkness as they approach, three large men brandishing steel and trying very much to assume the aspect of skilled assassins. I can't help but sigh as the brutes approach. In the darkness they are clumsy and ill-prepared for an enemy that fights back. I kill the first quickly, relying on a mixture of stupidity and fear to bring down the remaining pair. They slash wildly in the darkness, realizing too late that they are friend and not foe, having cut one another to ribbons while I watch from the shadows.

I bend down to pull a long knife from one of the dead men, delivering the mercy stroke to the man and his convulsing partner. The path to the Smokehouse den leads me through twisting city streets, and I breathe in the night air, revelling in the slight coolness which contrasts vividly with the blistering heat of the day. Here and there, I spy a lone soul standing watch beside a nondescript doorway: thugs sent to guard the entrances to unlicensed pleasure houses and gambling dens. I make sure to pass by a well-known Scorpion den on my way to the Smokehouse, picking up sufficient interest that one of the guardsmen follows me to my destination.

He waits at the opposite side of the street as I enter the Smokehouse through a high window. I know the building well enough to avoid the six men standing guard in the common room below. It is a simple thing to scale a wall, climb through an unsecured window, move to the doorway, and jam a chair beneath the handle to wedge the door tightly shut.

Throughout all of this, the bullish leader of the Smokehouse Brawlers lies snoring wildly upon his over-stuffed bed. I consider waking the man but have no need to visit terror upon such a petty monarch. He is merely a steppingstone, a necessary step along the path to the Scorpion. I harbour no special hatred toward the man. He simply acts within the bounds of his nature, as we all must do.

I cut the man's throat, pressing a pillow over his face as he bleeds out in gurgled silence. The deed done, I find an oil lantern nearby and spill some of its contents across the bed and the rest of the room. I light the lantern and dash it to the floor, slipping through the window and into the night as fire erupts behind me. I do not bother to observe the results of my actions. They are predictable and of little consequence. What matters is that word of this night's events will reach the Scorpion.

***

"It is a curious thing," I address Shadow as she sits opposite me in the parlour of Rook's stately home. "It seems that their most pressing quality is that of honour, or honesty at least. The Scorpion cares less about skill than loyalty."

She nods, picking at a heel of bread. "Yeah, I hear the same thing. That's what makes them so strong. It's not even their numbers, it's the fact that they're all so loyal. Shit goes down and they all know they've got each other's backs."

"Just so. I confess, I find myself admiring the Scorpion for it. Having worked with half a dozen criminal guilds these past months and finding nothing but predictable malice and jealousy, it sets the Scorpion Brotherhood in stark contrast."

"Have they approached you yet?"

"Not yet, but I am close. And what of you and the seven? Or *six,* is it?"

She drops the bread onto the table, scowling. "Fucker tried to keep the take for himself. The others found out, so I had to do something about it. Stupid prick. If he'd just been better at his job, I wouldn't have... Anyway, it's done, I guess."

She recounts the tale whereby the man known simply as *Four* sought to hold back a greater portion of his takings than was agreed. Shadow had acted swiftly, sending the man to the docks for a quick task and ensuring that he did not return. Her hands begin to shake as she speaks of the matter. I pour her a cup of ale and slide it across the table.

"This will steady your nerves."

She shakes her head. "It's my stomach I'm worried about, not my nerves. I don't get it. Four was a fucking prick. Just a real bad seed. You could see it as soon as look at him. I don't doubt that he deserved to be killed, probably a dozen times over. So, why the fuck do I feel like this? I haven't slept in a week, and I keep seeing the thing play over and over in my head. It wasn't like this with the Chieftain and his goons. I mean, I felt shitty for a few days, but nothing like this."

"The Chieftain's death was born of anger and retribution. You struck in the heat of the moment, out of an instinctual need to survive. But this second death was a matter of cool calculation. You ended a man's life by choice, for expediency's sake. The act was not coupled with fierce anger or the need to survive. Truthfully, this will live with you till your dying day."

She looks up at me. "Do you still remember your first?"

I shake my head. "Too much has been lost to me, little one. On a good day, I barely remember myself, let alone deeds long past. But I do remember the memory of that first death staying within me right up to the pit. Even if I cannot recall the memory itself."

"Ok, so how do I deal with it?"

"Give it time. As I have said, when you reach your seventh, the barb will no longer sting so viciously. In the meantime, busy yourself with your work. Tell me, how have the others reacted to the death?"

She shrugs. "Didn't give a shit. Especially because I divided his share among the others. They're cold fuckers. I can see some of them hoping that a few more get bumped off just so that their take goes up."

I nod. "There is a reason why I did not pick good souls for this task, little one. I had hoped that their gruesome nature would make your task a little easier when the time came to put them down."

"Didn't make it any easier with Four, but I get your meaning. Thanks, I guess."

I opt to change the topic of conversation. "Tell me, how has the enterprise gone these past months?"

"Well, we've raked in a tone of cash from the merchants and some of the crooked houses. I'm still going out to the lording manors every now and then, but it's kind of a dry well up there now. All told, we're pretty flush. I've sent most of it to Rook for safe keeping and put some of it aside like you said to. I think we're close to all-out war between the Scorpions and Slavers though. I mean, we're stealing shit all over the place, and no one knows who the fuck is doing it. Now everyone is at each other's throats.

Sooner or later, one of our crew is gonna bite it. I might not even need to kill them off."

We part ways and set about our business. Some part of me longs to take the girl in my arms and embrace her, to hold her while tears flow and her hearts bleeds. I hate myself for what I must do; for the evils she must endure to become the weapon she must be. I am no mastermind here. I, too, feel as though my actions are being played out according to some grander script, some grotesque cosmic design. I can feel the forces of darkness manipulating my steps, speaking words through my lips and shedding blood through my hand. Before the pit, I was no angel, but neither was I fully demon.

I head toward the tavern I have called home for the past few weeks, knowing full well what awaits me. Twin brothers, Edwin and Erwin, are merchants of high renown in these parts. They control a great portion of airship trade within the region and also head a criminal enterprise of no small consequence within the bowl city. I have worked with the merchants' crew for some weeks now, plying my craft with skill while I await their next move. I am well aware of a third brother, one Ermin, former leader of the Smokehouse Brawlers, who now lies dead, bled and burnt to a crisp by my hand.

Tonight, the twins will accost me. I will kill half a dozen men before they bring me to heel. They will take me to a secretive locale, ply me with drink and fellweed, then have at me with instruments of torture. The pain will be excruciating, yet my body will heal time and again. I know not what this realization will bring to the brothers. Perhaps consternation, perhaps great pleasure. They may torture me for an age or simply seek to separate my head from my body and be done with the matter.

The venture is not without risk, and it is for that reason that I have kept it from Shadow. It is my hope that providence will intervene before the twins can cause irreparable damage; providence in the form of the Scorpion.

I sense the men following behind me at a short distance. There are others on the rooftop and several lurking from hidden recesses and darkened alleys. I stop short in the middle of the street as the twins approach with a gaggle of hefty brutes, all wielding knives and cudgels. I stand with hands resting upon my shooting irons and the girl's words from months earlier come back to me. *Why is it, in a world with firearms, that the city guard wield sword and shield?* The thought makes me chuckle.

"Something funny?" Edwin asks, a cruel grin upon his face.

There are others now. I barely sense them at the edges of the darkness, behind the twins' men, deadly and ready to strike. I nod to Edwin.

"A friend spoke an odd truth to me some days ago," I say, flexing my fingers as the brutes fan out to surround me. "Something about bringing a knife to…"

I don't wait to finish the sentence, drawing both weapons to firing rapidly into the chests of the oncoming brutes. I twist and kneel as a cudgel blow from behind whistles past my head and fire a shot into the belly of its owner. I empty the irons and holster them in quick succession, leaving a heap of dead and dying souls with Edwin quivering beside the corpse of his brother. Three men crawl out from the shadows, waving their weapons tentatively as Edwin beckons them forth with frantic gestures.

I slide the thin-bladed throwing knife from my vest and walk toward the merchant.

"Now I can't say by what right you think to accost me in the night like this. True, I did kill your brother—a sin I have committed once again it seems. But I was nothing but loyal to Ermin and his Smokehouse thugs. I never once stole from the man, never once showed designs upon his station. Yet he sends three men to gut me in my sleep? Now I ask you, is that the action of an honourable man?"

He turns to run, and I throw the knife. It lands at the base of his neck, sending the finely dressed merchant to the ground where his head hits stone with an alarming crack. I turn to the remaining brutes, but, before I can act, shadowy figures emerge from the darkness and put the brutes down with speed and clean savagery. A tall figure walks toward me, dressed in a long duster and wearing a wide-brimmed hat. He smiles at me as he draws near, sheathing his blade and considering me with interest, taking special note to mark the shackles on my hands.

"The Shackle, no less," he says in a raspy voice with a thick accent I cannot place.

I nod.

"Well, sir, you are quite the shot now, aren't you? Ten men attack in the middle of the night, and you yet live? Simply fantastic."

He squats down and pushes Edwin over, reaching into the man's vest to pull out a small coin purse. He tosses the purse to a nearby colleague who snatches it effortlessly out of the air. All but the man in the duster and the black hat wear masks of wrapped fabric, their eyes painted black so that only the faintest hint of white can be seen.

"We've been watching you for some time, Shackle. It's a rare thing to find an honest man in our line of work. Yet, in you, I think that's precisely what I perceive."

I snort, motioning to the bodies lying in the street. "Thus far, honesty has caused me more than my fair share of trouble."

He waves the bodies away. "Petty thieves and charlatans. Men playing at games they cannot hope to understand. To date, you have worked for the lowest of criminal enterprises, plying your craft in the darkness as it were. Tell me, did you not think to offer your services to the Slaver's Guild? They would pay handsomely for a man of your talents."

I make a show of rubbing at the shackle on my left wrist. "I do not deal with those who would trade in human life."

He nods. "I see. That wouldn't have anything to do with your own incarceration, would it perhaps? A man pulls himself up from the slaver's pit, tends to avoid attentions of his former masters."

His words are spoken with a casual air, but there is a design within them. He is testing me with every nuanced question and each subtle movement.

"I have had my fill of bloodshed this night," I say, offering my hands in a sign of amity. "So, if you would be so kind as to say your peace, I will be about my business."

He laughs, a short, staccato rasp. "And what business would that be, sir? It would seem your former employers have a habit of ending their lives prematurely."

I shake my head, turning to leave.

"You are aware of the Scorpion Brotherhood, yes?"

His words pull me up short.

"We choose our title carefully, Shackle. We are a Brotherhood in truth, not just in word. We are bound together with bonds that run far deeper than simple greed or mere circumstance."

I nod. "I have heard as much."

He smiles. "Good. It pleases me to hear it."

He walks toward me, slowly pulling back the sleeves of his coat to reveal dual tattoos: a pair of dark scorpions upon the wrist. He stops a short distance from me.

"We, too, bear the marks of memory on our skin."

"And you would like me to join your fraternity?"

"I would."

"And if I refuse?"

He shrugs. "Then you may continue squabbling with fools and cutthroats. We will not force you to join our Brotherhood. Nor will we kill you without cause."

I pause, considering his words but not wanting to appear too eager. I must walk a knife's edge from this moment onward, entering the very maw of the beast.

"Very well. Then I will accept your invitation. As you say, I am currently without gainful employment and, if the Brotherhood value honest labour, then I have labour to offer."

He beams, reaching out to shake my hand.

"Splendid. Simply splendid."

The needle slips beneath my skin so deftly that I am barely aware of its bite, before the poison does its work and darkness swallows me. I have only enough time to offer the man a slight grin as I fall.

***

I am woken with a firm hand striking me across the cheek. The slap rings out in a dark chamber, the sound brining me back to wakefulness. I am bound to a chair, hand and foot, unable to move anything but my head. A woman stands before me, clothed in a simple shirt and dark pants. Her face swims before me, blurred and ill-defined as the poison reluctantly releases its hold upon my mind.

"You are a curiosity," the woman says, her voice deep and refined.

Delicate features resolve as my eyes come into focus. Long black hair tied in a plat hangs down her back, complementing dark eyes, high cheekbones, and lightly tanned skin. She has a beauty which is rare in this scarred and pitted world. But that beauty ends at the nape of her neck. Scars run the length of her arms, crisscrossing the flesh in a gruesome geography that speaks of violence and brutality.

I open my mouth to speak but cannot mouth the words. My head throbs and pulses with the beating of my heart.

"Let me tell you why you are here," the woman says, drawing close and running a finger across my cheek in an almost affectionate manner. "Despite your professed lack of ambition, you have taken great pains to make yourself known to the Scorpion. We have watched you for some time, and you have played your part well. Staging capture by the twins was a particularly deft manoeuvre, which is why we thought it best to cut the ruse short prematurely rather than let it unfold as planned."

So, instead of the twins, it is to be the Scorpion Brotherhood who torture me?

She leans in close, sniffing at me like an animal. "It took more than the usual dose to keep you sleeping. That alone intrigues me. Still, I have a task to complete, so it makes no sense to delay."

I try to speak a second time, but again I cannot force my mouth to form the words. It seems a curious torture technique, to render one's victim unable to speak before commencing the interrogation.

"You have a pretty face, so we shall begin elsewhere," she says, moving to a small bench at the opposite side of the room.

She returns with a thin blade, twisting the knife expertly about her fingers like a performer in a circus pavilion. She moves in close, cutting through the fabric of my pants to reveal the flesh beneath. For a moment, I consider slipping the bonds and putting an end to this, feeling power begin to swell from somewhere within. I decide against such a course of action. Perhaps, bound as I am to the torturer's chair, I might garner some important knowledge of the Scorpion?

The blade cuts only lightly, digging into the meat of my calf with exacting slowness. I bite down against the pain as the blade continues its long excruciation. The woman squats in front of me, the scent of vanilla bean drifting from her oiled hair. I feel a curious sense of intoxication at the scent.

"Now that *is* interesting," she says, leaning forward to wipe a hand across the bloodied calf.

She looks up at me, puzzled. "Very interesting indeed."

She stands, tears my shirt, and begins cutting a shallow groove into the flesh of my chest. Pain burns through my body, but I resist the urge to cry out. Again, she cuts with deliberate slowness, prolonging the excruciation with great skill. The cutting stops, and she leans in to consider her work. Once more the darkness within does its work and the cuts heal swiftly. She examines the wound closely, and once more the intoxicating scent of vanilla and sweat fills my head. I smell the sweat on her brow and feel the heat from her skin as she draws close.

"I wonder," she says, returning to her table and picking up a second implement. "Does the cutting truly cause you pain?"

She moves swiftly, driving an iron spike through my chest with frightful speed. The iron pierces flesh, driving past bone and into the organs beneath. I cry out, unable to hold back. It draws a smile from my tormentor. She grasps the spike with both hands and wrenches it free. The pain is excruciating, and I feel myself swaying in my seat. I have to fight to keep hold of consciousness.

There is a lesson here, Kane. Hold fast and learn the limits of your gifts, for such a thing may prove valuable in the days ahead.

She returns to her table, picking up an oddly shaped syringe and advancing on me. I barely feel the needle prick as she jabs me in the neck. Warmth floods my head, producing a strange, giddy sensation.

"Tell me," she asks, returning the syringe to its place, "are you a godling?"

I open my mouth, and the fetters which had previously kept me in silence seem to have fallen away. My words feel wooden and badly formed, but I speak, nonetheless.

"I am not."

She approaches again, wielding a gnarled instrument which brings to mind pliers or something similar. I feel my stomach revolt as she approaches, clutching the fingers of my right hand in the brutish device and twisting with such force that three fingers are detached from their places amid a swath of blinding pain. I no longer resist the urge to cry out, bellowing in pain at the sudden agony. To our combined surprise, the fingers reknit themselves swiftly, forming back into place within moments, the pain dulling swiftly. Soft emerald light emanates from the shackles at my wrists as my body heals.

"Truly remarkable," she says, smiling with something like genuine pleasure. "I had thought only the godlings possessed such skill at self-healing."

She returns to the table on the other side of the room, choosing her next implements with care. After a few moments, she approaches with a pair of long, thin blades. She kneels before me, her dark eyes considering me closely.

"Understand, Shackle, it is in our nature to be suspicious. You are not native to this city, and your skill is such that suspicions have been raised. It is important that you realize the pain will be inescapable. Whether you speak the truth quickly or hold out for a time, the pain will come, nonetheless."

It strikes me as a curious message to give a man laid out upon the torture rack. Not for the first time, I find myself wondering as to the true nature of this enterprise. Perhaps this is something more akin to an initiation ritual rather than an attempt to divine truth from lie? Perhaps they do not suspect my motives, but rather intend to prove my worth in the face of adversity?

The pain is blinding and constant as she cuts simultaneously into both legs, using the slow excruciation she has employed elsewhere. Knowing my inhuman capacity to heal, she cuts far deeper grooves into the flesh, causing blood to flow freely, pouring out across her hands and soiling her garments. Again and again, she repeats the torturous exercise, only relenting when her strength lets out.

My breathing grows desperate as she pulls the knives from their place, standing to full height and wiping a bloodied hand across her brow. She waits for a moment, her chest rising and falling as she labours for breath.

"Why have you come to Tullhaven?" she asks between deep breaths.

"To seek vengeance," I reply, weaving truth so as to make the lie more believable.

"Vengeance on whom?"

"The godling Tull and his kind."

"And how do you intend on executing this justice?"

"By any means."

She jams the blades into my chest, driving through flesh with surprising force. I cry out, gritting my teeth against the pain as she twists the blades.

"How do you intend to execute justice?"

"By—"

She pulls the knives free, placing a booted foot on my chest to provide the necessary leverage, then drives them home again. Once more I am consumed with pain.

"Speak truth, Shackle," she spits. "What do you intend?"

I let out a cry as she twists the blades. "To infiltrate the Scorpion Brotherhood… To bend them to my will and tear down the godling Tull and his Lordlings."

There is a sickly sucking sound as she pulls the blades from my body once more. Sweat pours from her brow as she smiles down at me.

"Now we hit upon the truth. So, you intend to use us for the execution of your vengeance?"

I nod, helplessly.

"Quite a bold plan, it must be said. And tell me, this charade with the twins, this nonsense with the Smokehouse, was this simply to garner our attention?"

I nod once more.

"Well, it seems to have worked splendidly. You know, I am tempted to drain your blood and see how far this gift of yours extends. Surly your body cannot keep producing so much blood indefinitely?"

The pain begins to subside, and I feel my lips twist into a grin.

"I have never thought to try it."

She smiles wickedly. "Well, perhaps it's time we did."

***

The food is simple but flavoursome: a simple broth with dark bread, cheese, and various nuts and berries. The woman sits opposite me at the table, watching me eat with interest, her mouth twisted in an amused smile. Dried blood clings to my torn shirt and breeches, its acrid stench mingling with the food somewhat.

"You watch as though you have never seen a man eat before," I offer, devouring a second piece of bread.

"And you eat as though you have not seen food in an age."

I shrug. "Servitude has taught me to eat swiftly, lest the opportunity pass and I be left to starve."

She nods, picking up a handful of nuts with her bloodied hands and dropping them one by one into her mouth in a manner which, in another place, might be considered seductive.

"This seems a curious way to treat a prisoner," I say. "To cut and rend the flesh with knives and then offer food and ale thus."

"It is not our usual custom. But then, you are not our usual recruit. Most who fall beneath my knife required days and weeks to recover. This gives us time to welcome them gradually to our cause. We test their resolve with iron and steel, then offer healing balms and unguents which sooth their agonies. With you, such lengthy pleasantries are unnecessary. I thought it best to offer you food rather than a hospice bed."

I wave a slice of bread in her direction. "My thanks. It seems that the repeated healing of my wounds creates a powerful hunger."

She smiles, leaning back in her chair. We are alone in the small dining room, but I sense the presence of at least three men nearby, bows drawn and ready to fire should the need arise. I count a dozen murder holes cut into the rock of the walls, hidden neatly behind kinetic lanterns and various furnishings. One misstep and I have no doubt my body would bristle with arrows.

"Tell me, how is it that you came across this curious ability?"

I shrug. "I spent a great deal of time imprisoned beneath the ground. Time enough for the mind to run and my body fall to ruin."

"And was it Tull that imprisoned you?"

"Not Tull, but one of his ilk. A godling to the northwest—the Red Queen."

She nods in recognition.

"It is said that the deep places beneath the red city run red with etheric effluent and the thaumaturgical discharge from countless aborted remakings. My cell itself was slick at the walls with etheric effluvia. I could feel it clawing at my mind and soul with unnatural strength. Perhaps, that very clawing has worked some change in me? Perhaps it has awakened the gifts you now see in me?"

"A matter of chance then?"

I nod. "I can think of no other explanation. In truth, my mind was so addled by the passing of so much time alone in darkness that I remember little of what transpired in that pit."

Dark intelligences whispering their profane utterances, taunting, tearing at mind and body, twisting flesh and thought, rebuilding man into something…other…

"And what of the limits of your gifts? Have you explored their length and breadth?"

I shake my head. "They come at a cost, you understand. I experience no little pain at their employ, so have not ventured to test their full limits."

"Tell me what you do know then. I have seen your ability to heal your own flesh, much as a godling might. What other talents has the pit gifted you?"

Her eyes are intense, but there is more at play here than the torturer's desire to obtain truth. I sense the hunger, the genuine curiosity behind her words. Once more I am struck by the woman's beauty. My flesh rails against her for the pain she has caused, yet I find myself unable to rally hate toward the woman. As her scent drifts across the table, mixed with thick broth and the remnants of dried blood, something stirs within me.

"I have strength beyond a normal man, and more speed than I had previously possessed. I have always worked well with shooting irons, but it seems that my ability in that regard has tripled after my incarceration. I can move through the shadows without being detected. I think that is the sum of my gifts."

I dare not mention those other, darker gifts that brood within. She sits in silence for a long while, allowing me to eat my fill. I sense the knife's edge of decision unfurling within her as my fate is decided. Should she see through the half-truths and determine me to be an enemy of the Brotherhood, I will likely have to kill my way through the entire Scorpion stronghold. Such a course will be unfortunate as there is much to admire about these rebels, much that I would like to explore further before executing Tull's contract.

"We are a Brotherhood," she says, sliding something across the table toward me, "not some petty guild to be wielded about by a paper despot. Work hard, earn your place, and you will share in our rewards. Make no mistake though, Shackle, we are led by the Scorpion and obey without question. In time, if you prove faithful, you may rise to great heights, but for the present you must content yourself to serve at the Scorpion's pleasure."

I pick up a small metallic ingot and turn it over to reveal a simple scorpion shape embossed into the iron.

"I have time," I reply, "and a great deal of patience. I will not seek to force my will upon others. I will serve until such a time as I am asked to lead. But make no mistake, the godling Tull will die by my hand, with or without the support of your Brotherhood."

She nods, smiling.

"I see the fire within you, Shackle. It is a flame we do not wish to put out, but it must be tempered if you are to become one of us."

She stands, stretching her neck to one side in feline fashion.

"You will be paired with a Brother for a time. Work with him, do your job well, and you may earn entry into the Brotherhood. If you are successful, you will say your oath and we will welcome you as one of our own."

I nod. "Well and good."

She motions to the dark recesses of a nearby chamber, and a young man with keen eyes and hard features steps into the light. He wears the usual Scorpion garb and rests a hand upon the hilt of a long dagger strapped to his side.

"Rikard will shadow you as you begin your service," the woman says, standing. "Ask him whatever questions you wish, and, unless he is bound by secrecy, he will answer. Work well, be honest in your dealings with us, and you will one day stand beside us in the Brotherhood."

***

I meet her upon the rooftops of the upper city. She moves so deftly through the darkness that I barely notice her until she is upon me. The shadows take form, and her lithe figure emerges beside me, sitting with legs dangling over the rooftop. She speaks in hushed tones, watching the darkening city below as the sun dips under the horizon.

"Been a while?"

I nod.

"So, you found the Scorpion yet?"

"I believe so, but no one calls him by that name. He goes by Claude."

She turns to me, a wide grin barely visible beneath her mask. "You're shitting me? Claude? Doesn't sound much like a criminal mastermind to me."

"I have my doubts that this is a criminal enterprise. The Scorpion are more than a Brotherhood just in name. They treat one another with respect, deal with dissension in their ranks swiftly but fairly and refuse to take work which might harm the common folk of the city. That is partly why they have been so successful; the common folk will never give them up because they are held in such high esteem."

"Yeah, but they deal in drugs and steal shit, yeah?"

"They do. But they also free slaves and channel money to the poor."

"Jesus. Sounds like there's some Robbin Hood shit going on there. You goin' soft on me, old man? You thinking of joining the Scorpions for real?"

"I merely say that there is much to admire about the group. There is honour to be found among its Brothers, and that honour keeps them strong. They are not driven merely by profit or the need to shed blood."

"You gonna be able to go through with the kill then? With the Scorpion, I mean?"

"In time. For the moment, I am content to learn all that I can. The Scorpion is a wise leader, and his followers demonstrate a profound loyalty."

"So, what's he like then, this Claude?"

I shrug. "He is a man of few words, but when he does speak, he talks with great eloquence. I do not think he was born to this life. He has a good mind for strategy and knows his people well. He has a little etheric power about him also; I have sensed it. When he talks, it is as if the ether works among the ears and minds of those who listen. Even the simplest command is undertaken with something akin to obsession."

"Sounds like you've found yourself a cult there, boss man."

I shake my head. "It is a criminal guild and nothing more."

"You keep telling yourself that, bud, when the bring out the naked virgins and sacred knives."

I let out a sigh. "And what of your own work? How does the thievery and general chicanery progress?"

She turns toward me suddenly, eyes sparkling within the thin slits of her mask. She reaches up to pull the mask from her face.

"I don't believe it?"

"What?"

"You...you almost cracked a joke. I mean, it was absolute shit, but that whole *chicanery* bit was the closest thing I've heard to a smart-ass remark in the whole time we've been together."

I shrug. "Perhaps you are beginning to make an impression upon me?"

"Giddy-up, cowboy! It's about fucking time."

The unabashed joy in her expression lifts my spirits a little, and I find myself verging upon laughter. She points a finger at my face, grinning inanely and making great sport of the matter. For the shortest while, we simply sit and laugh upon the rooftop, careless of our voices drifting out over the city below.

All too swiftly the laughter stops, and we assume our usual places once more.

"The crew is doing well. All six have brought in a healthy chunk of cash. I think we're gonna need to ease off a little on the thieving though because we're running out of new places to hit."

"And what of the Slavers?"

She smiles. "Man, we've had some fun with those bastards. They've got plenty of guards all right, but they're dumb as dirt, and it doesn't take much to distract them. Must have hit a dozen traders in the last week alone. We take out a few guards, set some of the slaves free, and then leave something there so it looks like one of the local gangs has done it. Funny as shit watching those fat bastard Slavers chasing their merchandise up and down the city."

Her expression darkens a little. "Half the slaves end up getting beaten or killed though, so I've lost my stomach for it to tell you the truth. Most of the poor bastards have just dreamed their way into this part of the Traumwelt, and that's their only mistake. Slavers pick them up and drag their asses down here so they can be bought and sold for the rich pricks up here on the hill. I don't wanna tell you what happens to most of them, especially the women. Makes me fucking sick."

"Which is why you have made a habit of killing Slavers?"

She turns to me, flushed with anger. "What do you expect? You want me to just leave them to it after what they do... After what they almost did to me?"

I hold up a hand to halt further argument. "I told you, when we began this venture, that your role was to breed chaos among the criminal guilds and gangs of the city. To put the chaff to fire and stoke the flames until such a time as we must take action. I told you to attack the Slaver's Guild and breed distrust between the lower city gangs. Killing Slavers will only add to that chaos, so no, I do not intend to chastise you for this."

The fire begins to dim a little in her eyes.

"I will warn you once again though," I continue, holding her gaze with my own. "The time will come soon enough when we must tear down this city and leave it forever in our wake. For the moment, you are an agent of chaos, a black angel wreaking havoc through the city streets. Once I kill Tull, though, you will need to become your namesake—a shadow, invisible and motionless."

She nods, but I see that the truth of the matter has not yet settled upon her heart. Fire still rages at the injustice she has suffered at the hands of the Slaver Chieftain and his men. That fire consumes reason and pushes her toward recklessness; a tendency which will need to be reined in before long.

"One more thing, and this will be a bitter pill to swallow. No matter how many Slavers you kill, there will always be more to take their place. No matter how many gangs we put to the sword, no matter how many scoundrels and thugs and cutthroats we bury in the red sands, more will arise."

"Then what's the point of all of this? Why don't we just take the money we've got and get the fuck out of town? We could find a nice quiet place and buy the whole damned thing; just buy us a nice house with a pool and animals and shit and take it easy until we drop dead from eating too much fruit?"

"You know that to be a lie, little one. We live in the Traumwelt. All there is, is struggle and strife. Even those who live at ease in this place do not hold their pleasure for long. It is the nature of the Traumwelt to bring chaos to order and tear down the structures we build with our own blood, sweat, and sorrow."

"So, why does it matter what we do if it's all hopeless in the end?"

The question bites hard into that narrow space within my heart which still beats with human need. For the briefest moment, I am overcome, unable to respond. Her words have unmanned me, laid bare the pointlessness of my life and the struggle which has consumed me.

"In truth, this place lacks the one thing that might give meaning to our lives," I say, not bothering to hide the sorrow from my words. "If man and woman could lie together and conceive. If father and mother could give birth to a child, that would offer some meaning to this chaotic world. One would strife to make things better for the sake of one's children. No price would be too great."

"Like Rook and his family?"

"Yes. That is it precisely. Rook is extraordinary above all men in this place because he has a reason for his struggle. He alone, perhaps among all the souls in this red desert, can be whole. He alone can strive and struggle for the sake of his kin. And yet…"

A memory surfaces, fleeting at first but growing more vivid as I close my eyes and let the darkness surround me. A small man, his features dominated by round spectacles and a permanent frown upon his face. A woman named Ellie… Husband and wife drawn together amid the arid streets of the red city.

"And yet the people who come to this place and make peace with their predicament…they find one another. They find solace and join to make new families. They adopt those few younglings who dream themselves into the red world. They become a new reason to struggle and fight for peace and justice. Even in this barren, lawless place, people still build families, communities, fellowships worth fighting to protect. People still live and laugh and love one another."

I see from the look on her face that my words have touched her. She smiles, nodding to herself. Yet my own words fail me. The memories that so swiftly blossomed have already begun to fade, replaced by the gnawing darkness at the centre of my being.

"You ask why we do this? I confess I am driven by a singular goal, but I cannot say why this goal possesses me such. I must fight the godling menace wherever I encounter it, for they are an enemy to peace and liberty. The death of the godling may not solve the ills which plague this world, but I cannot help but think that their deaths can only improve it."

We sit in silence for a time, contemplating one another's words. There is much more that I would like to say in that moment, but the night's darkness has begun to press in upon me.

"Our time together wanes. I must return to the Brotherhood and be about my work. Yet, before I leave, there is something I must ask of you, a question that burns within."

She grins, intrigued. "Ok, shoot."

"Most souls, on coming to this place, strive for a time to return to the waking world. Even if there are no means for them to return, they still ache for their homeland."

Shadow nods. "You want to know why I'm not interested in going back?"

"Yes, though it is not my right to ask."

"Yeah, it kind of is your right, dude. You saved me. You're my only friend in this shithole of a world. So, you *do* have the right. Thing is, I don't really know the answer. I suppose there wasn't much for me back in the waking world. I had a sister, but we never really got along. Truth is she's probably better off without me. I never had many friends, not really good ones anyway. There was an old

guy, a detective. I only knew him for a little while, but…
he was pretty cool. I like him. I wish I could see him
again, but apart from that I guess I don't really miss the
other world that much. Except for the food. Holy shit I
miss hotdogs and pizza and donuts and Coke… Yeah I'd
go back for the food in a second."

I nod. "Very well. For my part, I am thankful. I am not a
man given to displays of affection, little one, nonetheless…"

I cannot say what drives me to act thus, but I allow
myself a moment's freedom, moving toward the girl and
drawing her into a loving embrace. To my surprise, she
does not resist but seems to melt into my arms as we sit
together. We speak no words and shed no tears, holding
one another in silence for a few, brief moments. Like the
sparse trickle of water that sustains a cactus for many
months, that simple moment of kinship and affection
binds us together. Whatever the darkness has in store
for my future, I know with certainty that I will tear the
cosmos asunder for her sakes.

I will never utter the word, nor will she ever hear it. As
we sit in this moment, caught in a tight embrace, I see her
for what she has become, what she now is to me. *Daughter*.

12. Rise of the Cutter Cult

In my capacity as apprentice to the Scorpion Brotherhood, I am left to fulfil only the most meagre of duties. I spend my days guarding shipments of fellweed and other goods which arrive daily from the red city. By night I hone and polish blades, strip and clean all manner of projectile weaponry, and am permitted only a little time to eat and sleep. Feeling no need for the latter, I consider taking my leave of the Brotherhood dormitory to wander the night and clear my thoughts, but the halls and doorways are guarded, and I dare not risk showing my hand by using the curious gifts of my shackles to escape.

My fellow Brothers are civil enough in their dealings with me, but there is a distance between us which they appear in no hurry to close. I work as I am ordered, never complaining, completing each task to exemplary standard and not speaking unless I am spoken to.

As the days and nights move on in this fashion, I begin to reconsider my approach. Tull expects the head of the Scorpion, and I cannot delay indefinitely. On two occasions I have sent word to the godling of my progress, confirming that I have managed to infiltrate the Brotherhood and soon hope to learn the identity of the Scorpion and delivery his head as agreed. In truth I have been content to let the matter slide, learning a great deal from the manner in which the Brotherhood conducts itself. But of late I have learned little and seen nothing of Claude: the tall figure who seems most likely to be the Scorpion.

Matters begin to change with the dawning of the new moon and the emergence of the Cutter Cult in Tullhaven.

In the fertile grounds of tragedy and bloodshed, I begin to prove my worth to the Scorpion.

They strike first in the lower markets, two souls possessed of an unnatural lust for blood and chaos. A merchant's son of little renown and a street beggar are taken by a strange fever. It animates them, drives them toward sudden violence. They strike out indiscriminately at souls milling through the market squares, slashing and stabbing with naked blades, their eyes filled with red mist.

Confusion reigns throughout the market square as people flee from an unknown enemy. Blood pools about the ground amid writhing victims and the screams of horrified onlookers. I watch the madness transpire from a hidden vantage, a nook between the walls of two nearby buildings. I wait for the chaos to die down then complete the task for which I was sent, returning in the late hours to The Gilded Wren, whose basement I have called home these past months.

I am met, unexpectedly, by the Brotherhood's torturer, dressed in black, her hair platted, eyes dark and piercing. She smiles darkly as I enter my room, sitting upon my cot dressed in plain black garb.

"Am I to endure more time under the knife?" I ask.

She shakes her head. "That time is passed, provided you stay true to your oath."

I take a seat on the small stool opposite her. "I was unaware I had yet taken an oath."

She smiles. "Then you had best take care lest you unwittingly break it."

There is an ease to her words which sooths my mind, intermingling with the faint scent of vanilla and some other fragrance I cannot place. I find myself somewhat unmanned by the woman and have to remind myself of her function within the Brotherhood in order to bring clarity back to mind.

"If not for torture, then why are you here?"

She considers me for a moment, a wry smile across her delicate lips. Once more I feel the stirring of something within, the movement of strange forces that have not stirred in many years.

"What did you see in the market this day?" she asks, eyes sharply focused upon my own.

"I saw two men kill and wound without reason. Six, maybe more, dead at their hands."

She nods. "How did it begin? Did you see where the men came from?"

I shake my head. "I noticed them only once the bloodshed began. They seemed to act in unison, though their eyes were filled with a red mist, as though they had been taken by a fugue."

"They attacked with blades, yes?"

"Simple knives from what I could see. Though I did not have a clear view of the blades."

"And how were they apprehended?"

"Half a dozen city guard. They clubbed the men to death and dragged their bodies from the market."

She nods, suddenly lost in her own thoughts.

"You have seen this before?" I ask, already certain of the answer.

"Yes, several times. It seems to be growing more common of late. I had thought the Cutter Cult long since passed, but there appears to be a resurgence in Tullhaven."

"Cutter Cult?"

She nods. "A dark business. The red mist strikes without warning, consuming the mind and rendering the will useless. Those that are taken enter a state of possession in which their actions are not their own. Their sole purpose is to kill and cut with the naked blade. They turn on kin and comrade alike, striking out without reason to all who are near. They continue along this path until their body is damaged beyond repair. Then the mist recedes, and they are left to their misery."

"Why then, a cult?"

"There are some who believe the red mist to be a product of some deity or other. They use the blade in their sacraments, meeting in secret to worship their unnamed god. It is for these fools that the cult earns its name, though there seems to be no relationship between those who are stricken by the red mist and followers of the blade."

"Is it likely these blade followers would know the origin of the red mist?"

"They do not. I have had several of the wretches under my own knife, and they have proven utterly ignorant of the cause for this madness."

"How long has this blight been visited upon the city then?"

"A hundred years or more, though it has not been limited to Tullhaven. It comes and goes from time to time, growing periodically worse before vanishing. I believe we are in the throes of another swelling of bloodshed."

"How dire will it become?"

She shrugs. "None can tell. I have studied the red mist for many years and am no closer to divining its origin nor devising an effective means of combatting it. Though I have my suspicions."

"The godlings."

She nods. "It may be Tull himself for all I know. An aborted experimentation let loose upon the city for his own amusement."

"So, how do we combat such a thing?"

She stands, shrugging as she brushes past me. "If I knew that, we would not be talking."

Her hand brushes lightly against my cheek as she passes. She bends down, leaning in close and gently kissing my right ear. Her breath is warm and intoxicating upon the delicate flesh, and I find myself stirring toward her once more. I lift my head, but she has gone; vanished into the tavern above without a word.

I pass the night in sleeplessness, my thoughts a jumble with the events of the previous day and night. Though it is to the torturer that my thoughts most fervently turn. My mind rebels against all sense, playing over our conversation and lingering upon the woman's face like the product of some childhood fancy. The beginnings of infatuation blossom from somewhere within, overcoming the darkness which rules there.

As morning rises, Claude greets me in the tavern, smiling widely as I take my seat at the bench beside him. He is dressed in his usual garb, the wide-brimmed hat of midnight black and matching long-coat whose hidden pockets house an array of throwing blades and other weaponry.

"We have a task for you," he says without preamble. "One suited to your particular talents."

He spears a piece of sausage from his plate and devours it, continuing to speak. "The cutters are a grave threat to our operations here in Tullhaven. The city guard are ill-equipped to deal with such an enemy and lack the will to try. I want you to find the Cutter Cult in this city. Get to the truth of this red mist and report back. We must find a means of protecting ourselves or risk exposure."

"The red mist has taken those of the Brotherhood?"

He nods. "Two souls thus far. Not our best and brightest, but it is troubling, nonetheless. We depend on one another, as you well know. We cannot risk a Brother turning to sudden violence without warning."

There is more to his words than what he is saying, but I decide not to press the matter.

"May I ask why I have been chosen for this task?"

He smiles. "Call it a test if you will. Deal with this matter swiftly, help us put an end to the cutter threat, and we will welcome you into the Brotherhood as an honoured member."

He holds up his fingers and whistles in the direction of the hallway. Two figures enter the room; a mountainous thug named Mot and a wiry woman with a shock of brilliant white hair known as Lonnie. I have worked with both on occasion, and each has shown themselves to be a capable agent.

"These two will answer to you during this task. Work quickly and put an end to this madness."

With that he turns and strolls from the room, leaving me with Mot and Lonnie staring darkly toward me. I find myself somewhat amused at the circumstances which have led me to this place. Wheels within wheels and yet I feel no closer to slipping the noose around Tull's neck.

I point a finger at Lonnie. "Find out where the bodies of the cutters were taken. If they are still whole, examine them for signs of abnormality."

She nods and darts out of the room without a word. I turn to Mot, and the big man scratches his arm disinterestedly.

"Find out if there have been any other attacks throughout the city. Ask around to see when and where it has happened previously. Find me a map of the lower city and bring it here so that we can plot occurrences of the red mist."

He nods and lumbers out of the room. I am left to ponder my thoughts as the wheels of fate turn ever onward. I find myself set along a strange course of late. Am I now the hound of the Scorpion, sent to sniff out the Cutter threat simply to prove my worth to the Brotherhood? A voice speaks from the darkness within, urging me to forget the Scorpion Brotherhood and their petty concerns.

Kill the godling Tull and leave his body to the carrion birds.

I feel the impulse burn within me but fight against its dark urges. I will stay the course. Find the cause of the red mist, dismantle the Cutter Cult, and win my way into the inner circle of the Scorpion Brotherhood. I will take the head of their leader, present it to Tull and…

Even as I plan my next move, the darkness closes in, swamping me from all sides and dulling clarity. The phrase echoes through my mind again and again, driven by some urgent, otherworldly impulse.

Kill the godling Tull. Kill the godling Tull.
KILL THE GODLING TULL.

***

Of the two charges given me, Lonnie proves the most resourceful. She tracks the bodies of three Cutters to the city's carrion pits and braves the gruesome landscape to conduct her inspection.

"They all got blood in the eyes," she says, pointing to her own eyes in reference. "Cuts on the arms too, small ones. Ain't nothing else about 'em though. Just eyes and the cutting."

I nod, noting with interest the blood stains still on her hands and arms, an indication that she has wasted no time in returning with news of the Cutter corpses.

"Must'a been there a week or more. They was startin' to smell real bad."

Mot does not fare so well in his endeavours, citing a few snatches of conversation and hearsay regarding the existence of the Cutter Cult in Tullhaven. He mentions a few likely meeting places where the group may gather from time to time, but there is little confidence in his words.

Lonnie breaks in. "Word is they take the Cutters if they can get hold of 'em. Treat 'em like saints. When they hear that someone's gone cuttin', they try and take 'em alive and drag 'em to their temple. Don't mind if they get cut in the process. Some kind of blessing to be cut by one of the possessed."

Mot turns to her, confusion waring with sudden rage behind his eyes. She shrugs in response.

"Met a couple of cult Acolytes at the carrion pits. They was looking for the same thing I was, only they wanted to take the corpses back to their temple."

A smile broadens across my lips as the full import of her words sinks in. She walks outside the room, pulling Mot with her. They returned a moment later, Mot dragging a struggling soul in a hard embrace. He dumps the man unceremoniously onto the floor. The figure is a spindly character of middle years, wearing the livery of a palace footman and sporting several bruises to his face.

His hands are tied behind his back with heavy twine, forcing him to lean forward awkwardly on the floor.

"Figured I'd bring one of 'em back," Lonnie says, throwing something toward me. "He was wearing this. Some kind'a Acolyte's robe. They all wore them."

I nod. "And the others?"

She smiles. "Dead."

There is no haughtiness in her words, only an unshakable confidence in her abilities. She waits patiently as I examine the robe. It is thickly spun and free of device or insignia; a simple robe with a simple hood, much like any city dweller might employ anywhere in Tullhaven. Yet, as I turn the robe inside-out, the truth is made plain. Small, dull blades are sewn into the lining of the robe down each arm. The blades are not sharply honed but would cut the skin over time. I stare down at the prisoner, noting the bloodied grooves cut into his arms. I turn to the sorry soul, crouching down to meet his eyes. I see no defiance in him, only fear and confusion.

"Why do you cut yourselves so?" I ask, motioning to the marks on his arms.

He rubs at the puckered marks, smiling. "We abase ourselves before the blade and show our loyalty."

"Loyalty to who?"

He twists his head oddly to one side, genuine confusion written upon his face as though my question is incomprehensible. "To the Scythe."

"And what is this Scythe?"

His eyes shine at the mention of that name. "He is the giver and taker, the harvester of souls. It is he who keeps the balance in all things, who holds the cosmos upon the edge of his blade. The Scythe purifies the world through the glory of his blade."

"And where would I find this Scythe, if I was inclined to look?"

He seems genuinely ecstatic in response to the question, unable to see the truth behind it.

"He can be seen in the glint of every blade and knife-edge. He can be heard in the cries of the newly cleaved. Press the blade against your flesh as a sign of loyalty and he may come to you as your blood runs dry."

"Yes, but is he a person, a godling? What is he?"

The Acolyte sits dumbly, unsure how to answer the question.

"The Scythe is all."

I feel the ether begin to rise from within. My shackles take on a subtle blueish hue as Mot and Lonnie back away slightly, hands moving to their weapons. The ether drifts around me, flowing toward the Acolyte.

"Speak plainly. Where do you and your kind gather?"

He nods, smiling as his eyes grow glassy. "Beneath the Southmaw Meatworks, in the Temple."

"How many of you live in this city?"

"A hundred, maybe more. We are but one chapter of the great fellowship."

"Where may we find the Scythe?"

"Upon the wind and the edge of every blade. Within the hearts of the faithful."

"Is he a godling?"

The Acolyte shakes his head. "He is all."

Mot bristles. "The fool speaks in riddles. He knows nothing."

I ignore the brute and continue pressing the Acolyte.

"Tell me of the red mist, the turning. How are the Cutters chosen?"

He smiles. "In blood. They who are cut with the Master's knife give themselves over to the Scythe's will."

"Where do I find the Master's knife?"

"In the hand of the Master, of course. He chooses those who will give glory to his name. He lifts the downtrodden and exalts the lowly so that his power may be known."

There is no deception in his words, only delusion and religious zealotry. I hand the man back his robe and stand once more, motioning to the door.

"Let him leave, unharmed."

Lonnie nods, picking the man up off the floor and leading him from the room. Mot growls as the diminutive figure passes. Lonnie returns a moment later.

"Where to now?" she says.

I smile. "To the Meatworks."

***

We see no outward evidence of the Cutter Cult from where Southmaw Meatworks and a dozen similar establishments sit heavily upon the street. A large, squat building fashioned of the same moulded clay bricks as most of the buildings of Tullhaven, the Meatworks swells with activity. By the light of dim kinetic lanterns and etherically charged bulbs, shirtless men cut and carve at corpses of newly slaughtered beasts. Sheep and cows and creatures native to the Traumwelt are slaughtered and prepared for trade while blood runs through shallow gutters along the ground to the sewers below.

"Ain't no way in without causin' a stir," Lonnie says, motioning to the building below. "Reckon there's a tunnel down back heading into the sewers, be we ain't gonna reach it from our end."

The Scorpion Brotherhood control a vast network of disused sewers and tunnels which run beneath the city proper; used for the smuggling of contraband substances and the deployment of resources. Having spent several hours attempting to find a way through from those tunnels to the Cutter's temple, Lonnie concludes that no such path exists.

"We'll wait," I offer, crouching on the edge of the roof, watching the slaughterers do their work. "Wait here till dark. I'll return presently, and we will force the matter."

I receive a nod and grunt in turn from the pair, then take my leave and head away from the stench of slaughter, moving swiftly toward the upper city and the rear of the godling palace. I make my way through hidden paths and tunnels, using the godling's key to access the vast chambers below the palace. When I enter the room, Tull waits for me, wiping blood and grease from his hands with a cloth while a newly tormented body writhes and shudders upon his table.

"Ah, Shackle," Tull says, looking up from his work. "I confess, I half suspected that you had broken our agreement and fled the city."

"A man is nothing without his word."

He nods. "True though one could hardly scold a mercenary for turning tail with a small fortune. It seems the easier path, and your kind are known for such."

His words seem casual and easily spent, yet there is a strange correctness to them as if each and every sound has been carefully weighed and apportioned. I have the unnerving sensation of a mouse who has wandered into the lair of a cat.

"A man in my line of work must cultivate a reputation for integrity when it comes to dealing with patrons."

Tull drops his rag on the convulsing body in front of him, its pink flesh joined with various mechanical oddities and etheric manipulations. There seems to be a second creature—a diminutive Shadowspawn—grafted into the flesh of the poor soul. Dark, jagged limbs extend from the figure's abdomen, twitching and swirling in concert with moans of agony.

"A curious notion in your case, Shackle, as you have no reputation to speak of."

I nod. "I am hoping to acquire said reputation from my current venture."

"I see. Well, tell me, how does your hunt for the Scorpion fare?"

He moves to a small cabinet by the wall, pouring himself a drink, utterly unconcerned with the subtle agonies inflicted upon his latest patient.

"Well enough. I am engaged in a task which will see me inducted into the Brotherhood as a fully-fledged member. Once I obtain that status, I will move upon the Scorpion and return with your prize."

Tull nods, taking a swig of an odd iridescent liquid. "And you have obtained the identity of their leader?"

"Not as of yet. I have my suspicions but will need time to confirm them."

"Time, you say? Well, you seem in no great hurry to be about your business, Shackle. Given the nature of our first meeting, I had thought you a man of swift action and had paid you on precisely those grounds."

There is a barbed edge to his tone, but nothing malevolent. He toys with me, seeking to test me with his words.

"No mention of swiftness was specified in our agreement. I thought it best to proceed with caution, rather than bludgeon my way through to the prize."

Tull inclines his head a little, nodding slightly. He takes another sip.

"True enough. Were you to advance too swiftly, the Scorpion would likely take flight, and you would lose your chance to capture the scoundrel. Very well, take whatever time you need, there is no pressing requirement to act with haste."

He motions toward me with the glass in his hand, smiling. "Now, to the real business at hand here. You come to speak with me about the Scythe, yes?"

I nod, once more feeling like I am merely a pawn in someone else's game.

"I have been tasked with putting an end to the so-called Cutter Cult. Any assistance you could render would bring me closer to my ultimate goal."

"Ah, so you wish me to do your work for you then, eh? I pay you for your services and then you expect me to render assistance in the task for which I have already paid?"

"I seek to exploit every advantage in the execution of my duties."

He holds up a hand dismissively, a broad grin across his face. "Come now, Shackle, I speak in jest. Only a fool would ignore a valuable source of information for the sake of some misplaced notion of pride or honour. I will tell you all I know and then I must return to my work. Tell me, what do you know of the Cutter Cult thus far?"

"They are a religious sect that worship a figure known as the Scythe. They meet in secret and cut themselves as a sign of allegiance to their deity. Of the red mist, I know less. It seems to grip souls at random, turning an ordinary man into an indiscriminate killer. Those who are afflicted take to their fellows with whatever knives and blades come to hand. They cut and stab without intellect, slicing through whatever flesh is nearest, but with little efficiency."

Tull nods. "Explain."

"From what little I have seen, those taken by the red mist do not strike for the throat or upper leg. They do not seek to kill efficiently and do not wait to ensure that their victims are dead before moving on. Instead, they hack and stab with little thought, moving from one person to another until they themselves are brought down."

"And those who are taken, do they seem random?"

"They do, but there may be some greater plan at work here. It does not seem that members of the Cult itself are taken by the red mist."

"They are perhaps facilitators of the disease, rather than victims of it?" Tull asks, taking a seat at a large chair in one corner of the room.

I shrug. "I had hoped that you would be able to shed some light on the matter."

He nods, momentarily lost in thought.

"Very well. I suspect that this red mist of yours is not nearly so random a matter as you might expect. The figure known as the Scythe is known to me, though by a different name. He was once a lieutenant of the Warmaster; a godling named Avernath. The Warmaster serves now in the Red Queen's court, but for many years he was shadowed by a young warrior whose name I do not recall. Apparently Avernath grew fond of the young man, imbuing him with much of his etheric power. They fought many campaigns together and were said to be inseparable. As is often the case with such relationships, there was a falling out, after which the warrior fled into the red wastes, forever leaving Avernath's service."

Tull takes a final swig of the strange liquid in his glass, breathing in deeply as he finishes the drink.

"Some hundred years or so since their falling out, a figure emerged to the south—a fledgling warlord who eschewed all weapons other than the blade. Avernath's former lieutenant made a name for himself, and that name was *Scythe*. He gathered followers to his cause, fanatical devotees that invested their leader with supernatural significance, equating the figure with that most mythical of entities from earth's early history, the reaper…"

Even as the godling talks, I feel my stomach churn. The darkness within presses against my mind, threatening to burst forth in sudden violence, swelling in the presence of the godling. I feel the urge to strike out, to lay hands upon the godling and strangle the life from Tull. I fight back those dark urges, knowing full well that the time is not yet ripe. To strike now would be to show my hand far too early.

"He is a man then?" I ask, forcing my words through the darkness that threatens to choke me. "He can be killed?"

Tull considers my words. "He *was* a man though I cannot say with certainty quite what he is at present. He can be killed, I suspect, though the task will not be easy. He has become something quite…exquisite."

The corners of his mouth lift in a sly grin as he considers the subject. I feel the etheric force swell in response to his change of expression; a moment of unguarded joy where some hint of the godling's true power comes forth. The power washes over me, threatening to send me toppling to the floor. Its manner and magnitude are unfamiliar to me, and that brief moment of excess fills my heart with doubt once more.

Can the godling Tull be killed? Can any godling be killed?

"I see it coming," the godling says, oblivious to my reverie. "The Scythe and his followers will strike soon. They will wage war upon order and sanity, filling the streets with blood and undermining stability in this entire region. Word of their plague will spread like wildfire through the southern hamlets and even northwest to Rust and beyond. He intends to make a name for himself, Shackle, much as you intend to establish your reputation in my service."

"And yet, the coming bloodshed does not seem to trouble you?"

The godling nods, and I see, for a moment, the true depth of his obsession. "The coming bloodshed represents a true opportunity. The Scythe cannot help but reveal himself in the days ahead, and at that time you will have your opportunity to strike."

Tull stands to his feet, walking to the opposite corner of the chamber and opening a large chest. "I have a further request to make of you, Shackle."

He fishes a wooden box from the chest and walks toward me, brushing dust from its surface as he lays it out upon the bench in front of me. Upon the lid of the box sits the carved image of a snake devouring its own tail. Tull opens the box, removing a pair of shackles which seemed to have been carved from liquid obsidian. Their surface shimmers with an impossibly dark gloss, yet the material itself seems to bend and flex like leather.

"A truly remarkable device," Tull says, drawing something from the side of the strange black shackles. "In truth I have no idea as to its origin. I know only that the object does not derive from this world, nor your own waking world, I wager."

He slips a long, thin needle from one edge of the left shackle, then uses the needle to prick the flesh of his palm. A thin trickle of blood bubbles upon the surface, and Tull smears the blood upon the surface of the shackle. With a slow, metallic *click* the shackle opens. Tull repeats the process with the second shackle, then places the device back into its box.

"They are bound to me now," he says, sliding the box toward me. "I wish for you to capture the Scythe and not simply kill him. Wound him if you must but ensure that his heart continues to beat. Bind him in these shackles, and he will be rendered docile and ineffectual. He will remain thus until you return him to me here. Only I will be able to free him from his bondage."

The hunger in his eyes speaks the truth of his obsession. Tull *the Collector*.

"You intend to make a study of this Scythe?"

He nods, unashamedly. "I do indeed. Such a prize would make a welcome addition to my collection, but even more than that, a being such as he may unlock certain mysteries which are still unknown to me. Understand, Shackle, the Warmaster is not a figure to be trifled with. One cannot reason with such a brute. I have long admired Avernath and sought to better understand the source and nature of his power, but to date there has been no way to obtain such information."

He turns, lifting aside his tunic to show a long scar running down the side of his neck. "This represents my last attempt to discuss the matter with the Warmaster. He was…less than amicable."

I nod, feeling a need to be rid of the godling's presence. "And what will you pay me for this additional service?"

Tull considers my words. "Your fee will be doubled if you do this thing for me."

I make a show of considering the price and give my agreement, taking the box reluctantly and feeling it hum with power beneath my grip. Without another word, the godling Tull returns to his work, bending over the tortured frame of his latest abomination. As I leave the chamber, the room fills with the combined screeching of Shadowspawn and human host.

And with that meeting completed, my task becomes yet more complex. Wheels within intricate wheels; forcing me to tread carefully even as the darkness within rages and fits, calling for godling blood in a voice that threatens to overwhelm me.

***

When I return to the rooftop above the Meatworks, Mot and Lonnie are waiting, sharing a meal of dried meat and hard bread as they watch the streets below. It is Lonnie that speaks first.

"Ain't been much happenin' for the past hour. Closed up shop, they did."

I nod. "Did anyone new enter?"

She shakes her head, then catches sight of the dark box beneath my cloak. "What's that then?"

I shrug. "Nothing of great consequence. It seems the leader of the Cutter Cult is a minor godling, or something similar."

She nods. "Scythe."

"If we can cut off the head, the body will soon perish. If we can track down this Scythe and put an end to him, attending to the remaining cultists should prove relatively easy."

"If we can kill a godling, you mean?" Mot asks, his heavy brows darkening.

I nod.

"So, what's that then?" Lonnie askes, her eyes fall to the dark box I hold in the crook of my arms.

"A talisman of sorts," I explain. "It may help us if we run into this Scythe character."

"A talisman that'll kill a godling? Where exactly did ya snag that from?"

I throw her a smile. "Head into the Meatworks and see if you can find anything."

Without another word, she drops the dried meat and wipes her hands on her tunic, pulling a short blade and lockpick from somewhere on her person and dropping off the roof in a smooth, cat-like motion.

"Stand guard," I order Mot, slipping off the rooftop to land hard on the street below. I feel my arm jerk violently with the weight of the wooden box which contains the onyx shackles.

On reaching the Meatworks, I see that Lonnie has already found her way inside. I slip through the doorway, following her as she prowls through the dark interior of the slaughterhouse. The air is thick with the stench of dried blood and offal, the floor still damp with water used to wash away the day's murder in a crimson slurry that flows down channels cut into stone that lead to the sewers below.

We search for some time without result before Lonnie hits upon something. She draws me to the rear of the main building, to a metal grate in the floor which stands above a pool of fetid liquid that looks to be a mixture of effluent and blood.

"See?" she says, motioning to the floor beside the grate. Barely visible in the dark interior of the slaughterhouse is the top half of a boot mark, etched in crimson against the stone.

I lean over the grate, holding my breath so as not to inhale the vile stench. The opening is large enough for a man to enter, though the stench emanating from below makes such a prospect less than appealing.

"A tunnel, hidden beneath a well of blood?"

She nods, moving to the side of the grate and feeling along the ridge of the closest wall. After a few moments, there is a sound like the grating of stone against stone. Lonnie smiles, her teeth vibrant in the darkness. The well of blood and effluent beneath the grate drains away within moments, leaving a slick shaft with a metal ladder bolted to one side. I turn to Lonnie, motioning toward the grate.

"After you."

Her grin falters replaced by a barely concealed snarl. The grate is hinged and opens without difficulty. Lonnie makes her way gingerly down to the tunnels below, and I follow after, fighting the urge to wretch as my gloved hands press against the slick surface of the ladder rungs. Before we reach the bottom of the shaft, the mechanism up above which holds the well at bay moves back into place. A large stone block slides into a niche overhead, causing the shaft to shudder. We move quickly down the last few rungs, dropping to the ground in a dimly lit corridor with kinetic lamps hanging from the walls.

We follow barely visible footfalls down the narrower of two tunnels, Lonnie with blade and pistol drawn and I with the dark wood box and my holstered shooting irons. The tunnel twists and turns, leading us through a complex path which branches out here and there in all directions. Were it not for the slick footprints in the earth, we would be unable to follow our prey and would likely lose ourselves within the labyrinthine underbelly of the city.

"How long do these tunnels stretch?" I ask.

Lonnie shrugs. "It's said there was once a city beneath Tullhaven. Stretches all the way to Rust."

"Surely not."

Even as I speak, we enter a large underground chamber which branches out to a dozen different tunnels, each carefully cut into rock and earth, with a worn plaque hanging above each entrance. The copper plaques are pitted with age, turned mottled green and battered by years of neglect. We cannot read the writing, nor make sense of the strange symbols which adorn the entrances to each tunnel, but the tell-tale footfalls of our prey lead us to the south.

After a short while we come to a smaller chamber, lit with vibrant crimson light and crowded with a dozen or so souls all dressed in simple robes. At the head of the group stands a gaunt figure clothed in crimson. The figure brandishes a long, curved blade and smiles wildly as he addresses his flock.

"We stand upon the cusp of midnight, dear friends. For the Great One hones his blade in preparation for the coming night, and we, his servants, must be steadfast and true. Fear not the cudgel of the ignorant masses. Fear not the misbegotten ruler of the Haven, nor his cruel militiamen. For the blade-that-cuts will sunder truth from lie and we, the faithful, will inherit…"

The robed figure continues his sermon as Lonnie and I position ourselves at the rear of the group, hidden by a pair of roughly hewn pillars which stretch from floor to ceiling. As we watch the Cutter's rite continue, a book is produced and placed upon the stone table at the front of the chapel. A candidate is selected from among the gathered faithful. The young man bears his arm while blood is drained into a small copper bowl to be used as ink upon the pages of the large volume. The bled candidate returns to his place, lauded by his fellow cultists with cries of encouragement and appreciation.

The leader of the congregation begins to pen words into the opened volume, speaking the words with each stroke of his stylus. The words seem to contain little of consequence, recounting how two of the cultists had attempted to recover the bodies of a recently "blessed" individual who had been taken by the red mist. The cultist in question—the self-same man who was chosen to give blood in service to the book—is praised for his efforts though no mention is made of the where the recovered bodies have been placed.

I turn to Lonnie. "Go to Mott and be sure to mark the path. Bring a dozen Brothers and be quick about it."

She nods, vanishing into the tunnel with speed.

I stay cloaked in darkness, observing the ceremony with mild interest. Something worries me about the words that are spoken, the deeds which are recounted.

Despite their professed service to the Scythe and their love of blade and bloodshed, there is nothing murderous to their words. These men are content to observe the falling of the red mist, to celebrate the cutting of flesh and the professed coming of their messiah, but there is little direct intent here. The cultists are not ordered to kill or maim. On the contrary, the bestowal of the red mist and its consequent violence is hailed as the domain of the Scythe and not to be undertaken by human agency alone.

I watch and listen, waiting for Lonnie and the others to return.

***

We raid a dozen Cutter temples, scattered throughout the city in varying sizes. To each temple there stands a chaplain of sorts; one man chosen from the ranks of cultists to stand at the head and speak for the temple itself. Though their numbers are small, the religious apparatus of the Cutter Cult is surprisingly sophisticated. Each temple holds a copy of their holy script: a book penned in blood to which the meagre exploits of each local chapter are added with the passing of each cycle. Ceremonies and rites are held regularly, sacraments taken, and secret vows sworn with blood and binding words.

It is the vast religious edifice that underpins the Cutter Cult which proves somewhat perplexing. To hear Tull speak on the matter, the Cult and her progenitor are newly formed, perhaps fifty or sixty years in the making, a derivative of one soldier's falling out with the Warmaster. Yet there is a theological depth to the ramblings of the cultists which speaks of long years of religious tradition.

In addition, despite its love of blood and blade, the cult does not actively do harm to the general populous. Sacrifices are drawn from the cult itself, and the harm inflicted is delivered by each cultist's own hand.

Several of the temples themselves, while only rudimentary in structure and ornament, hark back to the earliest days of the city, and hint toward older locales from which the Cutter Cult derives. The older temples sit nestled among vast networks of underground tunnels that predate the city of Tullhaven. Each temple seems set aside for the purpose of worship; not merely as empty buildings which are now occupied by the Cutter Cult, but as ancient chambers that have been used for cultic rites for years beyond memory.

Of the underground city, little is known. Whilst mapping its multitudinous tunnels and chambers, we discover arcane machines of unknown design, whose function can only be guessed at. We find an aged library with books and scrolls of such age that they turn to dust when touched by human hands. We find crowded tombs and arcane inscriptions, intricate carvings and works of ancient art. But of the original citizens of this city, there seems to be no evidence. Even the withered remains of the dead offer no answers, other than the fact that the city's denizens were likely human.

With each new temple we discover, each cultist interrogated, the godling's words are proven less reliable. Of the Scythe, there is little tangible evidence. It is to the principle of death, of finality, that the Cutter Cult owes their theology, rather than a belief in a tangible, physical being. Thus, when they speak of the Scythe, they speak of a messianic figure, prophesied to bring judgement to the Traumwelt and usher in an age of enlightenment and prosperity.

I sit and ponder these thoughts as a young Brother approaches. I cannot remember the pup's name, but the crooked nose and scarred features of the lad mark him out in my memory. He is quick-witted and dependable, despite his youth.

"What news?" I ask.

"Two more attacks," the Brother says, wiping sweat from his brow. "First outside Tull's palace and another in one of the Slaver dens down by the Burns. Same as the others. Red mist in the eyes. A couple of people cut down until the city militia can get it under control."

"Was the cult involved?"

He shakes his head. "They tried to pick up the bodies but got driven off by the militia."

Having delivered his message, the boy nods and returns to his duties. I turn to Lonnie. "I think perhaps we are looking to the wrong cause here. Tell me, is there an apothecary or a poison smith among the Brotherhood ranks?"

She nods, leaving without another word. In her absence, I study the many sheets of paper upon which I have scribbled notes and drawings. If there is a deeper logic at work behind the Cutter Cult and this red mist madness, I cannot find it. I have spent a great many hours wrestling with these pages, but still I feel the truth sitting just beyond reach.

When Lonnie returns, it is with the torturer in tow. The woman approaches wearing a wry smile. She runs her hand across the scattered papers at my desk, picking a scrap of text from the pile and examining it casually. Once more I am struck by the woman's cruel beauty, by the scent of vanilla and the seductive air that seems to accompany her.

"You are an apothecary?" I ask.

She drops the scrap of paper, sliding into a seat opposite me. "Of a sort. Why?"

I shake my head. "Perhaps it is best that I speak with Claude first, before following speculation?"

She smiles, leaning forward a little, her eyes sharp and dangerous. "I will not ask you again, Shackle. You called for an apothecary, and I have come. Now tell me, why?"

I see it then, perhaps for the first time. I see it in the way she carries herself, in the supreme confidence she exhibits; the authority of her words and the deference all others in the Brotherhood seem to give her. All this time and I have had it wrong. Claude is not the Scorpion. No, she sits before me now, with eyes like a hungry wolf.

"I do not think that the Cutter Cult has caused this latest spate of bloodshed. In fact, I would go so far as to suggest that the red mist and the Cult are not related in the least."

She leans back in her chair, pulling a small stiletto from her coat and picking absently at her fingernails. "And what makes you say that?"

I motion to the papers scattered before me. "Consider what we have learned about the undercity. It is vast, ancient, and home to a great many secrets. The temples these cultists use for their rite seem to have been built for the purpose, yet I doubt that they were designed for this latest incarnation of the Cutter Cult. All evidence suggests that the cult derives from an older religion; one which was very much in use when the undercity was at its prime."

She nods, circling the blade of the stiletto in the air. "Go on."

"The cultists themselves are largely harmless. They speak of blood and steel, but their words are largely a matter of metaphor. While they may lurk in shadows and keep their cult secret, they pose little threat to the people of Tullhaven and the ruling interests of the city. These are the poor and wretched, the doltish and weak, those who cling to their religion for the significance it gives them. They feed off the violence of the red mist, yet they themselves are not violent in nature. Indeed, the slavers and merchants prove more violent and disruptive to the city when filled with drink."

Scorpion lets out a deep breath. "I would count it a kindness if you could come to the point some time before the sun rises."

"The Cutter Cult has not caused the red mist. It has merely experienced a resurgence in the wake of the recent violence. The Cult itself, I would say, has ancient origins but has only recently come to associate itself with the red mist. So also, this figure of the Scythe is more deified idea than concrete entity. I would wager that the progenitor of the Cutter Cult has long since passed on; perhaps in the years when the undercity was still alive and well?"

"So?"

"So, if we treat the red mist on its own merits, other possibilities emerge. It has occurred from time to time over the years. Rising for a short time, claiming a variety of victims with little in common, then receding. Yet, if the histories I have read are to be believed, there is more of design than coincidence to the red mist phenomenon.

You see, I have witnessed plague first-hand. I have seen it ravage half the world and eat through whole cities and villages without mercy. Such diseases burn through chaff and wheat alike, consuming all in their path until there is no more fuel to be burnt. Only then, once there is no more to consume, does the scourge die off."

Scorpion nods, tapping her knife lightly against her chin. "But the red mist is far more precise, more selective?"

"Yes. It may appear haphazard in the early days, but when it reaches fever pitch, it ends abruptly and seemingly without reason."

"You sense design behind the mist?"

I nod. "Agency, yes. I believe that the mist is not a matter of chance or some random infection. I believe it is caused by tangible means and controlled to some extent by its author."

She smiles. "You suspect poison?"

"Perhaps…or some etherically charged affliction. Note that it seems to strike most commonly in pairs and not larger groups."

"I know of no poison or agent which could cause such sudden violence. There are a great many substances that do harm to the individual, but I cannot think of any that would cause a man to… Wait, in pairs you say?"

She stands abruptly, calling Lonnie over from the corner of the room. She whispers something to Lonnie, and the other woman departs at pace, climbing the stairs up to the tavern proper. Scorpion moves toward me, walking around the table to sidle up beside me, her body pressed lightly against mine. Her hand draws my chin upward, and I am caught in a deep, impassioned kiss. No words are spoken, no explanations given. After a moment, she breaks free, sauntering back to the other side of the table without a word.

Lonnie enters the room, carrying a small tray of food. She places it on the table in front of me as Scorpion takes her seat on the opposite side.

"You have seen this dish before?" Scorpion asks.

I give the plate a cursory inspection. The meal is a mixture of corn chips and fried meat which sits within a bowl of stale bread.

"I believe the locals call it Two Shoes."

She nods. "And they do so because it is always intended to eat in company. It is very rare to see a single soul sit down to eat this particular meal. It's bad luck, you see."

As she talks, she breaks off a piece of corn chip and dips it into the meat, savouring the taste as she leans back in her chair.

"This dish is served in a hundred ale houses and brothels throughout the city. A dish served to a pair of patrons."

"So, if our poisoner were targeting a meal such as this…"

"It would explain your pairs of red-misted lunatics."

I lean forward to take a better look at the meal. "Corn, meat, spices. The poisoner could have tainted one of these at the source."

She shrugs. "Or they are poisoning ready-made food at taverns and alehouses throughout Tullhaven. If the latter is the case, then it is likely we are dealing with a cadre of poisoners, rather than an individual."

I nod. "The results are too specific to suggest that they are poisoning the source."

We discuss the matter at length, soon coming to a plan of action. In the weeks that follow, the Scorpion

Brotherhood question a hundred tavern owners and merchants. Sale of Two Shoes is forbidden in those taverns and ale houses run by the Brotherhood, and we see that rumours of the poisoned dish circulate broadly throughout the city.

The number of red mist incidents drops so dramatically that it confirms our suspicion. Yet, after weeks of toil, we come no closer to learning the identity of the poisoner. The Scorpion and I meet regularly—too regularly. Without warning I find myself snared within her arms—lovers entwined in a fevered embrace while the city begins to burn around us.

Just as we think ourselves growing closer to the answer we seek, the red plague strikes a brutal blow, felling two dozen market goers and leaving a bloody trail throughout the upper west side of the city. A nightly curfew is enforced by the city militia, and several of the larger merchant houses begin withdrawing funds and personnel from Tullhaven. Violence erupts in the street as local gangs fight for supremacy amid the uncertain state of the city. Tull's puppet issues a series of decrees and expands the size and reach of the militia, paying double for the services of those who will patrol the streets.

It seems that the sudden passion I share with Scorpion grows in concert with the swelling of violence and fear throughout the city. We do not speak during the act, but simply devour one another; giving way to animal passions. She makes no secret of our coupling, and the Brotherhood seems content to leave the matter be. For my own part, I am adrift at sea; grounded only by the constant gnawing in my gut, the ever-present need to bring death to the godling Tull and his ilk.

I meet with Shadow and Rook several times, apprising them of the situation and instructing them to be cautious in the volatile days ahead. Through some curious gift, the girl senses my coupling with Scorpion. I admit nothing, but her wry smile and constant verbal jabs speak of some secret knowledge in that regard. There is nothing of jealousy or concern in her manner; only a sense of pleasure and what might well be pride. Of Rook, little has changed. The big man fulfils his role in court and keeps his wife and child far from prying eyes. He stores the pilfered gems and gold Shadow has acquired and waits in readiness for our plan to come to fruition.

All the while, though, I dare not admit it to Shadow, I feel myself begin to unravel. I am too many things to too many people, and the darkness within only grows with time's passing. So it is, that when the red mist strikes again, I am unprepared for what follows.

***

"You are a curiosity," Claude says, pulling a thin lockpick from his jacket and bending down at the doorway.

I shrug, my mind split between a dozen different thoughts. "No less than yourself, I should think?"

He lets out a short breath. "Come now, gunslinger. There is little mystery to me. I am a man of some skill with weapons and more with the command of those who use them. I admire loyalty and abhor injustice. For these reasons, I have come to serve the Brotherhood and, by extension, the Scorpion."

I cannot help the grim smile that alights upon my face. "And that is precisely the mystery. To find a good man in this world is a rare thing indeed."

He cocks his head in my direction. "And do you not think yourself a good man, gunslinger?"

"A weapon does not consider if it is good or bad. Nor does the hand that wields it," The words come from an old memory I cannot properly place. A man, a teacher of sorts, gruff and well skilled in violence.

Claude laughs, his voice muffled beneath his kerchief. "Very well, gunslinger. We will stow this talk of good men and curiosities until we are both well plied with liquor."

I nod. "Agreed."

The doorway gives way, and we enter, quickly and quietly. Though I do not understand the means by which the trick is performed, I see its evidence in the silent steps that follow us inside the large tavern. Through some etheric means, Claude has masked our steps and words, such that we can move unheard through the night. This is the third tavern we have inspected, and there are half a dozen more we must attend to this night, so Claude moves swiftly.

We head to the tavern larder where stores of salted meat and produce are housed. A flicker of light spills out from the room as we approach, accompanied by sounds of movement. Claude pulls a long dagger from his coat, and I do likewise. He motions to the left, and I move in the direction indicated. We approach the room crouched, brandishing dark blades.

I see a tall man, clothed in simple robes. He holds a small glass vial in one hand and is set to drop its contents into a large vat of dried meat. With terrible speed, Claude advances on the man, driving his blade up into his chest while clamping a hand around the vial. I look left and right for signs of the intruder's accomplices, but the stands alone.

Claude holds the poisoner, driving his dagger home as the man's lifeblood spills out onto the floor. He does not cry out nor utter a sound, but dies quickly in Claude's arms, his body giving a slight spasm as it slumps to the ground. With due care, Claude presses the stopper home upon the poisoner's vial, waiving it in my direction.

"Well, my friend, it seems we've found our poisoner."

He takes a step, leaning down to examine the man. I hear the faintest crack as his boot crushes a second vile that lies beside the dead poisoner's body. Dread fills Claude's face as a crimson mist rises from the broken vial. He clasps a hand over his mouth and nose, walking slowly through the mist toward me. Several, terrible moments pass as the mist slowly fades. Only when the last of it has gone does Claude uncover his mouth. He smiles, shaking his head as he hands me the second vial. I slip the object into a pocket."

"We should examine the body," I suggest. "But that can wait until morning. I'll send for Mot and Lonnie. They can clean this up and—"

Claude stands with a curious expression. He stares at his hands, now shaking slightly as though taken by some palsy. He looks up at me, eyes red with the demon mist. Whatever evil is contained in that vial, he has inhaled an undiluted portion of it. His muscles begin to spasm as the crimson rage takes him. In that final moment, he knows what must follow. He pulls a dagger, driving the blade into his chest with brutal finality as his eyes remain locked upon mine. He staggers, but that last moment of lucidity vanishes too swiftly. Of a sudden, he is a mindless brute, slipping on his own blood as he lunges for me with the blade wrenched from his own chest.

I step back, out of the larder and into the common room of the tavern. Claude drags himself on hands and knees, desperate to cleave flesh with the bloodied dagger in his right hand. With the last vestiges of strength, he claws at the floor, making sickly sounds which barely approximate speech. I am spared the final blow, as his strength finally gives way and Claude's body breaths its last.

Thus dies the last good man in Tullhaven, and I am sickened by the sight. I consider the poison resting in a vial in my pocket, the robed figure who died far too easily in the nearby room. I know not what drives such sentimentality, but I am moved to attend to his body. I pull the jacket from his corpse and retrieve his hat from the larder. I bind his body with hessian bags and carry him from that place, back to the inn where Scorpion awaits news of the night's events.

She does not weep to see his body, but I can sense the agony its sight causes her. I speak of our encounter at the tavern and advise that I have sent men to acquire the dead poisoner. When they return, she inspects the body in gruesome detail which I watch from a distance.

"The man was mute," she says. "his tongue was cut out, and there are markings cut into his flesh."

I move a little closer, inspecting the curious symbols cut into the man's body.

"Have you seen their like?" she asks, her voice hard-edged and ragged.

I shrug. "Symbols of etheric significance, I would guess, though I cannot read their meaning. It matters not, however. I know who we seek. I know who has brought this misery upon us."

Her dark eyes set upon me like a hawk's gaze. "Who?"

I return her gaze. "The godling Tull."

My words seem to cause her physical pain.

"And how do you know this?"

I shrug. "I have had dealings with several of the godling's servant these past months. There is an aura about them, an etheric taint. It is as though their proximity to the godling changes them in some way. Also, Tull is fond of making his servants mute or blind. It may seem rather circuitous, however—"

She holds up a hand. There is no rebuttal, no defiance in her eyes. Even as I prepare a lengthy explanation, I see that she accepts the truth of it.

"But there is more," I continue. "The godling is not the lunatic hedonist who dwells within the palace. He—"

"He lives beneath the palace and performs ghastly experiments with flesh and shadow. Yes, gunslinger, we are aware of this."

Her words take me back a little.

"We have lived in this city for many years, gunslinger," she says. "Do not suppose that you know more of its secrets than we do."

Something in her voice hints at another secret I had thought hidden. I decide to take my chance and let the bones fall as they may.

"Then you know that I work in service to the godling Tull? You know that I was sent to infiltrate the Brotherhood and kill the Scorpion?"

She smiles, her lips hard-edged. "Why do you think I kept you so close? Better to keep a viper at hand than let it slip out of sight and strike from the shadows."

I nod. "Better to kill the viper and avoid the trouble altogether."

She moves closer, placing a hand on my chest. "You are not the first mercenary Tull has sent to find me, gunslinger, and you will not be the last. Better I keep you to hand than end your life and be forced to wait for another."

"And what do you intend to do with this viper?"

She leans forward, kissing me gently and leaning her head against my chest. "I have a gift, Shackle. Whether of etheric origin or simply a matter of heredity, I do not know. I can see into the heart of a man and know his true desire. I see through lie and artifice to the truth of intention. That is why I have been able to build this Brotherhood without fear of internal strife or betrayal. I choose only those whose hearts I see the right qualities in."

"And what qualities do you see in me?"

She places a hand upon my chin, looking up with eyes that seem suddenly filled with sorrow.

"I see turmoil. Black horror and grave pain vying for control. I see sorrow and madness and rage. I see something that might be love. Not for me, but for another, a youngling to whom you have become something of a father. But mostly, I see the death of the godling Tull sitting as the very prize of your heart's desire. You wish him dead, he and all his kind, and you will stop at nothing to bring this to pass, no matter the impossibility of the task."

She lets out a long sigh. "I cannot see if this desire is of your own making, or the design of some other, but it rules you, Shackle, and you are slave to its whims. Whatever you were sent here to do, your singular goal is to kill Tull, and that in itself makes us more ally than enemy."

"Very well. Then that will have to serve as our pact then."

She moves away from me, lifting the vial of crimson poison from a cushion on the bench and holding it up to a nearby lamp. "And what are we to do about this then? We have the weapon. We know the identity of the culprit, but we have no means of exacting vengeance. In truth, I had suspected Tull, but had not means of proving that suspicion. Even so, we are powerless to act against him."

"Perhaps. Or perhaps the time has come to be done with shadow puppets and intrigues? Perhaps your vengeance and my heart's desire may soon be sated."

"You intend to confront him?"

"I intend to kill him."

She muses upon my words, worry etched across her brow. "I cannot offer men to aid you in this. We have already lost Claude and—"

"I need no aid."

Her eyes narrow. "Your gifts—the healing and such—there is more at work within you than I have seen with my own eyes, yes?"

I nod.

"Sufficient to kill a godling?"

I shrug. "We shall see."

She nods, sitting at a large chair by the doorway and examining the crimson vial once more. I move to the corner of the room and pull the dark wood box from its niche beneath a small cabinet. I feel the etheric power of the onyx shackles vibrate within the box as I move toward the doorway. Scorpion holds out a hand before I pass by, pointing to the long jacket and hat hanging over a nearby chair.

"Take his clothes. Wear them in memory. It is a foolish custom, but you were there with him at the end, and it is our way."

I move to speak but think better of it. I take up the coat and hat and prepare to take my leave.

"He was very fond of you, Shackle," the Scorpion says, tears streaming down her cheeks. "He thought you a man of principle and honour."

I nod but find no words to offer in return.

13. A Terrible Truth

I stand once more in the depths of the godling temple. While a false nobility frolic in the vast halls above, Tull persists at his vile work. Machines of strange design are grafted to human flesh, blended with etheric shadow and pressed into new and horrific forms. Covered in blood and oil, the godling smiles as he catches sight of me.

I drop the dark wood box to the floor, allowing the imbued shackles to spill out. Tull wipes his hands on a rag, approaching with mild amusement.

"Am I to import some significance to this gesture?" he asks, kicking at the broken box with one foot.

I feel the power within me begin to surge, fuelled by an etheric rage which I am forced to press down beneath the surface. I advance on the godling, heedless of the danger such a move might provoke.

"You sent me on a fool's errand. There is no Scythe, no godling pretender who stands behind the Cutter Cult and their misbegotten beliefs. There is no sorcery at work within the red mist, only a rabid poison that devours the mind and turns its victims into mindless savages."

Tull nods. "And you feel perhaps that I have done you ill?"

"I have wasted a great deal of time searching for phantoms and devils, when the true devil lurks within these very walls. It is *you* who has unleashed the red plague upon this city. I think it likely that the very poisons which have caused this madness are brewed here, in this chamber."

The godling's eyes narrow. "I see. And what precisely do you seek? An apology perhaps? Or is it simply the satisfaction of confronting me on the matter?"

I feel a dark ire rise within me. "I am not a fool, godling, so I do not appreciate being treated as such."

He raises a hand. Sudden pain rises in my throat, cutting off my breath and pressing like iron clamps about my neck and chest. I am driven backward against the wall, my heart pounding, excruciating pain clawing at every fibre and sinew of my flesh. I cannot help but let out a cry of pain as the invisible bonds do their work. I gasp for air, clawing helplessly at the invisible force that crushes breath and life. Bones crack and splinter within my chest as blood wells from within.

As my vision begins to blur, Tull releases me from this sudden bondage. I fall in a heap upon the ground, clutching at my throat and heaving with breath.

"You use that tongue far too casually in my presence," the godling says, taking a step toward my crumpled form. "I did not doubt that you would return to me though I confess that I had not thought you so stupid as to insult me to my face. Many men have died for far less. Indeed, I am perplexed to see that you have endured."

Tull looks down at his hands with a curious expression. He bends down, staring into my eyes as though searching for something.

"There is strength within you, gunslinger, but of an entirely different order to that which I first supposed. You have something of the gift about you."

His expression lightens. "So, once again I am forced to rethink my plans concerning you. You have fulfilled part of your contract, so I will permit you a brief explanation."

He bends down, picking up the onyx shackles and hefting them with a grin.

"As you say, there is no Scythe. Not in the sense that I described at least. It is true that the Warmaster once lost his most faithful disciple, and that figure did indeed flee to the red wastes. Some have even attributed the red plague to figure though, as you no doubt suspect, the Cutter religion is far older that the Warmaster's wayward pet. You have seen the old city, so you know of what I speak. So, why did I send you after the Cutter deity?"

He waves a hand across the face of the onyx shackles, and, momentarily, the chamber fills with etheric power. Tull smiles and lets the shackles fall to the floor.

"In truth, I simply wanted you to take the shackles with you. They have no power in themselves, understand, but I imbued them with a whisper charm, a means of hearing your words and those of your compatriots among the Brotherhood. Scythe was merely a necessary ruse to ensure you kept the charmed shackles nearby. Through their etheric whispers, I have learned a great deal these past weeks."

A cold chill stabs at my heart as I unravel Tull's words. I scour my memories, recalling the last time I met with Shadow.

"Yes, I have learned a great deal indeed. Two things most notably. Firstly, it appears that you have found the Scorpion. I confess I am not familiar with the woman, still it is clear that your suspicions are correct. She is indeed the leader of your Brotherhood and thus the goal of our compact. Kill her and you will earn your final reward and may leave this city and go about your business."

He draws close, kneeling down so that our eyes meet.

"Kill the Scorpion and our bargain is done. I will forget your recent transgression and leave you and the girl to your own devices. Ah, now I seem to have your full attention. Yes, I know of the girl and of your false prince, Rook. I see the plans unfurl within your mind, gunslinger; how you would win my trust and then plunge a dagger into my very heart. For this alone I had thought to kill you this night, yet you have survived a blow which would kill any ordinary man, and I confess I am intrigued. For one who has lived as long as I, such a thing is a rare gift. So, I grant you this one chance. Fulfil your part in this bargain and the girl will go free. Fail, or attempt to betray me, and I will bring her to my table and make of her a wretched obscenity—a thing of metal and misery, blood and bile."

I stare into the godling's eyes and feel teeth clamp about my heart once more. I do not voice anger, nor question his words, for their truth is written plainly upon his face. He has the girl, and I have no choice but to play his game. He will kill me; of that, I am certain. But first, as the cat takes its pleasure with a mouse, he will toy with me a little longer.

"Go," Tull says, standing to his feet and waving me away. "Finish this business and return to me. Do it quickly, do it well and you shall win your freedom. You and your little thief."

I stand slowly, my body still racked with pain.

"It makes little sense," I offer, twisting my neck to one side and feeling it give a satisfying crack. "You know the identity of the Scorpion. Doubtless you have known for some time, despite my efforts. Why not kill her yourself?"

Tull walks slowly toward the closest of his experimentations, bending down over the body of a young man whose limbs have been severed and replaced by mechanized monstrosities that hiss and hum, leaking oil and blood in equal parts while the senseless figure thrashes against his constraints.

"Yours is a short-lived species," he says, picking up a small metal device with one hand and tapping it gently on the interior of one of the mechanized limbs. "You are born too swiftly, emerging from your mother's womb a full year before your proper time. You live and die so swiftly that your passing makes no contribution to the larger cosmic landscape. You must build upon the work of your ancestors to have any hope of making progress."

Tull twists his left hand, bringing thin threads of etheric energy to life. The threads wind their way toward his victim's limb as he tinkers with intricate mechanisms, his face a mask of studious concentration.

"We of the godling race are a different matter entirely. We live too long and experience far too much of the same. I myself have lived ten thousand years, in one form or another. I have seen all that mankind has to offer. I have journeyed beyond the mortal realm and tasted the rarefied air of a thousand worlds. For such as I, novelty is the only true pleasure that can be drawn from this existence. The experience of something genuinely unexpected is to be savoured above all else, for such moments are increasingly rare."

He looks up from his work, pointing a bloodied implement toward me. "You are one such novelty, gunslinger. And it is for that reason alone that I have allowed you to live this long. Even in that first moment when you found your way into my sanctum, I recognized your unique nature—the darkness that wars within you, the power brewing below the surface. I confess, I had thought to kill you immediately, but could not bring myself to act in the face of something so tantalizing. There is a power within you, gunslinger, which is older than time itself. The darkness that broods behind your eyes is of an order of power that can barely be comprehended. Yet, it lies locked within the vessel of your flesh, hidden away for some unknown purpose."

I take a step closer, feeling the power stir within me as he talks. "That does not answer my question. Why send me to kill the Scorpion? Why not act yourself."

Tull smiles. "Why scent your tea with honey? Why fill your bath with petals and lemon? Because a life without pleasure is no life at all, gunslinger. It pleases me to send you forth, to place you upon the board and watch the game unfold. For it is all a game, gunslinger. The city above ebbs and flows to the tune of those pieces I have put in place. I move the pieces sparingly, allowing matters to unfold with natural abandon. For, if one understands the nature of man, one can predict the movements of every piece upon the board. Consider the so-called red plague. This is little more than a distraction, a catalyst for change in the hope of producing new and vaguely interesting reactions. Yet, each piece still acts within the confines of their character. Even with the threat of sudden, inexplicable doom, the pieces continue down their set paths."

He takes in a deep breath, and I sense something of genuine frustration behind his words.

"I play the game because it pleases me, because there is the slightest chance that a piece may not behave as it is supposed to on the board. There is a miniscule opportunity for my predictions to go awry; for something genuinely surprising and new to surface. And, to a godling such as I—one for whom the natural world has so little to offer—novelty is the finest of liquors. Were I to act myself upon the board and execute simple victory, then what enjoyment could I derive from the process? To kill the Scorpion myself is such a definitive action that it denies the chance of novelty. But if I send another in my place...there is a chance."

"By that logic, you must adhere to the rules of the game, yes? If I kill the Scorpion, you will allow me and the girl to go free?"

Tull nods, returning to his work without another word. I read the lie in the gesture. He may not kill us outright, but why would such a creature give up his prized game piece so swiftly? He will toy with us until our novelty wears out, and then dispatch us without a second thought.

As I walk from the chamber, my eyes cannot help but linger upon the dark monstrosities strapped to the godling's tables: poor creatures that mew and moan beneath his blade. I would kill the girl myself before I let Tull kiss her with his knife. There are no options left to me. I have to act quickly, and there is but one acceptable path left to me.

I must kill the godling Tull.

14. To Kill a Godling

I find Rook standing upon his balcony, wearing a grim expression. He clutches a long blade in one hand and is stripped to the waist as he was when we first met.

"How fare your wife and child?" I ask.

"They sleep in peace," the giant answers, his words somewhat curt.

"And how goes your courtly intrigues?"

Rook turns toward me, wearing a heavy scowl. "Fickle men play at parlour games while children live in squalor at their feet. They prance and primp and spend their nights feasting beneath the shadow of the puppet king."

The big man lifts his blade, twisting its edge slightly. "Each night I carry this blade beneath my finery, comforted by the steel against my thigh. I imagine myself laying waste to those gilded halls and cutting the throats of every frilled dandy who makes his coin on the backs of dead slaves and indentured servants. This dream alone is what keeps me sane during the endless feasts and celebrations I am forced to endure."

I put a hand to the brute's shoulder. "You need not dream, my friend. The time has come to act and act with speed. Ready your wife and daughter to flee the city this night. They may take whatever servants and wealth which can be moved without suspicion. Send them north and to safety but remain in the city yet another day and night, for I have need of your arm and blade."

"The godling?"

I nod. "He has the girl and intends to kill us both. I am to kill the Scorpion and lay her corpse at Tull's feet, but I see no truth in his eyes, only deception. He will kill us both or consign us to perpetual misery as one of his misbegotten horrors."

Rook's eyes narrow. "You wish me to find the girl?"

"No, I dare not risk it. The godling will likely have her sequestered somewhere within the palace, close at hand so that he can make sport of me upon my return."

"You intend to kill the Scorpion then?"

I shake my head. "There is no profit in it for me, and it buys me no time."

"What then?"

"The game is lost, and I have but one final card to play. I risk death for myself and the girl but see no other choice but to proceed."

Even as I speak the words, their truth is made plain to me. A certain stillness settles upon my soul as I speak— the peace of the damned who no longer fear the future.

"I will enlist the aid of the Scorpion and her Brothers. I will march upon the palace with all the rage I can muster and kill every living soul that stands before the godling. I will let loose the hounds of chaos and set the tinder to flame. By the next night, I intend to stand before the godling and deal death."

Rook nods, wearing a stoic expression. "They say the godling cannot be killed."

"That they do."

"And what role do you wish me to play in all of this?"

"A simple matter. Merely unleash your wrath upon the Slaver's Guild and, in turn, upon the godling's court. I will convince the Scorpion to give you ten good men. With them, you shall cut a bloody path through the Slaver's camp, enlisting whatever help you can find among the slaves themselves. Do not tarry but move swiftly. Once the work is done, return to this house and don your finest garments. Gird yourself with iron and enter the palace in preparation for the nightly feast. Then, my friend, let your blades sing their finest song. Kill the puppet king and his entourage and, once this is done, flee the city and find your wife and child."

"And what of you, gunslinger? What of the girl, Shadow?"

The girl's face appears momentarily in my mind, and I feel a tug of pain from somewhere within. I do not pull away from the sensation but embrace it. The pain is real; it tethers me to the moment and brings clarity of thought.

"We will likely die, but that is a better fate than the godling would wish us."

"You intend to force his hand? To fall upon his sword and save yourselves from his excruciation table?"

I nod. "Just so."

"There is little hope in such a plan."

I turn to the big man, seeing the genuine concern in his dark eyes. "This world is not for us, Rook. It is for you and your kin. Whatever comes in the night that follows, you must flee this city and cling to your wife and child. Do this and we are well remembered."

The giant's hands grasp me, pulling me close into a tight hug. I feel my bones creak within his monstrous embrace.

"I will do as you ask, gunslinger," he says, "and perhaps, with luck, we shall meet again?"

"Perhaps."

***

I find Scorpion where I left her. We speak for long hours, then couple until the sun rises and the city begins to stir.

"We strike at dusk?" she asks, running a finger over my chest.

"At the tolling of the Evenbell. If the attacks are properly coordinated, you should cripple the Slaver's Guild and her compatriots beyond repair. It will leave the Brotherhood in a position of strength in the years that follow."

"Unless the godling takes it upon himself to seek retribution and kill us all?"

"There is no gain without risk."

She leans back, pouting. "This is not risk, it is insanity. It goes beyond poking the bear between the eyes. We are set to walk headlong into the flames."

I take her head in my hand, drawing her close. "Then why did you agree to follow me in this?"

She grins, moving a hand up my thigh. "You made a persuasive argument."

"Speak plainly. Why will you follow me in this?"

She does not answer but moves from the bed to pour herself a cup of ale from a nearby tankard. Candlelight kisses her naked form, glinting off the scars which crisscross her flesh.

"You do not see it," she says, turning slowly toward me. "You have a quality that inspires others to follow you. Perhaps it has always been thus, or perhaps such loyalty is a product of your gift?"

She points to the shackle on my left wrist.

"Claude was of a similar ilk. He, too, inspired trust and loyalty."

I shake my head. "I am not of a kind with Claude. I make no claims on such character."

She shrugs, sliding back into the bed and moving close. "Men will follow a bloodthirsty brute just as fiercely as they will a priest that eschews violence. Both can inspire loyalty."

"Is that what I am then, a bloodthirsty brute?"

She lays a finger across my lip, trailing it down my jaw and through the hair of my chest. I feel myself stir once again at her touch.

"You are a man with a talent for violence, but that does not make you a brute. You wear these shackles for the strength they give you, but they are a curse as well. You carry your prison with you, gunslinger. The darkness follows your every step."

"You offer an ambiguous answer to the question."

She smiles. "You are an ambiguous man. A contradiction."

"A great many souls will perish this night. The city will burn—"

Her lips halt my words, and she catches me in one final embrace before slipping from the bed and clothing herself.

"For a chance to be rid of the godling, I would risk every last Brother. You will have your chance, gunslinger. End this madness."

She returns to me, holding a small leather pouch in one hand. "I had thought to offer you the finest poison I could concoct in the hope that it might bring low the godling. In truth, however, I could not hope to brew a poison viler than this. Perhaps it will slow him somewhat?"

I take the pouch, seeing the crimson liquid swirling in the small glass bottle within.

"All will be made ready," she says, turning from me and heading out the doorway, her boot heels marking a crisp march up the stairs and out into the tavern common room.

I lay for a time, my thoughts caught in a maddening squall. I feel power stir from somewhere deep within, from the dark recesses ruled by those *other* forces. They whisper of strength and confidence.

Kill the godling Tull...sever the godling's head...cut his ribbon...end the godling...

Here, on the cusp of action, the voices grow more insistent. I feel etheric power pulse through the shackles upon my wrists, filling me with power and the will to act. I stand to my feet, fighting against the voices as I don my clothes. I press them back, bargaining for their silence with the promise of this night's bloody truth.

Tonight, it ends, one way or another.

***

With the tolling of the Evenbell, madness descends upon the bowl city. From my perch atop Rook's rooftop, I watch the violence unfold like a brutish pageant. The Slavers are hit first, their compounds softened with explosive concoctions that shake the very foundations of the city. A dozen pillars of thick smoke soon rise from the lower city, marking out the Slaver compounds like pins upon a map. Scorpion's men attack in silence, their brutal art making full use of the confusion. They kill overseers and merchants alike, freeing slaves as they go and adding to the chaotic milieu.

To the right I hear a voice booming above the din: Rook, bellowing with each mighty swing of his blades. I cannot help the smile that alights upon my face. Whatever else this night holds, I have given Rook his vengeance and seen his family safely from this city and its violent end. That thought pleases me a great deal as I head down toward the city streets and make my way toward the palace.

Gunshots fire in the distance, splitting the night air like the crackling of feast-day crackers. More explosions rock the city's foundations, tearing into the guild halls and compounds of the Scorpion's rivals. In one night, she seeks to end all opposition and intends to wrest control of Tullhaven from the godling and his compatriots. In one night, he will rise to be the most powerful force within the bowl city. I am under no illusions as to the reasons for her cooperation. For all her words of inspiration and loyalty, I could see the avarice in Scorpion's eyes—the hunger for domination, for power. She seeks to use me just as I seek to use her. We play our game, each aware of the other's true intentions.

To the north, still more explosions cut through the night air as the militia barracks are set to blaze and its inhabitants are cut down to a man. I know enough of the Brotherhood to know that they leave nothing to chance. They will use every resource to its full capacity. They will fight to their last breath, and they will overcome whatever resistance stands before them.

I confess a begrudged admiration for the Scorpion Brotherhood and their leader. Never before have I seen such dedication to a cause, such inspiration in the followers of a single leader. Except, perhaps, in the case of poor Litmus...

The crack of gunfire close by pulls me from my reverie. I round the corner to find three militiamen standing in the road, weapons aimed at a dark figure hidden by shadow nearby. Even from a distance, I can sense the bloodied outline of Rook hunched in a doorway. I feel etheric power rise as the shackles at my wrists begin to glow red in anticipation of the coming violence. For a moment, I consider using my shooting irons, but the darkness within compels me to bring etheric power to bear. I can no longer refuse those whispering voices.

I walk at pace toward the militiamen, feeling the power continue to grow as I draw near. One of their number sees my approach and levels his weapon at me. There is a sharp crack as the weapon discharges, and I feel the bullet brush my cheek. A second militiaman, filled with panic, attempts to draw and fire, but before he can manage it, I am already upon them.

I punch the first militiaman in the chest, hitting the fellow with sufficient force to crush his ribs and turn his organs to pulp. His body is thrown backward, to the astonishment of his fellows, just as I grab the second guard and punch out at his throat. The third man drops his rifle and starts to run. A heavy blade sings from the darkness and buries itself in the militiaman's back, sending him to the ground in a bloody heap. Rook emerges from the darkness, advancing on the man and ending his life with a swift jerk of his hands around the militiaman's neck.

He turns to me, blood covering his half-naked form. He looks every bit the demon, clothed in blood and darkness, yet it is with fear and hesitation that he looks at me.

"Well met, friend Rook," I offer, pressing against the etheric energy which still boils in my blood. "How goes your engagement with the Slavers?"

Rook seems to settle a little. "Satisfying and long overdue. I left your compatriots in the Brotherhood to their work, but there will be nothing left of the Slaver's trade in this city by morning."

I nod. "More will rise. They always do."

Rook shrugs. "Perhaps so. But for this night, no Slaver will go free."

He points to the two bodies lying in a heap before me. "You have grown stronger it seems?"

I turn to consider the bodies of the militiamen. Both are dead. "Indeed, it seems so. Let us hope it is enough to cause Tull a little strife."

We continue up the street toward the palace, encountering a dozen or so militiamen and dispatching them with relative ease. I feel the power ebb and flow with each new step, built upon a growing hunger that will only be sated once I am in the presence of the godling Tull.

"Once we reach the palace, make a short end to the aristocracy and do not linger. I cannot say what power the godling may release when he is confronted, but you would do well to be out of the city and away from this place."

Rook nods as we round a corner and approach the palace steps. He motions to the score of guardsmen stationed by the palace entrance.

"There are other paths into the palace. I am curious why you chose to enter so brazenly?"

I cannot help the crooked smile that comes to my lips. "The time for subterfuge is done, Rook. The time for restraint has passed."

The first spear shafts barely miss me, hurled from the steps above by well-trained guardsmen. The shackles at my wrists swell with etheric power, filling my vision with crimson light as a second wave of spear thrusts hits home. One of the spears hits my chest, forcing me back a step. Yet the steel tip of the weapon does not penetrate skin. Crimson light crackles around my body, dissuading the projectiles from their true path by means of an etheric ward.

I break into a run, pressing my advantage as the guardsmen stare at one another in disbelief. It does not take them long to recover their wits, but I am on them far too quickly, my legs given unnatural strength and speed by the etheric gifts flooding through my flesh. I drive my fists into the throng, battering three men to their deaths within a single heartbeat. Swords are drawn, and I am forced to block a series of thrusts and swings with nothing but my bare arms. Yet the shackles do their work once more, and I feel no pain as the sword-blows rain down upon me.

I snatch one of the blades from a guardsman, spinning to club the man about the head with his own weapon. His kindred draw close, intent upon skewering me with their blades. I lunge at the closest man, throwing his body into those standing behind. I drive my fists into chests and faces, battering my combatants without the use of tool or weapon. There is nothing of elegance or thrift to my movements, merely the brutish slapping of bare fists against flesh. The power I am lent gives each thrust of my fist inhuman properties. The enemy falls like straw puppets, and, before long, the palace stairs are slick with blood and guardsmen lie strewn across the thoroughfare as though discarded by some bloody-minded Titan.

In the distance, Rook has advanced up the vast stairway. He dispatches a pair of guardsmen by the main portico, nodding toward me as he moves on. Even from this distance, I can sense the unease in the man. He is eager to be rid of me. Eager to be far from the inhuman forces at work in my flesh. I follow after, making my way toward the inner tunnels that will lead me to Tull and my fate.

Screams peel out from every corner of the palace as servants flee the vast structure. Here and there, I see a dead guardsman, cut down with the precise strokes of Rook's blades. I feel etheric power swell within me as I draw closer to Tull's chamber, growing in intensity and causing my vision to blur somewhat. I recall encountering a group of guardsmen, but do not witness the moment of their demise. In one heartbeat they are torn down, yet I do not recall the act of violence which brought them low.

I am moving now, through tunnels and secret passages. I work my way through the bowels of the palace, following a trail of dead bodies as I work my way toward Tull. At first, I think the bodies signs of Rook's passing, but a momentary glitch in perception suggests otherwise. I am walking, surrounded by a crimson nimbus of light… Two souls attack from the darkness, approaching with drawn blades from hidden niches… I drive my fists into their heads… Their blades crack and shatter against my skin…

The power throbs with each beat of my heart. It is as though I am carried through the underbelly of the palace, rather than walking. I no longer feel my feet, nor do I experience the deaths of those I encounter along my path. Perhaps a dozen more soldiers? A scullery maid too, and several other servants killed for the simple crime of being in this place, at this time. I do not feel the blows I inflict, nor hear the cries of terror which greet me. I am a passenger of sorts, confined to the murky interior of my own body while some other force animates my flesh.

I cannot count how many souls die by my hands, just as I cannot say by what path I reach the godling's chamber. Nonetheless, amid the blood mist and carnage, I find myself standing before Tull, wreathed in crimson fire. The godling does not bother looking up from his work.

"I take it by your current fugue that you do not wish to fulfil our bargain then?"

I open my mouth to speak, but the words are lost to me. Tull looks up, smiling. He wipes the gore from his hands and approaches me.

"You are lost at sea, yes? You thought to use your gifts against me, to harness the etheric power of your trinkets and bring them to bear against a prime godling?"

He taps a finger atop my leftmost shackle, and I feel it shimmer and twitch at the touch.

"But now you learn that there is a price to pay. Each time you employ the ether, it takes something from you. To draw upon so much power so swiftly, it would turn a strong-willed man into a blithering simpleton. It says something of your strength of will that you yet stand, gunslinger. In truth, I applaud you. Were you not so hell-bent upon my destruction, I could make good use of you."

I press the words from my lips, forcing each sound as though swimming against a brutish current.

"Release the girl and let us…leave."

Tull shakes his head, as a disappointed father might chastise his son.

"You understand so little, gunslinger. In time, with the right instruction, you may become a valuable piece upon the board. For the moment, however, you are slave to your inner passions; passions which blind you to the truth."

He waves a hand toward the shackles at my wrists. "All of this, this power, is but a drop in the ocean, gunslinger.

You have been given your gifts only recently, so you do not understand their nature. You cannot wield what you do not understand. Nevertheless, I am willing to teach such a skill. It will take time, but I see potential in you."

I force myself to move forward, reaching for the godling with impossibly slow hands. Tull laughs, taking a step backward.

"Truly, you think yourself able to contend with me, gunslinger. You are a child wielding a stick. You know nothing of the ether with which you have been so recently endowed. But as for me and my kin, we were born to the ether. It imbues our every fibre. It pulses through our very blood. You threaten me with sticks and stones when I could crush this city within my palm and turn your bones to ash with a single thought."

"The girl…" I manage, driving my feet slowly toward him. "Release the girl and…I will remain…"

Tull steps backward, circling around the nearest table, upon which some unfortunate soul lies in silent torment.

"My dear boy, you seem confused as to the nature of our relationship. The playing piece does not make demands of the player."

He lifts his hands, and the table twists on unseen mechanisms. It rises, lifting its hapless victim into a forced stance. The creature standing before me is a twisted thing of flesh and iron, a grafted monstrosity with swollen limbs and the evidence of gruesome agonies across its pallid flesh. Great welts of red flesh punctuate the junctures where machine and bone are connected, weeping fetid streams of yellow puss. Amid the whirring cogs and pistons that surround its pitted skull, I see twin eyes staring back at me, painfully human and familiar.

"I have already taken the girl," Tull says, "just as I will take you. She is as yet unfinished, so you should not be alarmed at her current incarnation. The girl will once again be a thing of beauty, but the process of melding shadowspawn with human flesh is a delicate matter. Her flesh requires a degree of strength which machine and grafted bone supply."

I that moment, the etheric power falls from me like a discarded robe. I fall to the floor, eyes suddenly filled with tears.

"Yes, gunslinger. It was all for naught. I knew of your stripling from the moment you first entered my chamber. Daisy, is it? Or am I to call her Shadow? She has an unnatural strength to her; different to yourself, but no less fascinating."

Confusion and sorrow war within me as I gaze upon those sorrowful eyes. The creature before me is an abomination, yet I sense the girl within, and it breaks some part of me to see her thus. The godling continues to speak, but the words are lost to me. In that moment of deepest darkness, clarity dawns once more. The singular phrase which has led me to this place rises from somewhere within. I do not fight it but welcome the cold shadow that rises around me. Darkness swirls about my shackles, filling the chamber with power.

Kill the godling Tull

The imperative draws me to my feet, hands outstretched. The shadow seems alive as it dances about my hands, thick tendrils snaking toward the godling and wrapping around his throat. Tull's expression changes as the shadow cords take hold. He flares with etheric power, becoming twice his usual size and shimmering with etheric light. He struggles against the cords of shadow that bind him, screaming as the chamber begins to quake around us.

My eyes stay fixed upon the girl, upon her eyes, which seem so familiar yet strange in their current place. I speak no words, but simply let the darkness take hold. A thousand whispered voices fill the chamber as darkness swallows all. Distantly, I hear the godling shout words of desperation, but their substance is lost to me.

Kill the godling Tull

The chamber is filled with shadow and that whispered imperative. As the darkness swallows me, I feel no sorrow, no regret, only the warm comfort of oblivion.

15. South

I am blind for a time, feeling only the barest scraps of sensation. I hear the sound of water dripping, of flames licking hungrily. I feel myself carried, dragged across the ground.

The whispers have ceased their incessant prattling, and where before I had felt raw, unbridled power, I now feel an odd vacancy, as though some part of my soul has been spent.

The screams follow next, accompanied by the sharp crack of gunfire and the din of warfare. I am carried back, in my mind's eye, to the wars of old—memories without colour and life. It is as though I am being dragged through the landscape of memory, brought back to earlier days and earlier wars, yet I still cannot see.

I find myself curiously alert in my newly blunted state, searching the narrow vista of sensory impressions in an effort to piece together a clear picture. I remember the night's violence, storming the godling's palace, confronting Tull...the girl, twisted and...

**

Time bends...darkness wanes, and I find myself waking to brilliant daylight.

I am carried on the back of some beast of burden, laying prone with the crimson sun beating down upon me from above. Slowly I recover my wits, sitting upright and waiting for my vision to clear. The crimson sands of the red desert move slowly around me. I am seated in the rear of a small cart. It rumbles across the road, filling my ears with the rhythmic patter of falling hooves and cartwheels.

"Welcome back to the land of the living, gunslinger."

I turn to see Rook sitting at the opposite end of the cart, his face split with a broad smile as he whittles upon a piece of wood.

"The palace?" I ask, my throat hoarse.

"Burned to the ground, along with half the city. I know not what you did, gunslinger, but the city of Tullhaven will never stand proud again."

I tap a hand to my chest. "You found...found me?"

He nods. "Amid the rubble, yes. It was a wonder that I found you at all. When the palace fell, I was caught upon one of the lower ramparts. The earth fell about me, and I was forced to run the gauntlet while towers toppled, and the earth belched fire. As the madness ended, I found you laying at my feet, surrounded by rubble and flame. I pulled you from that place and took you from the city."

I turn, looking in the direction of Tullhaven. Though the city itself is hidden by the vast bowl in which it rests, pillars of smoke still stretch up to the heavens. We must be a day or more from the city.

"They will rebuild," Rook says, "but never so grand as before. It will not rise to its previous heights, but Tullhaven will always stand in some form or other. Though perhaps we shall know it by another name?"

"The...godling?" The words cut their way out of my throat.

Rook shrugs. "I cannot say, gunslinger. I saw no sign of Tull when I pulled you from the palace. Perhaps you have indeed managed to kill the godling as you said you would?"

He hands me a small water skin, and I drink greedily.

"We are headed northeast to the outlying territories. I and my kin will seek to build a life for ourselves in one of the hamlets near the outer rim. You are welcome to join us if you wish. Or, if you have a mind to continue on your way, I will arrange for your share of the wealth to be prepared for departure."

I move to speak, but the big man holds up a hand to stop me.

"One more thing, friend gunslinger."

He leans forward, pointing behind me to the head of the caravan. I turn, squinting to see amid the brilliant morning sunlight. Two wagons ride ahead, along with a handful of riders on plain mounts.

"Look well, gunslinger," Rook says. "She rides at the head of our band."

A figure sits atop the furthest mount, slight of frame and boasting some kind of rifle which stands proudly erect from the saddle. Even from this distance, I know her.

"How can this be?"

Rook laughs. "Another miracle, by all accounts. The Scorpion made a gift of her. She was waiting here with my wife and child when I fled the city. She had suffered somewhat at the hands of Tull's guardsmen, but there is strength in her."

"I saw her…saw the thing Tull had made of her."

"I cannot say what you saw, gunslinger. But see for yourself. Shadow rides at the head of our caravan, alive and unmolested by the godling."

Even as he speaks, the girl spins in her saddle, staring back toward us. For a moment we stare at one another. Then, as if to dispel the ghosts of doubt, she lifts a hand and waves. I find myself raising my own hand in response, my heart swelling at the sight. Her words are carried on the desert sands, tickling my ears as they reach us.

"About time you woke up, old man! How 'bout you get off your ass and help a girl out?"

***

The caravan heads southwest, further from the smoking carcass of Tullhaven. I speak at length with Shadow, piecing together the events of the past weeks as best I can. She speaks of her brief time imprisoned by Tull, of torture and mental manipulation, then freedom gained by the blood of the Scorpion Brotherhood. In turn, the girl asks more questions that I can answer. I speak of the final confrontation with Tull, of the red rage, the dark shadow, and the voices.

I find no condemnation in her eyes as I speak of the whispers that have driven me to face Tull. She listens with interest as I speak of the consuming darkness, the embrace of terrible power and the price I pay for its use.

"You think he's dead?" she asks.

I shrug. "I cannot say. I think it likely that he is either dead or incapacitated. Tull does not strike me as the kind of figure to take such an affront lightly."

She nods. "Yeah, that prick would ride halfway across the world to get you back for fucking his shit up."

"At least, I am somewhat quiescent."

She narrows her eyes. "In English please, professor!"

I tap a finger on my chest. "The voices are quiet. I no longer feel the urgent drive to act."

She nods. "So, the puppet masters have taken a break, yeah? Well, you gotta be happy with that. I knew something was wrong back there. The way you were always going on about Tull. It just didn't make any sense. Why pick a fight with someone you haven't got a hope of beating?"

"Indeed."

"Ok, so what now? Do we go with Rook and his family? Do we try to track down another godling and start this shit all up again? What's next?"

I do not answer immediately, but let her questions settle in my mind.

"I do not know. For the time being, let us content ourselves to accompany Rook and his kin."

She leans in close, smiling.

"Yeah, I'm not buying it, princess. You're planning something, I can tell. Spill it, grandpa. What are you thinking?"

I smile. "Not yet, little one. The time is not ripe."

"Oh, come on, you can't go saying shit like that. Just give me a hint!"

I let out a slow breath, enjoying the light breeze that brushes past us.

"Not yet, but when the time is right, I have unfinished business in the Red City."

16. Postscript

He appears to me in a dream: the old man, sitting upon a large rock, surrounded by vast, empty deserts. Within the dream my actions are my own, yet I feel compelled to sit before the old man and hear his words.

"Welcome, Idrus Kane of the shackled hand," the old man says.

I sit in silence, awaiting the words that must surely come.

"You have taken your first step, gunslinger. You have pit yourself against the godling Tull and triumphed where countless others have failed. Now that the godling slumbers, you must gather your strength, for he will seek bitter vengeance, and you will not know the hour of his coming. Follow the outlander and his kin. Make your home among the outlying baronies and learn all there is to learn. Teach the girl all you can, take her with you to the very cusp of this world and back again, but beware that the thread you carry for her does not pull you under."

The old man leans forward, his gnarled face looming above me.

"You cannot save her, gunslinger. Nor can you bend the will of this world to your own designs."

I attempt to speak, but without success.

"In the days ahead, you must fight the coming shadow, but beware. You cannot hope to prevail alone. Gather unto yourself allies and compatriots who will fight as you fight, for only in the company of others can you hope to keep the darkness within at bay."

He leans back, sitting upright upon his rock and sharing a crooked smile.

"Head to Baronsville, gunslinger, and learn your lessons. Gird your mind, for the days ahead will be fraught with terror and sorrow. Fall, and the fate of two worlds falls with you. Prevail and you shall have your vengeance."

***

I wake from a rare moment of slumber. The old man's visage lingers in my mind's eye, though it is now a distant thing. I cannot recall the moment when I drifted into my reverie. So many weeks have passed since I have felt the need for sleep that it leaves me groggy and somewhat unsettled as the morning light gently kisses the caravan.

As my mind readies itself for the day ahead, I see the small train of wagons heading off into the desert wastes, with Rook and his beloved at the head and several ex-slaves and servants manning wagons throughout.

The darkness within has grown quiescent, and I am permitted a brief moment of pleasure as I see Shadow emerge from the wagon ahead. She slinks from the cart, clothed in her black thief's garb and holding a curious rifle she seems to have acquired during the previous night's adventures. She walks toward me, walking alongside the wagon as the train lumbers slowly along.

"Hey, boss," she says, grinning. "You must have been shattered. I can't remember the last time you actually slept right through the night."

I nod. "Just so. It appears my encounter with Tull has taken a great deal from me."

"Man, I still can't believe you did it. I mean, you fucked up a godling. That's pretty impressive, you know?"

I allow the briefest of smiles. "Indeed."

I keep the warning from the night's dream to myself. Better that she enjoys this brief moment of peace than have her thoughts weighed down by the truth.

"We kind of kicked ass back there," she goes on. "I mean, I also got my ass handed to me, but overall, we did it. Killed Tull, burned the fucking Slavers to the ground and, from what I hear, tore three kinds of shit out of the nobility."

She motions to the front of the caravan where Rook walks alongside the first of the wagons, his broad frame lumbering gently.

I nod. "It was the best of all possible outcomes. In truth, I find myself somewhat at a loss. I had thought us destined for the charnel pit. The godling Tull, he showed me a vision of you...a horror."

"Yeah, Rook said. I think he was just trying to fuck with your head. Probably would have done something like that with me in the long run, but the worst I got was a couple of bruises and a bloody lip. They just shoved me in a cell until the Scorpion found me. She told me to give you something you know, the Scorpion."

That catches my attention. Shadow jumps up onto the cart and shuffles up beside me, laying her newfound weapon down beside her. She moves uncomfortably close and presses a hand against my chin so that my eyes look straight ahead. I feel the gentle touch of her lips against my cheek.

"I figure she wanted me to kiss you on the lips, but there's no way in fuck we're going there."

She blushes a little, uncomfortable with our sudden proximity.

"She was a remarkable woman," I offer.

"Yeah. Kick ass."

I smile a little. "She will likely rule that city within the week."

We sit in silence for a time, listening to the gently creaking of the wagon wheels as the train moves gently onward. Here and there, the sounds of conversation can be heard from further ahead, along with the clattering of pans and supplies as the morning's meal is distributed.

"You see those slaves?" Shadow asks, pointing to a group on the cart ahead. "Rook took all the servants and slaves from his house and picked up a few extras too. They treat him like a king."

"Indeed. I can think of no man better suited to the task."

She nods. "We did a good thing here, man. I mean, sure a lot of people died and probably a lot more will, but we made a difference to these people. Saved them from slavery and God knows what else."

Even in my current state of delirium, it is difficult to share her sentiment. We may have saved a few souls from the fire, but countless innocents will die in the days ahead.

"And what of your own instruction?" I ask. "What of the seven given over to your charge?"

She shrugs, her expression growing more serious. "Down to five by the time it all went bad. I had to kill that crazy bitch, Seven out of self-defence. She tried to cut my throat while my back was turned. Didn't even offer a reason when I pinned her. She just smiled like a twisted fuck and tried to stab me through the fucking chest."

"So, you put an end to her?"

"Yeah, I did, and it was fucking horrible. She didn't die quick like the other guy. She was slippery as fuck, so I had to keep cutting on her, and she just wouldn't give up. In the end I had to hold her and just wait for the blood to drain out of her. That's how Tull caught me. Fucker had goons waiting, and I was stuck in the warehouse killing Seven when they jumped me. If it wasn't for her, there's no way they would have caught me."

I nod. "And what of the other five?"

She shrugs. "Gone. Probably hiding somewhere in the city or fuck knows where."

"That is to be expected. Still, you have a further five kills ahead of you."

She nods, the memory of her last victim still painfully vivid in her mind's eye. "Yeah, I figured." Shadow leans over and picks up the rifle lying beside her. "But I've got a plan for that. Figure it's a hell of a lot easier to do it from a distance. So, I'm gonna stick to using Big Betty here when I can."

The rifle looks to be of specialized build, made for long-range combat and modified with various mechanized and etheric devices that likely enhance the range and accuracy of the weapon.

"A fine thing, and well crafted," I offer, taking the weapon from her and examining it closely. I feel the thrum of etheric energy vibrating from within the stock of the weapon.

"Where did you manage to secure such a weapon?"

She smiles. "I swiped it on my way out of Tull's place. It was hanging on a wall opposite my cell with a bunch of ammo. There were other weapons too, but this baby caught my eye. I made a deal with myself that if I ever made it out of there alive, I was gonna swipe it."

I hand the rifle back to the girl. "And so, you did."

She nods. "And so, I fucking did."

"Have you had occasion to use it yet?" I ask.

She shakes her head. "Not yet, but I figure something will pop up before long. If there's one thing you can count on it's that the Traumwelt will try to fuck you over pretty quickly if you give it enough time."

"Indeed."

I point behind her shoulder to the cloud of dust emerging at the horizon. She turns, squints to see through the desert haze. Whether by etheric sight or some other gift granted by my shackles, I see the pack of Needleworgs approaching from the west. A hunting party, hungry for blood and fixed on our scent. I am about to offer a description of the threat when the air between us is split with the half-crack of a muffled gunshot.

One of the Neddleworgs falls to the ground, trampled by its fellows as the pack charges toward us. Shadow aims the rifle a second time, grinning as she goes about her deadly business.

"Looks like it works," she says, firing a second time and felling a second of the beasts.

Not for the first time, I find myself impressed by the girl and her prowess with ranged weaponry. I stand to full height and motion toward the oncoming threat. Rook and the others of the caravan follow my hand and stare out toward the oncoming pack as Shadow kills another of the beasts.

"It's incredible," she says. "Hardly any kickback, and most of the sound is muffled. I think you can even change which direction the gunshot sound goes off to. Kind of like throwing your voice, I guess. Takes a while to shoot though, but that's ok."

The muffled sound of gunfire rings out again, and another of the approaching beasts falls. They are less than a dozen now, but only moments from reaching the caravan. I jump to the ground and see Rook and several of the others circle toward us with weapons raised. I feel the familiar power of etheric energy swell as my shackles begin to glow red. I rest each hand upon the shooting irons at my belt and take in a deep breath.

It begins.